MURDER IN
SHADOW

D0862995

Anne Cleeland

ARTEMIS
—PRESS—

ISBN: 0998595624
ISBN 13: 9780998595627

For George Grandison, who defends the powerless; and for all others like him.

1

It was past time to settle all lingering problems; he'd been unwilling, up to now, but the child would soon be born.

Detective Sergeant Kathleen Doyle stood beside Officer Gabriel as they reviewed the remains of the decedent, a man of approximately forty years who'd met a bad end, here in the Lambeth borough of London. The victim lay crumbled against an overturned ashcan, having attempted to avoid his fate by fleeing up this back alley. He was wearing an expensive suit—which probably explained why he wasn't very well-versed in the evading of criminals—and he looked to have been dead for some hours. A bloody wound on his left temple indicated that he'd been coshed, and even his shoes had been stolen.

"It all seems a bit smoky," Doyle remarked thoughtfully, as she surveyed the scene.

"How so?" her companion asked. "Seems a straightforward robbery-murder."

But she shook her head. "No—I don't mean the crime. DCI Acton is the senior investigatin' officer, and he's not here. DI Williams is the crime scene manager, and he's not here, either—faith; we don't even have an evidence officer, to throw a fig leaf of dignity over this investigation. Instead it's only you and me, which is a case of the blind leadin' the blind, with all due respect."

The young officer raised his brows in amusement. "I beg your pardon?"

"We shouldn't be the ones standin' here," she observed slowly. "And yet, here we are."

Gabriel's amused gaze returned to the body, splayed out before them. "I imagine we can perform a patched-up investigation, if we put our minds to it. Just remind me what happens first."

Smiling at his tone, she pulled her mobile. "First, my friend, we beg for help. Let me text DCI Acton on the sly, and see if he's finished at court." On this particular investigation, Chief Inspector Acton was serving a dual role as the senior investigating officer and also as Doyle's husband, sworn and sealed. Hopefully, she could wheedle him into pulling rank and taking charge of this crime scene; Doyle had never been the ranking officer on a homicide before, and she had a sneaking suspicion that it involved a lot of paperwork.

Gabriel crouched down to take a closer look at the corpse, and she cautioned, "Don't touch anythin'; the SOCOs will give you the edge of their tongues if you muck up the scene before they get here." Gabriel wasn't up-to-speed on crime scene protocols, because he was a transfer from counter-terrorism, on loan to the CID. A recent corruption scandal had come to light, and many of Scotland Yard's upper management were currently cooling their heels in prison, or awaiting trial. And—no doubt as a result of this sorry state of affairs—it was left to the lowly Doyle and the inexperienced Gabriel to try to sort out this poor fellow's murder. Doyle, however, couldn't shake a nagging suspicion that she was being kept busy whilst something much more interesting was happening, elsewhere.

She texted Acton, "How goes it, R U available?" Acton had mentioned he'd be testifying this morning—although he hadn't mentioned the specific case. It seemed odd that he'd been tied up so long—oftentimes the Crown Court would accommodate the police by allowing them to be on call, since the mills of justice tended to meander a bit and there was no reason to keep law enforcement off the streets. But there was something strange about his absence that she couldn't quite put her finger on—perhaps it was because usually, he kept himself within an arm's reach of her.

The answer came through. "Sorry, not yet finished. After lunch, perhaps."

"Ok. In Lambeth w/ new case." It wasn't necessary to tell him, of course; Acton would know exactly where she was since he kept track of her, using her mobile's GPS. Her husband was a well-respected chief inspector, but in truth, he was a bit nicked—although no one knew of it, except for the wife of his bosom. And it wasn't the good sort of nicked, where the person stood on tables and said outrageously funny things, but a rather a dark sort of nicked, where a black mood would settle in, a great deal of scotch would be consumed, and then questionable people would suddenly disappear off the streets.

Acton was something of a vigilante, and tended to dispense his own version of justice whenever he felt that the justice system—the one they were sworn to uphold—was lacking for any reason. Fortunately, Acton's nicked-ness had caused him to fixate on his red-headed support officer, and after rushing her into marriage he now spent a great deal of his time obsessing about her, rather than obsessing about who needed to be killed, next. Not the most ideal of situations, but—all in all—an improvement.

Resigned to her fate as this scene's ranking officer, Doyle looked up to review the entry into the alley. "All right, then; we'll start with the basics, and ask the PCs to cordon off the alley at both ends to set up a perimeter. We should clear a path for the coroner, too—are the SOCOs on the way?"

Gabriel nodded. "Yes. They're a bit shorthanded, unfortunately."

This was only to be expected, as their entire department was being run ragged, what with trying to handle the usual major crimes caseload alongside the massive corruption cases that were getting themselves prepared for trial. "Well, let's start takin' video and gettin' the lay of the land. D'you happen to know which case it is, that Acton's testifyin' on?" Unlikely that Gabriel would know, but it was still bothering her, for some reason.

"No, but here are the SOCOs." Gabriel indicated the Scene of Crime Officers, who were piling out of their van and looking a bit harassed.

She shook off the uneasy feeling and straightened up, in an attempt to give the forensics people the impression that she was capable and competent. "Good—let's get the prelim done, and hopefully we can rope in some DCs to canvass for witnesses. Otherwise, we'll have to do it ourselves."

As was always the case when a murder occurred in a public place, a small group of gawkers had already assembled outside the cordon, and it was always possible that someone had heard or seen something suspicious, even though the murder seemed hours old. Mentally, Doyle girded her loins; she never enjoyed having to sort through a wide variety of agitated persons, all eager to tell the police every uninteresting detail about their day, thus far, and with half of them positing wild conspiracy theories about why the decedent had been done in. She hated canvassing, and with good reason.

"I'll be happy to canvass—I don't mind."

This was true—she'd already noted that Gabriel could turn on the charm, when needful, and he seemed to have a gift for worming his way into places that usually barred their doors to all persons constabulary. It was no doubt a useful skill when one worked in counter-terrorism, and Doyle should watch and learn; she tended to be impatient with witnesses, and half-inclined to beat them with her baton. "Thanks, Gabriel; and if you could sweet-talk someone into confessin' before I have to type up a protocol, I would truly appreciate it."

Gabriel smiled and pulled his tablet. "Don't worry—I can work an entrapment with the best of them."

This rang true, and Doyle reminded herself that Gabriel was a sharp one, as she watched him walk away. Best keep it to mind, and best watch her tongue—she was the opposite of whatever a sharp one was. A dull one, perhaps—although she kept managing to land on her feet, despite this unfortunate drawback.

She then turned her attention to the SOCOs, and felt a twinge of sympathy as she watched them reluctantly pull on their bunny suits. It was unlikely the forensics people would be able to process anything of interest; any evidence found in an alley like this one was automatically compromised, and any barrister worth his salt would argue that the suspect's DNA—even if they managed by some miracle to collect it—didn't mean he was anything other than an innocent passerby, in the wrong place at the wrong time.

As there were no bullets, they couldn't count on helpful ballistics, either. If they were lucky, the cosher may have dropped his weapon, or left something else behind that could offer up the whisper of a lead; otherwise it appeared they were in for a long and fruitless slog.

The supervising SOCO approached her, and Doyle said in her best presiding-officer voice, "We're short an evidence officer and a CSM, but let's start preparing for the coroner's arrival, and try to get an ID." Although the crime appeared to be a simple stranger-robbery, the victim's identity and recent dealings may help to shed some light; she mustn't overlook the possibility that this was not a random crime.

"Yes, ma'am." The woman pulled on her gloves, eyeing the victim. "Poor bloke. At least we know someone's going to miss this one. The last one I worked is still a John Doe in the morgue."

Doyle could only agree. "Yes, goin' by his clothes, this one does seem well-heeled—except that his shoes were stolen, so I suppose he's heel-less, instead. Mayhap he wandered into the wrong place, and paid the price for his foolishness."

But the SOCO was more cynical, having seen many a robbery-murder. "He may have wanted to buy drugs, or something worse." She paused, assessing the corpse with a practiced eye. "His feet are big, and his shoes would be expensive; maybe we should check in with the local pawn and second-hand shops. The killer may have already tried to cash in."

"An excellent idea." Doyle made a note. "I'd have never thought of it."

The SOCO shrugged. "We did it with the John Doe. It went nowhere—he wore an ordinary size, and wasn't rich enough to have anything but ordinary shoes."

But Doyle found that her scalp was prickling, and she raised her head. "The John Doe's shoes were missin', too?"

The woman shrugged, as she tested the visual recorder on her tablet. "It happens. After the wallet and the watch, sometimes the shoes are next in line to be worth something."

Why, there's something here, Doyle thought in surprise, as the woman carefully approached the body. Doyle was Irish, and—thanks, no doubt, to some long-dead ancestor—she was a bit fey. Mainly, it meant that she could read the emotions of those persons in her vicinity, but it also meant that she could usually tell when someone was lying. In addition, there were those occasions—such as right now—when her instinct would prod her, telling her that she was missing something important. The shoes? she thought in surprise; what about the shoes?

Her thoughts were interrupted by a ping on her mobile, and the screen identified the absent CSM, Inspector Williams. Unfortunately, the SOCOs were still within earshot, so Doyle was forced to be civil rather than berate him like a fishwife, which was her inclination. "Why, hallo, sir. Very nice it is, to hear from you."

Williams wasn't fooled by her tone. "Sorry, Kath; I'll be there as soon as I can. Anything of interest?"

"Rich man, coshed and robbed in a shabby alley." Doyle frowned. "Where are you, that's more important than bossin' me about, here?"

"You're more than capable of bossing yourself."

"I'm a foot soldier, Thomas—born and bred. I need direction."

"Then you'll have some as soon as I get there; I'm in the middle of dealing with a witness on the Santero case. Just secure the scene and any surveillance feed—there must be CCTV, in that area."

She made a face, because reviewing surveillance feed was her least favorite thing to do, right after canvassing for witnesses. "Do we have any PCs who are available to help?"

"Check with the desk sergeant, but unlikely, I'm afraid."

"No rest for the weary, then. Acton says he's hung up in court—what's the case, d'you know?"

"Sorry—got to go, Kath."

"All right, then; cheers."

Doyle rang off thoughtfully, and frowned at the screen for a moment. Williams seemed a bit constrained, and he'd side-stepped a straight answer about Acton's case—faith, Acton himself was being overly-vague about it. With a pang of alarm, she remembered that Acton had voiced his private opinion that the Anti-Corruption Command unit—the unit he was working with, in prosecuting the massive corruption rig—was itself corrupt. This was alarming to no small extent; if the watchdogs were also bent, it meant that it was a very dicey situation for her husband, who was busily ferreting out all their dastardly secrets. Hopefully, he was not fleeing up his own alley, somewhere.

Trying to hide her uneasiness, Doyle stepped forward to interrupt the SOCO, who was discussing blood spatter with her photographer. "I'm sorry, but I'm not very tech-savvy, and I'd like to find out how long it will be before the DCI arrives. I don't want to bother him again—can you trace his location from his phone call?"

"Yes, ma'am." The woman lifted Doyle's mobile, and touched the screen a few times. In a moment, a map appeared with a highlighted indicator. "Palace of Westminster, ma'am."

Doyle frowned slightly. "Palace of Westminster? Is that the address for one of the Crown Courts?"

The SOCO gave her a look, as she handed back the mobile. "No, ma'am. That's the address of Parliament."

"Parliament?" Staring at the woman in surprise, Doyle slowly sheathed her mobile. What on earth would Acton be doing at Parliament—and testifying, to boot; he'd been telling the truth, when he'd told her he was needed to testify. Suddenly, she lifted her gaze to stare down the alley, unseeing. "Holy *Mother*," she breathed.

"Ma'am?" The SOCO was fast losing patience and small blame to her; she was not used to dealing with third-tier law enforcement personnel, and Doyle was about to cement the woman's low opinion of her.

"I'm afraid I must go," she announced hurriedly. "The coroner is comin', and Officer Gabriel will secure the scene, until the CSM gets here."

"Are you all right?" the woman asked in mild alarm. Doyle was heavily pregnant.

"A family emergency," she explained vaguely, as indeed it was. The chickens were coming home to roost with a vengeance, and it appeared that the fair Doyle's foolish husband was attempting to keep her well-away from the fallout. Good luck to him; pigs would fly.

As Doyle hurried away as quickly as she was able, the SOCO called out, "What do I tell the chief inspector, ma'am?"

"Not to worry," Doyle threw over her shoulder. "I'll see him before you do."

2

Oftentimes, the problem was that it was too simple. He mustn't be complacent, and assume everyone will behave just as they ought. Indeed, a challenge would be welcome, occasionally, just so as to make it interesting.

Doyle sped to the Westminster address, hailing a cab and turning off her mobile in the hope that Acton wouldn't see that she was coming. It hardly mattered, though; if the hearing was underway, there was nothing Acton could do to prevent his bride from storming the gates.

Acton held an ancient title—a barony—which only supported the public's good opinion of him in that it was considered a boon if an aristocrat actually did anything remotely useful with his life. Unbeknownst to his admirers, however, there'd been a bit of chicanery several generations back, and an imposter had been put up as Lord Acton when it had looked as though the estate would have to be sold to pay taxes. The false Lord Acton had married an heiress, and by doing so, had saved the day.

Sir Stephen Waite, Acton's second cousin, was Acton's current heir, and it should have been Sir Stephen's grandfather who inherited the estate, instead of the imposter. Thus far, the issue had been simmering beneath the surface, since Acton had long been a bachelor, and Sir Stephen stood as Acton's current heir. But the fair Doyle had unexpectedly turned up to marry Acton out-of-hand and then—in true Irish fashion—had promptly gotten herself pregnant. Now that Sir Stephen was about to be cut out of the succession altogether, matters had come to a head, and he must have filed a formal claim to the effect that he was the rightful Lord Acton.

It was a doubly unexpected, because it seemed that Sir Stephen had jumped the gun. Doyle had seen her son in a dream, once, and had informed her husband that the boy would have green eyes. This had caused Acton some concern, since apparently there were brown eyes as far as the eye could see in the Acton family tree—with the exception of the imposter, and Doyle's mother. You'd think that Sir Stephen would have waited for Edward to be born, so as to add this factor to his claim— but, of course, he wouldn't know about the green eyes in the first place; until Edward was born, only Doyle and Acton knew.

Acton had mentioned the possibility of Sir Stephen's challenging the succession, and he'd also mentioned that such matters were determined by some committee of lords in Parliament—thank all available saints and angels that Doyle had been paying attention, for once. I'll outsmart him, she thought with a small sense of triumph. He thought he'd keep me out of this mess, but I'll be there with bells on—nothing like a pregnant bride to inject some drama into a dull-as-ditchwater succession proceeding.

In truth, Doyle didn't care about the title either way. Being hardscrabble Irish, she was not one for tiaras or hereditary honors, but it was important to Acton, who was very fond of his estate and not at all fond of his vile cousin. Of course, matters were complicated by the fact that there'd indeed been a switch, when Acton's great-grandfather had substituted the imposter.

With a growing sense of alarm, Doyle realized that Sir Stephen would not have brought a claim in Parliament unless he'd dug up some decent evidence to support it, and so she urged the cab driver to hurry. If the ground was about to be cut out from under Acton's feet, she needed to be there to support him—not to mention he might run amok, which he was wont to do when anyone crossed him, with the disappearance of a certain psychiatrist serving as an excellent case in point. She'd be needed to hang on to his coat-tails until he could calm himself down, and re-think any stray impulse he might have to lay waste to a roomful of peers. After all, he was also in the line of succession to inherit an earldom; it wasn't as though they'd be forced to sell apples on the street corner, for heaven's sake.

Since Acton had said he hoped to be finished by lunch, she'd best hurry along and find wherever the hearing was as quickly as possible. Therefore, she was rosy of check and a bit out of breath when she was directed to the committees corridor, and after hurrying down the marble hallway with as much speed as her bulky form would allow, she paused outside the hearing room door to take a deep breath, and then quietly slip within.

Her gaze was drawn immediately to her husband, who was seated at a table at the front of the room, and apparently in the midst of giving testimony. He met her gaze with all appearance of surprise, and then gestured in an apologetic manner to the elderly presiding officer who was seated near him, on a dais. "I must beg your pardon, my lord; my wife has made an unexpected appearance—"

Miserable, conniving, black-hearted gombeen, Doyle thought in a gathering fury, as the sixteen members of the committee turned around to view her with open curiosity. *I've a good mind to rend my garments and divorce the flippin' sassanach on the spot.*

The elderly chairman looked upon her with extreme interest, as he motioned to the attending clerk. "Of course, of course; please see to it that our visitor is seated comfortably—"

The clerk hurried forward to escort Doyle to one of the chairs that lined the walls, and as she was seated, she could see that Sir

Stephen was eying her a bit sourly from his position at the petitioner's table.

As Doyle tried without much success to calm herself, the chairman viewed her pregnant form with polite concern. "May I offer water, madam?" Leaning forward, he offered a dry little smile. "Although, perhaps you've sworn off water, forever—I could scarce blame you." He then chuckled as though he'd said something very witty, and all persons present dutifully chuckled in sycophantic appreciation of his extreme cleverness. Some months ago, Doyle had jumped off Greyfriars Bridge into the Thames so as to rescue a fellow detective, and now she was something of a hero, since the papers had played up the incident to be much more than it truly was and nobody—*nobody*—could just let it *go*.

"No—no, thank you, sir." Doyle had a hard time maintaining a civil tone, as she was still coming to terms with the fact that her husband was a serpent-in-the-garden.

"May we continue, my lord?" asked Acton's counsel, in a polite tone.

"Proceed," nodded the chairman, although his gaze strayed briefly to Doyle.

He'll want a snap, she thought with resignation; they always do.

Acton's counsel took up the threads of his interrupted examination. "And your father, sir—the previous Lord Acton; he disappeared, and was pronounced dead by the High Court?"

Acton bent his head forward slightly. "After the appropriate amount of time, yes."

"Did the police conduct an investigation?"

There was the smallest pause, before Acton offered in a neutral tone, "My father's death was not believed to be a homicide, at that time."

Good one, thought Doyle, listening with grudging approval. Create the implication that—on second thought—perhaps our petitioner, here, did him in.

Counsel paused for a few beats, apparently deep in thought, and then turned to ask Acton, "Do you have any idea, sir, what happened to your father? Why he disappeared?"

"None," said Acton, who'd killed his father himself.

"Did your father ever mention a—a discrepancy, in the succession?"

"Never."

Doyle had to refrain from wincing at this out-and-out untruth. In point of fact, from what Acton had hinted, his father had been a miserable excuse for a human being and a bit mad—although Acton was a bit mad, himself, so his assessment may or may not be wholly accurate. In any case, his father had threatened to expose the succession-hoax, and had blackmailed everyone he could about it, until Acton—a young man, attending university— finally reached a had-it-up-to-here flashpoint and had murdered the wretched man. She wondered, for a moment, what had finally tipped the balance.

"When were you first made aware of Sir Stephen's claim that it is he who is the rightful heir?"

Acton frowned slightly. "Sir Stephen is my current heir and will remain so, until my son is born."

With all appearance of regret, counsel spread his hands. "I beg your pardon, sir; that was a clumsy question. When were you first made aware that Sir Stephen believed he should be the right- ful Lord Acton of Trestles?"

"Only recently."

Counsel nodded, and then paced with his hands clasped be- hind his back. "And yet, Sir Stephen has been residing at your estate, all this time?"

"Indeed."

Counsel paused to look up. "Has he contributed, in any finan- cial way, to the upkeep of the estate?"

"He has not."

Good one, thought Doyle again; portray him as an ingrate. Create the impression that the claim was brought by Sir Stephen only as an attempt to cling to his free ride, now that he's about to be booted out.

The chairman could be seen to jot a quick note before he glanced over at Doyle again, and offered his small, dry smile. Doyle realized that she should probably return his smile, and did so.

"Respondent rests, my lord."

"Ah—well, then." Recalled to the task at hand, the chairman checked his notes. "Has the next witness arrived, as yet?"

Sir Stephen's counsel stood. "Not as yet, my lord. I believe there are traffic concerns."

"Well, then; let's adjourn for an hour—it's nearly lunchtime." The chairman rose rather hurriedly, and it soon became apparent that his intent was to speak to Doyle, as he made his way toward her chair.

This was an annoyance, as Doyle was itching to berate her devious husband, but she swallowed her temper and tried to give all appearance of cordiality, as she greeted the elderly man. Out of the corner of her eye, she noted that Acton had made a beeline toward her also, no doubt hoping to prevent her from shoving the presiding officer aside so that she could lay into him like the rough end of a jack-saw.

With courtly charm, the chairman took her hand. "May I say that it is a pleasure to meet you, madam. I clipped all the newspaper accounts of your heroic action." He then leaned in to confide, "I must confess that I feel an affinity; my dear wife was a redhead."

"Of course, she was," said Doyle, and then belatedly realized that she probably shouldn't be flippant. "That is excellent."

"It would not be at all seemly, just now," the man confided, after having apparently forgotten that he was still holding her hand, "but after this matter has concluded, perhaps I might have a photograph?"

"Right," Doyle agreed; and then, because she should boost Acton's stock even though she'd just as soon strangle him, "I'm the one that's honored, my lord."

The elderly man smiled with genuine pleasure, and then appeared to recall himself as he released her hand, and walked away with a stately tread.

3

She was breathtaking when she was angry.

D oyle could scarce contain herself until the chairman was out of earshot. "Well, he's hand-picked, husband, and well done, you. Do they send all the retired judges over here, thinkin' they can't muck it up too badly?"

Acton didn't respond, but instead gently took her elbow and leaned his head down to hers, as he steered her out of the room. "Please don't be angry, Kathleen."

"Of course, I'm angry, you underhanded *knocker*. Should I've held a handkerchief to my pale lips? Honestly, Michael."

"I thought it might be helpful if it appeared that I was trying to protect you from this distasteful situation."

This was self-evident; Acton had wanted the pregnant bridge-jumper to make a dramatic and alarmed appearance, and she'd answered the call like a bucket boy to the fire bell. After taking a steadying breath, she continued in a low tone, "I don't like feelin' like I'm bein' manipulated, Michael. You're as bad as the stupid ghosts." Unfortunately, Acton's dead ancestors tended to goad her into taking action when she'd rather not, which was most of the time. For example, there was a knight at Trestles who was fit to be tied about something, but as she didn't speak medieval-ghost, she was at a loss as to exactly what it was.

Acton soothed, "Let's have a bite to eat in the cafeteria, and talk it over."

She eyed him with deep suspicion because ordinarily, Acton would rather starve than eat in such a public place. With a mighty effort, she calmed herself—best not to start a donnybrook, here in the hushed hallway—and allowed him to lead her away. "Well then, be warned; I've half a mind to take up a chair and brain you with it, which wouldn't help your cause."

He made no response as they retreated down the corridor, but instead smiled benignly at her, no doubt because they were the object of many a covert stare.

Pinning on her own smile, Doyle admitted under her breath, "No; there I'm wrong. We could brawl like Sailortown shants, and it wouldn't matter in the slightest. I'm heroic, you're heroic, and Sir Stephen is a fool indeed if he thinks he's goin' to get anywhere with this." She glanced up at him. "Is he goin' to get anywhere with this?" May as well ask; no doubt Acton had taken his own assessment.

"No. He will not succeed."

It was the truth, but she leaned in and warned in low voice, "I know you think you're bullet-proof—what with this sorry excuse for a chairman, and your bridge-jumpin' wife—but Sir Stephen's counsel's got a cat-at-the-cream-pot attitude, Michael, and it makes me uneasy. He's got somethin' up his sleeve."

"Then we shall see. I remain confident."

"You're always confident," she complained, as they entered the crowded cafeteria. "It's wearyin', is what it is."

Solicitously, he seated her at a table whilst the diners in their immediate area began to whisper in excited, low voices. "I wasn't at all confident that you'd marry me. The fear of failure kept me awake at night."

She quirked her mouth, as he seated himself across from her. "Serves you right; I should have kept you guessin' for more than twenty minutes."

"The worst twenty minutes of my life."

Because she couldn't help it, she began to laugh, and then rested her head in her hands. "You're killin' me, here, Michael. Please tell me straight-out what's afoot."

Acton lifted the menu to examine the offerings. "I think it's obvious. Sir Stephen has brought a spurious claim to the title, and he will fail in his attempt."

She took a guess at what "spurious" meant, and peered through her fingers at him. "That won't wash, Michael. It's me, remember?"

He lowered the card, and amended, "I'd like to settle all pending problems before Edward is born. It would be best if this unpleasantness was resolved."

"Unpleasantness" being his aristocratic way of referring to the unfortunate fact that Doyle had been the victim of a shooting, and it was as yet unclear whether the shooter had conspired with Sir Stephen to make certain that Edward was never born.

Tentatively, she ventured, "Are you sure they're goin' to resolve it in your favor?" After all, the imposter-heir had indeed been substituted many years ago; perhaps Sir Stephen had managed to come up with some solid evidence, after all this time.

"I am."

This was the pure truth, and she considered him for a moment, her brow knit. "I trust you, Michael—I truly do; but please keep in mind that you're bearin' false witness, all over the place." Acton was going to be confirmed as a Roman Catholic shortly, and Doyle held out a faint hope that the occasion would not prompt the earth to open up and swallow her poor church whole.

"I will make it right. I promise."

With a sense of resignation, she took up her own menu card and reviewed the items. "And—aside from the minor point of mortal sin—let's try not to forget that the CID is flailin' underwater, whilst we're over here at the palace, fussin' over stupid bloodlines. I had to dump a very interestin' murder in poor Gabriel's lap so as to hotfoot it over to this little holy show."

This caught his attention, because Acton liked nothing better than an interesting murder. "Oh? I understood it was a simple robbery-gone-bad."

Frowning, she fiddled with her silverware. "It looked to be so—the usual case, where the villain coshed the victim a bit too hard. But there's something there, Michael—" She paused, thinking. "It has to do with how his shoes were stolen."

As her husband tended to respect her intuitive abilities even more than she did, he accepted this rather disjointed explanation without a blink. "Oh? How so?"

She looked up at him. "I don't know why it's important, but it is. The victim was a wealthy man—we don't have an ID, as yet—but he was in a seedy alley in Lambeth. Why? And the SOCO said that there was a John Doe in the morgue, and that his shoes had been stolen, too."

Acton watched her. "And you don't think these are random, unconnected crimes."

"No—no, I don't," she said slowly. But I don't know what it is I'm thinkin', here."

"Williams is the CSM?"

"Yes, but he's wasn't at the scene—he said he was runnin' down a witness who was willin' to talk on the Santero case." A practitioner of the Santeria religion had been arrested for murder, but the CID was having problems building a case because those witnesses who would be most likely to grass were too afraid of the suspect to testify. There was not much protection the Met could offer, when it came to the fear of evil curses.

Crossing his arms, Acton considered this for a moment. "Let's find out who handled the John Doe case and have a look at the file—that would seem to be the place to start. Let me know as soon as we have an ID on today's victim." He checked his watch. "We'd best eat something; we've only another half-hour until we resume. I'll fetch you a spinach salad—it's quite good, here."

She made a face. "I'm not one for salads," she reminded him, although he certainly should know this, by now. "Who's the next witness?"

He offered in a neutral tone, "I believe my mother is scheduled to testify."

Horrified, Doyle stared at him in abject dismay. "Your *mother*? Saints and *holy* angels, Michael—what is she goin' to say? Mother a' mercy, but this could get nasty."

But Acton did not seem to be the least bit out-of-curl when presented with this possibility. "Indeed."

Doyle tried with little success to reign in her extreme alarm at the prospect of the dowager Lady Acton holding forth on the House of Acton's secrets. "There's such a thing as bein' too confident," she warned. "Do we know her aim, in all this?" Acton's mother was a thoroughly unpleasant woman who hated her Irish daughter-in-law with the heat of a thousand suns. Not only that, but she also appeared to be very fond of the vile Sir Stephen.

"We shall soon see. Let's share the salmon, shall we?"

He didn't wait for an answer, and Doyle watched in bemusement as he went to fetch the food, thinking that her poor husband was distracted indeed, if he didn't remember that she hated seafood. Of course, it was no small surprise that he was distracted—what with having to defend his title on the one hand, and trying to out-fox the crooked ACC on the other. She should try to be a better helpmeet to the man; shame on her for sulking, and adding to his troubles.

With renewed resolve, she smiled on her husband when he returned, and palmed a packet of saltines to eat later.

4

She had a low iron count, at the last doctor's visit. He'd been assured that this was normal, and that no additional supplements would be necessary, but it was worrisome.

One back in the committee room, Acton saw Doyle re-seated in her chair against the wall and then went over to take his place at the respondent's table, with his counsel. Doyle noted that the two men didn't speak, which was probably because they were well-prepared for each and every contingency. Acton's counsel was a sleek, clever man who was very much enjoying his task despite his slightly bored appearance. Uneasily, Doyle wished she knew what made Sir Stephen's solicitor exude such an aura of confidence—mayhap Acton's mother, the dowager, would claim that Acton was not her son, or something. Nothing would surprise her, with this miserable bunch.

The chairman took up his position on the dais, and immediately directed another friendly smile at Doyle. Doyle smiled back, and reflected that the man was surely too old to make an advance, which was just as well because she was not about to sacrifice her virtue on the altar of Acton's stupid estate.

Sir Stephen's counsel rose. "The petitioner would like to call the dowager Lady Acton, my lord."

"Proceed."

The clerk opened the door to the hallway and called for Acton's mother, who paused in entering the room to remove her gloves, her expression faintly bored. Looking about her with a full measure of discreet disdain, she then made her way toward the front table. Upon spotting Acton, she nodded to him in polite greeting. If she saw Doyle, she gave no indication.

Doyle watched with grave uneasiness as the dowager was sworn in, since it was yet unclear whether Acton's mother and Sir Stephen were in cahoots. It seemed unlikely that the dowager would willingly conspire to relinquish her own title—and the exalted standing that went along with it—but perhaps Sir Stephen had bribed her in some way, or had brought other pressure to bear.

Sir Stephen's counsel began asking questions, which the dowager answered in a tone that left no doubt as to the general inferiority of all persons present.

"—and did your husband ever reference a discrepancy in the succession?"

"My late husband," the elderly woman declared in a frosty tone, "had a great many animadversions to report, most of which were directed toward his assorted relatives."

Not a clue as to what she just said, thought Doyle.

"Yes, ma'am—but did he mention the succession?" counsel prompted.

"He may have," the dowager conceded. "I know he'd quarreled with his own father over the matter."

"So—you are aware there was some controversy?"

There was a small pause. "I'm afraid I cannot say, one way or the other." This was a lie.

Counsel nodded, and then waited a few beats before asking, "Do you have any explanation as to what happened to your husband? Is there any chance he yet lives?"

Acton's counsel rose. "Objection, my lord; this matter has already been resolved by a High Court proceeding."

The chairman skewed his gaze to the examiner, who explained, "The prior proceeding did not touch upon the succession issue, my lord."

"I'll allow a limited inquiry." The chairman shifted in his chair as an excuse to shoot a covert glance at Doyle from beneath his bushy white brows.

Sir Stephen's counsel continued, "Is it possible, ma'am, that he was so distraught over the burden of knowing he was not the true titleholder that he killed himself?"

"Objection—this is pure speculation." Acton's counsel stood with a show of extreme disapproval.

"Sustained," said the chairman, who leaned forward to admonish, "I'll not give you any more leeway, if you're only going to pull tricks."

"I beg your pardon, my lord. Nothing further." Sir Stephen's counsel withdrew in a chastised manner, but Doyle knew that he was nonetheless satisfied, because he'd gotten his point across.

"Response?" The chairman turned to Acton's counsel.

"I've a few questions, my lord," Acton's counsel acknowledged.

"Five minutes," said the chairman, who then leaned back in his chair, and steepled his fingers.

Saints, thought Doyle, as she watched with extreme foreboding. Here we go—I hope they know what they're doing; she's as much a viper as Sir Stephen, and God only knows what she'll be willing to say.

Acton's counsel rose, and appeared to be deep in thought as he paused before the dowager for a moment, his head bent. But to Doyle's surprise, he didn't ask any further questions about Acton's late father. Instead, he asked, "Ma'am, have you ever met a man associated with the d'Amberres, of France?"

Doyle blinked. Now, this was out of the clear blue sky.

She could sense that Sir Stephen's counsel was suddenly wary, but he rose negligently to object, "I fail to see the relevance, my lord."

"I'll allow," said the chairman, who'd glanced up from trying to put the lead back into his mechanical pencil.

The dowager knit her delicate brow. "Yes. I met a man, when he came to visit at Trestles—he was a *comte*, I believe. I cannot recall his name, just now."

"Was the gentleman's name Philippe Savoie?"

Doyle closed her eyes in acute dismay.

Again, the dowager frowned slightly. "Perhaps. I cannot recall for certain."

Acton's counsel turned to face the assembly as he asked the next question. "How are the d'Amberres related to your husband's family, do you know?"

There was a sudden, still silence, and for the first time, the dowager seemed wary. "I believe the d'Amberres are distant cousins."

"Are you aware that Mr. Savoie—the gentleman whom you met at Trestles—has a claim in this matter?"

Sir Stephen's counsel shot to his feet. "Objection; my lord—"

"Objection on what grounds?" asked Acton's counsel, spreading his hands in mock-confusion.

Flustered, Sir Stephen's counsel amended, "May we be allowed a short break, my lord?"

"Five minutes, stay in place," intoned the chairman, who then leaned back in his chair so as to contemplate the ceiling.

Holy Mother of God, thought Doyle, who slowly let out the breath she'd been holding. It looked as though they were indeed putting up Philippe Savoie—of *all* people—as the supposed true heir. Savoie was a Frenchman, and a criminal kingpin, to boot—not to mention a friend-of-sorts to the fair Doyle, based on past favors. Previously, she'd got the uneasy feeling that Savoie was somehow involved in the fight over Acton's estate, but Acton had assured her that there was nothing to worry about. And now—incredible as it seemed—it appeared that she'd been right, and that Savoie was indeed involved. Only—only, it was clear that Sir Stephen's people had been caught by surprise. Which left only one explanation—

Whilst Sir Stephen could be seen whispering furiously to his counsel, Doyle let her astonished gaze rest on the back of her husband's head. It was Acton; Acton must be the one who was putting up Savoie as the true heir. But that was *completely* ridiculous—surely Acton wasn't going to hand the title over to Savoie, just to spite Sir Stephen. And besides, what Englishman in his right mind would hand over the ancient barony to a French blackleg like Savoie? For heaven's sake, the man was a known criminal, and on the Watch List—it all made no sense, whatsoever.

Sir Stephen's counsel rose and said, "My lord, we've been taken by surprise, and would request a recess to research this matter. The fact that counsel has never mentioned the existence of this individual—"

"Objection," said Acton's counsel, in dignified protest. "The lineage is no secret, and this committee is attempting to ascertain the identity of the true Lord Acton. My client would be as disadvantaged as Sir Stephen, if Mr. Savoie's claim proves valid."

"Then we'll hear from Mr. Savoie, and get to the bottom of this," said the chairman, who shot an openly apologetic glance at Doyle. "Any further questions for this witness, or shall we adjourn?"

"Only five minutes more, my lord," said Sir Stephen's counsel.

The chairman sank back into his chair with unfeigned disappointment. "Proceed."

Doyle watched Sir Stephen's counsel approach the dowager, and almost felt sorry for the man. Obviously, Acton had some plan afoot, and Sir Stephen had lost all control of the narrative, which now portrayed Acton as being more-in-sorrow-than-in-anger with his pesky cousin, and his pesky cousin looking like a first-class grifter, which—to be fair—he was. Not to mention it seemed evident that even if he won the case, Sir Stephen was slated to be second-in-line after Philippe *flippin'* Savoie. Sir Stephen's counsel had better come up with a game-changer—and fast—or all was lost.

With a solemn expression, Sir Stephen's counsel stood before the dowager. "Do you have any reason to believe that your son—" here, he turned to gesture toward Acton "—is not the true Lord Acton?"

"I do not," said the dowager, at her most regal.

"Then, do you believe there are any impediments that would prevent his wife's son from supplanting Sir Stephen as the heir to the barony?"

"I do," said the dowager.

Astonished, Doyle slowly straightened in her seat, as a hush fell over the room.

"And what is that impediment, if I may ask?" Counsel turned to face the assembled committee members, so as to draw attention to the answer.

"I am not certain that my son is legally married to—to this young woman. It is unclear whether his first wife yet lives."

There was a stunned silence. Now, there's an excellent game-changer, Doyle conceded, and wondered whether she should pretend to faint.

5

It was regrettable that the claim was so salacious, but the temporary unpleasantness would be well worth it. The more salacious the claim, the better.

"So; I'm an adulteress," remarked Doyle. "Didn't see that one comin'."

Acton was driving them from Parliament to the morgue, and he took her hand with a small smile. "Come, now; you of all people know it is not true."

After having been re-called to testify about his supposed first marriage, Acton had categorically denied that he'd married the young woman in question, but was then presented with a record from Holy Trinity Clinic, supposedly showing that the young woman had given birth to a son, and had claimed to be married to Acton at the time.

Doyle had not been alarmed; she knew—in the way that she knew things—that Acton was not the marrying kind, and indeed, his courtship of her fair self—if one could call it that—only supported this sure knowledge. Aloud, she said, "I suppose it wouldn't hurt to say it, though."

He squeezed her hand. "I've never married anyone but you. I will never marry again."

"That about sums it up, I suppose."

"They're hoping for the best," he soothed. "I am certain it will amount to nothing."

But she eyed him sidelong, having put two and two together, and having come up with one wily husband. "Yes; they thought they had you stymied, what with this first-marriage business, but—in a *truly* amazin' turnabout—Philippe Savoie shows up as the true heir from generations ago, and his claim would trump everyone else's."

"Amazing, indeed," Acton agreed.

She turned to look out the window, trying to decide whether she should let him know that she was on to him—honestly; no one ever explained to you that marriage required so much in-house detective work. At the hearing, Sir Stephen's counsel had explained that the record of birth had been recovered from the archives at the clinic, and that a verifying copy had also been found amongst the archives at Lord Aldwych's estate—Aldwych being Acton's great-grandfather.

Doyle decided she may as well come down on the side of honesty—not that it ever seemed to do her much good—and noted, "If I'm rememberin' things right, Savoie killed the records keeper at Holy Trinity Clinic, but was never prosecuted for it."

"Savoie had immunity," Acton reminded her.

"Then he's a lucky man, I suppose. Considerin' he also killed the archives-keeper at Lord Aldwych's estate—the other place where a copy of this birth record was unearthed."

"An extraordinary coincidence," he agreed, and it was a lie.

"You don't believe in coincidences," she reminded him in a dry tone. "I wish you'd tell me what's afoot, here, husband, and I wish I didn't have to keep askin' you to."

He glanced over at her. "I am afraid you are too honest." He squeezed her hand in apology.

"It's a failin'," she agreed.

There was a small silence, and apparently he realized that a further explanation was required. "There is the possibility that you would be called upon to testify, and I dare not take the chance of telling you ahead of time what has been planned."

"Bein' as I've a tendency to gabble in a panic."

He tilted his head. "Not at all; instead, you are refreshingly forthright."

Making a wry mouth, she looked out her window. "That's because you're supposed to tell the truth and shame the devil, Michael."

"I'm afraid this situation is a bit more nuanced."

Little point in pursuing this particular subject, even if she asked him what "nuanced" meant. "I thought a wife couldn't testify against her husband."

"That's only in criminal proceedings," he explained. "And even in that case, there are exceptions."

She glanced over at him. "Then it's lucky, we are, that no one's thinkin' about drummin' up a criminal proceeding or two. It's got to be fraud at the very least, for your grandfather to pretend he was not who he truly was, and take over the title."

There was a small silence. "I'm afraid it was not my decision."

Shaking her head slightly, she looked out her window again. "That won't wash, husband; you'd have done the same thing—only instead of marryin' an heiress, you'd have probably robbed the Bank of England, or somethin'."

"I wouldn't have stood idly by," he agreed.

After shifting in the seat so that she was more comfortable, she decided that she didn't want to hear another dose of Acton-law-breaking logic, just now—she was already flush to the gills. Aside from his side-trips into vigilante justice, she'd a strong suspicion that Acton was involved in some sort of illegal gun-smuggling rig, although she'd never confronted him about it. She'd seen hints—and knew there were illegal guns in the safe at their flat—but decided she'd leave it for now; his murdering-people problem seemed much more pressing than his gun-running problem, and one small step at a time. "Well, at least tell me whether your first wife is slated to make a dramatic appearance—or is that another thing you don't want me to know ahead of time, so that I won't have to do any play-actin'?"

"No, the young woman they refer to is dead. She caught my interest, for a time, when I was at university." He paused. "They are not aware that she is dead, however. I am certain they've attempted to find her—and any child she may have had—but have come up empty. Therefore, Sir Stephen hopes to remain my heir until I can obtain a divorce from my first wife—no simple thing for me to accomplish, since she is missing, and there is a title at stake."

Yet again, she eyed him with deep suspicion. "Lucky, it is, that Sir Stephen discovered these long-hidden birth documents— faith, both of them at once—and was given a good reason to bring this wretched claim."

Acton made no comment, but instead reached into his inner jacket pocket. "Would you like some dried apricots? I have a packet, here."

Thoroughly astonished that her husband would carry around a packet of dried apricots— much less offer them to her—she barely refrained from recoiling. "No, thanks—I'm not very hungry."

"They're quite good," he cajoled. "Just have a taste."

But she was too busy frowning out the windscreen, and thinking over these latest revelations. "Whatever happened to the pretend-first-wife, Michael? How can they know who she is, but not know that she's dead?"

There was a small pause. "I am not certain," he said slowly, "that I wish to tell you."

Glancing at him in surprise, she caught a glimpse of black anger, quickly suppressed, and so said gently, "All right, Michael. But remember that it's a hardy banner, I am."

"I am sorry," he said suddenly, "to have to put you through all this."

"Never had a nicer time," she assured him, and lifted a corner of her mouth. "And the chairman is smitten, I think—another notch on my belt. By an enormous stroke of luck, his dear departed wife was also redheaded. Fancy that."

"We're coming up to the morgue; have you discovered anything further about the Lambeth robbery-murder, and the missing shoes?"

And—just like that—the subject is changed, she thought. "Gabriel phoned to say they got an ID straightaway because the girlfriend had called in, very worried. Of all things, the victim was a QC, from the Inner Temple."

"That," said Acton slowly, "is of immense interest."A Queen's Counsel was a deserving and experienced barrister who'd been awarded the title for exceptional work. It meant the victim was an elite member of the judicial system, and explained his fine suit of clothes even as it didn't explain what he'd been doing getting himself killed in a Lambeth alley.

Watching her husband's distracted reaction, Doyle ventured, "It opens up more questions than answers, I think. Seems a bit strange, that someone like him was knockin' about in such a place."

Acton was silent for a moment, thinking, and she stayed quiet, respecting the process until they parked. "Are you thinkin' the QC's murder may be connected to the ACC's corruption cases? That it's a shadow murder, of some sort?" A shadow murder was one committed in the hope that law enforcement would think it was the work of another murderer.

"It is an unusual victim, in an unusual place," was all he offered, but she knew that his attention had been caught for some reason.

A few minutes later, they were standing with the district coroner in his chilly morgue, looking over the remains of the John

Doe that the SOCO had mentioned—the other victim who'd been found without his shoes.

"Coshed. No ID, and no leads," said the coroner. "In another two days, he's set to be cremated—we got a judge's order."

"He may be a traveler," Doyle offered. "He looks to be in good shape, so he's not homeless. If he's a traveler, that might explain why no one has ID'd him."

"I believe," said Acton, "that instead he is a pawnbroker, from Fremont."

Doyle looked up at him in surprise, and then scrutinized the corpse, wracking her brain and noting the tattoos on his arms. "Oh—oh, that's right; the witness we spoke to about Giselle's murder. Her ex-husband, right?"

"William Blakney, I believe."

"I'll cancel the cremation order," said the coroner, who made a notation on his tablet.

6

It appeared that Blakney's death was something he hadn't foreseen.

Doyle was at home with her feet up, researching the dead pawnbroker on her laptop and mostly coming up empty. She called out to Acton, "Blakney had a record—minor stuff, like possession of stolen goods. Nothin' that stands out, but I suppose we can assume he's consortin' with criminal types, since that goes along with the pawnbroker-in-Fremont territory."

"Usually, that is the case," Acton agreed.

Doyle's scalp prickled, and she tried to decide why this would be. In a casual tone, she asked, "D'you think it has anythin' to do with the turf wars that we were investigatin', back when we spoke with him? Mayhap someone had some unfinished business."

Acton was sitting at his desk, and raised his head to gaze out the windows for a long moment. "Perhaps. Or he may have tried to extort the wrong people. Or he may have known too much. There are too many unknowns, as yet, to attempt a working theory."

Mental note, Doyle thought; don't ever be a pawnbroker, because there are too many reasons to be getting yourself murdered. "Why were the shoes missin'?"

"I'm afraid I cannot wager a guess."

"Perhaps, madam, the killer wished to dispose of incriminating evidence." Reynolds, their servant, was preparing dinner, and had been listening to the conversation.

Doyle lifted her brows, and typed a note. "Good one, Reynolds. Mayhap there was somethin' on the shoes that would have been helpful for forensics, and the killer didn't want to give the game away."

"Both victims were murdered in place," Acton pointed out. "And neither one in an unusual setting."

"Oh, that's right." For Reynolds' edification, she explained, "The posh QC was fleein' a robber, up an alley."

"Or perhaps he wasn't," Acton offered.

At sea, Doyle lifted her head to look at him. "Perhaps he wasn't? He was knockin' over ashcans, in his haste to get away."

Acton looked out the window again for a long moment. "Where did the fatal blow land?"

The penny dropped, and Doyle stared at him. "On his temple—bashed him hard enough that he'd have gone down like a plumb. So, he wasn't fleein'—unless he was cornered, or somethin'. Saints, Michael—let me text Gabriel and Williams; the scene might have been staged."

"That is a possibility." Acton walked over to open the oven door, and look within. "Ah, spinach casserole; one of my favorites."

"Is it?" she asked in surprise. "Didn't know that. Faith, you marry someone, and you think you know 'im."

Acton straightened up. "Let's have some, shall we?"

Doyle gazed upon him incredulously. "Never say spinach casserole is what's for dinner?"

"I thought we'd have something light, tonight."

She watched with acute dismay as Reynolds carefully removed the casserole from the oven. "Are you certain we don't have a spare pig's knuckle, lyin' about?" Doyle was not one for vegetables—except for mash, of course, and then only when it was accompanied by a fine pile of greasy bangers.

"Hush," Acton smiled, as he invited her to join him at the table. "You'll hurt Reynolds' feelings."

"Reynolds doesn't have feelin's, do you Reynolds?"

"Certainly not, madam."

Acton decided to change the subject, as he signaled for the servant to serve up the casserole. "What else have you discovered, with respect to Blakney's murder? Anything of interest?"

Doyle contemplated the leafy mass of vegetation on her plate with deep suspicion. "Unidentified John Doe, found off Emert Street. Williams was the CSM, although there wasn't much of a follow-up—he was probably too busy, poor man, and there was nothin' to go on, anyway. The judge signed off on a cremation order with no further ado."

This was understandable, unfortunately; if there was no ID and no leads, the CID tended to put its resources to work elsewhere—particularly as the aforesaid resources were stretched thin, after the corruption scandal had laid waste to many of their ranks. "The m.o. looks similar to the QC's murder—an ambush, then coshed and robbed. Shoes taken, as I mentioned."

Suddenly struck, she paused in taking up her fork. "Faith, Michael; it should have been an easy thing to ID Blakney, since his prints are on file for his pawnbroker's license, and he had past criminal convictions. It's a shame that no one ran his prints, but I suppose they were waitin' for someone to report a missin' man."

Tentatively, she took a bite of the casserole and then suggested to Reynolds, "I think a pat of butter wouldn't go amiss."

"I believe," said Acton firmly, "that we are out of butter."

This was not true, and Doyle fixed her scornful gaze upon her husband. "I'm not goin' to sacrifice butter, too. I already gave up coffee, and a body can only bear so much."

"Very well, then," Acton conceded, and signaled to the servant.

As they ate the buttered spinach, Doyle eyed her husband covertly, having the feeling that he was secretly pleased about something. "What's next?"

"That," he said thoughtfully, "is a good question."

She lifted a brow in amusement. "Never say you're stymied—I'll not believe it."

He tilted his head. "We need more information. Let's wait until we have a preliminary on the QC, to see where we are, and what is needed."

"All right. I'll alert Williams and Gabriel that these two murders may be related. Should I wait until we've somethin' more concrete, or should I put that in the report now?"

"Now, by all means," he replied, and her scalp prickled, although she didn't understand why it would.

That night, Doyle had another one of her dreams. They happened occasionally—strange, vivid dreams, usually featuring someone who was no longer alive, trying to convey a message that never seemed to be very straightforward. Since she always had a hard time concentrating on these occasions, more often than not the dreams were a source of frustration and disquiet—although they'd saved her life, once, so there was that.

This one was no different; Doyle dreamed she was standing in a darkened, outdoor area, and the wind was blowing even though she couldn't feel it. Before her stood a familiar figure, impeccably dressed, and regarding her with an impassive expression.

Doyle could scarce believe it, and had to force herself to be civil. "Dr. Harding; you've got some nerve. Best watch yourself, else I'll give you another dose of excessive force." The man was Acton's former psychiatrist, and he'd been knee-deep in the recent plot to do away with the fair Doyle.

"Little good it would do you," the man replied. "I'm not alive, if you haven't noticed."

"Oh—well, I suppose I'm sorry for it." Best not inquire into the particulars of how that came about; Acton was not one to let the grass grow under his feet, when it came to acts of bloody vengeance.

"You can't just trust him."

With a mighty effort, she frowned, trying to focus. "Trust who? Acton?"

"Not this time."

Although it hardly seemed necessary, she replied with some scorn, "You're the last person that I'll be takin' advice from, thank you very much."

"And you've forgotten about Elena."

She stared at him in confusion. Elena was Detective Sergeant Munoz's sister, and she'd recently been rescued after having been coerced into sex slavery. "I haven't forgotten about Elena; she's doin' fine, now—well, all things considered. She's married to Inspector Habib."

"You've forgotten the whole point," he insisted. "Try to think."

"I can think as well as the next person," she retorted, stung. "And I like Aiki much better than you. Where's Aiki?"

But there was no response, and she was staring at her bedroom wall, trying to still her fast-beating heart.

"All right?" murmured Acton sleepily. He pulled her back against his chest, and as was his habit, absently began stroking her arms.

"Just tryin' to get comfortable, Michael; sorry I woke you." Because the last needful thing was to let Acton know that his dead psychiatrist—the one who'd tried to kill her—was haunting her dreams, and telling her not to trust her husband.

7

He wasn't certain whether he should just allow it to play out, so that a valuable lesson was learned.

Doyle was seated at the deli which was located a few blocks from headquarters, and waiting for DI Williams to come meet her. She'd asked if they could meet off-campus, which was what she tended to do when she needed his advice on non-official matters. She'd been puzzling over Harding's middle-of-the-night message, and had finally realized what he'd meant. As much as it pained her to admit it, the dead man was right—she'd missed something important.

Williams came through the door, dressed in his shirt-sleeves since it was a fine day outside. He was tall and blond—and nearly as clever as Acton, which was truly saying something. He could probably be counted as Doyle's best friend, even though they'd had some uncomfortable moments because he carried a torch for her fair self. Nonetheless, he'd been in her corner, time and again, and the unfortunate fact that he acted as Acton's henchman in carrying out her husband's dark deeds did not change the fact that she trusted him. He was the only person, aside from Acton, who knew about her perceptive abilities, which was a measure of just how much she did trust him.

After spotting her, he came over to pull up a chair, and she noted with a twinge of sympathy that he didn't seem his usual self—looked a bit pulled about, he did—but this was only to be expected; they were all being run ragged until more foot soldiers could be enlisted to fight the good fight.

He smiled, and reached for the coffee she'd bought him. "Hey."

"Hey, yourself. I'm that grateful that you're willin' to consort with a bigamist."

He set the cup down, and contemplated it. "I think, technically, you're not the one who's the bigamist."

"Why, that's an excellent point, DI Williams, and I do feel much better." She hadn't been certain that he knew about the succession hearing, but it seemed clear he was up-to-speed on the latest doings in the wretched House of Acton.

His next words only verified this. "I don't know if it's a good idea to draw me into this, Kath."

She made a face, and took a sip of his coffee—technically, she'd given it up, but sneaked a half-cup, here and there, just so as to stay sharp. Pregnancy had a way of making one un-sharp, and she needed her wits about her, what with Acton pulling strings in the background and Williams being all guarded about something, although he was doing his best to hide it.

As she gave him back his cup, she said lightly, "Not to worry, I don't want to spend another minute thinkin' about the stupid succession—and Acton has another title to spare, anyways, so it all seems a bit greedy, to us lowly peasants."

Williams raised his sharp gaze to hers. "Acton has another title?"

Belatedly, she remembered that this may not be a piece of information that was intended for public consumption and so she hastily disclaimed, "It's complicated, but that's not what I was wantin' to talk to you about. Remember Dr. Harding?"

He accepted this rather disjointed change of topic with an ironic nod. "I do."

Of course, he did. Williams had punched the good doctor out, and then—for good measure—had framed him for assault. "Yes; well, did we ever figure out what Harding's motive was, when he tried to shoot me? It's not as though he acted alone, but Acton has never mentioned him again."

Immediately, her companion was wary—probably because he knew very well why Acton did not speak of Harding. "Why are you wondering about him? Has something come up?"

Glossing over the fact that something had indeed come up in the form of an unwelcome spectre, she replied, "I just wish I knew what Harding's motivation was. Was he tryin' to bump Edward out of the succession, or was he tryin' to bump Acton off the corruption case?"

But Williams was too wily to be caught giving out state secrets. "I don't think it matters, Kath, and I wouldn't ask too many questions."

She blew out a frustrated breath. "No. And it would be little use, anyway; Acton is the grand master of not answerin' questions that he'd rather not."

"Tell me about Acton's other title."

She looked up at him, a bit irritated because he'd been no help with her Harding questions. "Why on earth do you care? It's *such* a passel of nonsense, and Acton won't tell me whatever it is that he's cookin' up."

"I think," Williams said slowly, "that the succession necessarily impacts your safety—yours and Edward's—so Acton is making sure no one is motivated to attack you again."

With a mighty effort, she shook herself out of her sulks, and acknowledged that this was a fair point. Williams always made good points, but in doing so didn't make her feel like she was a dunce, which was greatly appreciated. "I know—I know that's at the root of it all. I'm just out of sorts, I suppose. It comes from havin' been cut out of the loop, bein' as I'm the weak link."

"I suppose you'll just have to trust him, Kath."

Reminded of Harding's words on this subject, she retorted a bit too forcefully, "Of *course* I trust him, Thomas, it's just—" She frowned, trying to put her instinct into words. "He's bein' all Holmes-y, and holdin' his cards very close to the vest, but he seems—I don't know, he seems—troubled, I guess is the word. He's a bit troubled, but he doesn't want me to see that he's troubled." She paused, debating whether to say more, since she shouldn't be speaking about her marriage with anyone else— faith, she didn't even speak about it with herself. "Acton figured out that the QC's murder was staged, but I got the impression that he wasn't sure that he wanted to let anyone else know that it had been staged."

Williams frowned in turn, and fiddled with the sugar packets. "Perhaps he wasn't certain it was staged, and that's why he hesitated to mention it. The victim may have turned to make a stand and then been struck, which would explain the location of the wound."

Doyle nodded without comment. This would have been a decent argument, had it not been clear that the body was positioned in such a way so as to make it appear he was in the act of flight. And as Williams—of all people—should know this, Doyle diplomatically changed the subject. "Actually, I wanted to talk to you about somethin' else."

He glanced up. "Oh? What's up?"

"We've forgotten somethin' important, in all the fuss. Elena Munoz was forced into the sex ring—but why Elena?"

This was indeed a good question. In the course of investigating the corruption rig, they'd discovered that the villains were blackmailing others into compliance by threatening to coerce their female relatives into sex slavery. One such victim was Detective Sergeant Munoz's sister Elena, but it had not occurred to anyone to wonder why Elena had been seized.

Williams's expression grew grave, and he nodded. "Good catch. It must have to do with Munoz—right? She's in the CID, and it can't be a coincidence. They must have been trying to control Munoz, in some way."

Doyle leaned forward, and lowered her voice. "But d'you see the problem? If the villains tried to contact Munoz after Elena was grabbed, she's never mentioned it." Reluctantly, she added, "And recall that Munoz was recruited to work for the Anti-Corruption Command." The very same ACC that was orchestrating the takedown of the corruption ring—and who Acton thought were involved up to their necks.

He thought about this, a slight frown between his brows. "And?"

Doyle tried to remember what she was supposed to know and not supposed to know, and then gave it up. "Acton thinks that the ACC is bent, too, even though they're supposedly the ones doin' the investigatin'."

Unsurprisingly, Williams lowered his head in alarm, and glanced around. "You can't just say things like that, Kath."

She eyed him. "What do you think?"

He pressed his lips together. "I'm not going to tell you what I think."

She crossed her arms, and leaned back to sulk. "I don't think it's fair that I have to be the weak link, all the time. It's someone else's turn."

He crossed his arms in turn. "I don't think it is possible to say the right thing, so I will make no response."

With a sigh, she conceded this point, and leaned forward again. "All right—then just listen to me, and I'll try to come up with a workin' theory. Let's assume the ACC is bent, even though it dare-not-be-spoken-aloud." She paused, contemplating the linoleum table top. "So—mayhap someone from the ACC wanted Munoz to infiltrate the corruption investigation, and find out what was goin' on. They'd got wind that the jig was up, and were wantin' to find out how much was known so they could decide whether to flee the scene."

But Williams pointed out the obvious. "Why wouldn't they know already? It was the ACC's investigation, after all, and therefore they'd be infiltrating themselves. That doesn't make much sense, Kath."

This was irrefutable, and she raised her head to gaze out the windows, thinking. "No, it doesn't. But I think it's important that we find out why Elena was seized." She met his eyes with some reluctance. "Should we assume Munoz has been compromised?"

He let out a long breath. "Perhaps you should discuss this with Acton."

Slowly, she shook her head. "Acton wants me well-away from whatever's going on."

"Then stay away, Kath."

With another sigh, she confessed, "I can't. A ghost is plaguin' me."

He regarded her with an expression that was equal parts astonishment and amusement. "A ghost? Really?"

Smiling, she shrugged. "It's complicated."

"I'll bet. Is your ghost acquainted with any of my ghosts, from the Santero case?"

This was of interest, and Doyle was more than willing to be distracted. "Oh? Never say you've your own ghosts?"

"The Santero sends out *orishas* to wreak revenge, and so no one is willing to grass on him."

Doyle stared at him. "Well, that's impressive. Faith, none of the ghosts I've met are half so useful."

"Then I guess the Santero's got more pull than you do."

Doyle was aware that her instinct was prodding her to pay attention, which was no hardship since she found the subject of great interest. "Tell me how it all works—faith, it's hard to believe this type of thing is taken seriously, in this day and age."

"Basically, it's a lot like voodoo."

She had to laugh. "I like the way you make it sound as though I'd know all about voodoo, Thomas."

He smiled, and explained, "It's another primitive religion based on black magic, curses, and animal sacrifices. A Santero is in the manner of a priest, and is believed to control the *orishas,* so that they do his bidding."

Suddenly struck, Doyle said slowly, "So—is this one of those things where you need a personal item, to put a curse on your victim?"

He shrugged. "I suppose that's part of it, yes."

"Like—like shoes, for instance?"

There was a slight pause, whilst he regarded her with a glimmer of amusement. "I hope you're not going to tell me your working theory is that these murder victims were coshed by *orishas.*"

She made an impatient sound. "I'm not sayin' it's *truly* ghosts, Thomas—for heaven's sake, ghosts can only do so much. But it could easily be the suspect's minions, makin' it look like supernatural mumbo-jumbo. And that would explain why everyone's afraid, and no one wants to cross the Santero—it's all smoke and mirrors."

But once again, Williams pointed out the flaw with this working theory. "That doesn't make a lot of sense, Kath. There's little point in stealing an object for a curse, if the victim you stole it from is already dead."

"Oh—oh, of course." Frustrated, she leaned back, and rubbed her eyes with her palms. "Faith, I'm comin' up against brick walls on all sides—it's annoyin', is what it is. And I suppose I shouldn't be surprised that everyone is tryin' to dupe me, since I'm as dupable as they come."

Williams regarded her in surprise. "Who's trying to dupe you?"

Her eyes slid to his. "You are."

His gaze fell to study his hands, clasped on the table. "No comment."

There was a small, tense moment, and then she touched his hand in sympathy. "All right, Thomas; I'll not hound you about whatever-it-is that I'm not supposed to know. Let's speak of mundane matters, instead. How's our Miss Percy?" Morgan Percy was the junior barrister on the Santero's defense team—a clever and rather ruthless young woman whom they'd met in an earlier case. It was clear that she was mightily attracted to the worthy DI Williams, which was an interesting situation, since they were currently on opposite sides of a notorious murder case.

Doyle had the impression that Williams was attracted to Percy, but was put-off by a few glaring gaps in the girl's moral character—which, to be fair, appeared to include major crimes-committing. It was a bit ironic, though, because Williams thought nothing of helping Acton with his dark deeds, but balked when it came to Percy's. She didn't press him on it; they'd quarreled on the subject in the past, and she'd learned her lesson.

"Miss Percy is doing an excellent job of defending her client."

She heard the nuance beneath the words, and sympathized. "We have to keep the system honest, Thomas; even the Santero is entitled to a defense."

"Not when it's so clear that he's a soulless brute, Kath."

Diplomatically, she made no response, but wondered why her scalp prickled.

8

It would not go amiss, perhaps, to make it clear that he was aware of the circumstances surrounding Blakney's death, but not make it clear as to what was to happen next.

Because she needed to follow up on the Munoz angle, Doyle made a point of stopping by the other girl's cubicle, once she'd returned to headquarters. After having saved Munoz by jumping off Greyfriars Bridge, Doyle was now in the uncomfortable position of being linked with the other girl in the public's eye even though they weren't necessarily friends. The situation was equally resented by Munoz, who was—to be fair—Doyle's superior in every measure of detective work, but had to suffer the ignominy of being the one who'd needed rescuing.

Doyle rested her arms across the top of Munoz's cubicle and tried to think of how to find out what she needed to find out. "Hallo, Munoz. How're things?"

Munoz looked up, immediately defensive. "What do you mean by that?"

Belatedly, Doyle remembered that Munoz was currently involved with the notorious Philippe Savoie of Watch List and inheriting-Trestles-from-Acton fame, which was not a particularly good career move for a DS at the Met. Although, apparently—if Doyle was keeping her plots and counter-plots straight—Savoie was Acton's plant, and hopefully wasn't truly attempting to turn Acton's ancestral estate into a hideout for underworld misdeeds.

To test out what was known, Doyle offered heartily, "It's all rather awkward, actually. If you marry Savoie, you'll have to file my initials off all the silverware."

With an impatient gesture, Munoz tossed her hair back over her shoulder. "What are you *talking* about, Doyle?"

Doyle took some comfort in the knowledge that Munoz was a fellow weak link, and shrugged. "Just teasin'. Don't get all bristly."

Her mouth pulled down, the girl turned back to her typing. "I'm not serious about Savoie—I can't be."

This was a relief, and Doyle ventured, "Yes—well, it's unlikely that he's reformed. That kind of tiger doesn't change his spots."

"Tigers don't have spots, Doyle. They have stripes."

Doyle frowned. "Which is the one that has spots?"

"A cheetah."

"A leopard, too," added Doyle, trying to make up for her lapse.

Munoz pulled her mobile, to check her messages. "No, those aren't spots, on a leopard."

"Well, be that as it may, Munoz, its unlikely Savoie's reformed his notorious self."

The other girl added with heavy irony, "Not to mention I had a fling with his brother."

"There is that, of course. I suppose things could get awkward, when everyone sits down together for the Christmas goose."

Munoz paused, and lifted her gaze for a moment. "He's got a sweet little boy."

"He does—we saw him at the church, that time."

"I don't think the mother is in the picture. He never mentions her."

And with good reason, thought Doyle, but aloud she said, "I suppose that makes things a bit easier for you."

The beauty tossed her head. "I'm not serious about him, Doyle."

"Right-o," said Doyle, and drew her own conclusions.

Pointedly, Munoz began packing up her rucksack. "I have to interview the girlfriend on the QC case, so I've got to go."

Doyle was instantly outraged. "Why wasn't *I* given that assignment? That's *my* case."

As Munoz stood, her gaze rested for a significant moment on Doyle's protruding belly. "I think Gabriel's worried that you're sick, or something. He told me that you had to leave the scene this morning in a hurry."

"No—I wasn't sick; somethin' came up, and I had to leave." Doyle saw that an opening had been provided, and took it. "Since Gabriel was mistaken, I get to come along with you for the interview. That's only fair."

But Munoz could not look upon such a plan with enthusiasm and made a face, as she brushed by Doyle. "I hate it when we work together—everyone expects me to appreciate you."

"Don't let that throw you off," Doyle offered as she followed the other girl down the aisle way. "Treat any such suggestion with open scorn."

"Don't tempt me." With poor grace, the girl spoke over her shoulder. "You can come, but I have the lead."

"Grand. Do we think the girlfriend's a suspect?" This was a reflex question—usually, murderers were someone close to the victim, and a girlfriend would be carefully scrutinized before she was ruled out.

Munoz pointed out, "Seems unlikely in this case, since he was coshed and robbed in an alley."

Stubbornly, Doyle persisted. "Remember that we think the scene was staged. And she could have hired someone to cosh him, if she didn't want to get her hands dirty."

"All right; I'll keep an open mind. Just try not to say anything stupid."

With an effort, Doyle bit back a retort and remembered that she was here to do a bit of probing. "I'm surprised you're available to help out, in the first place. Weren't you workin' on an assignment for the ACC? Are you still undercover for them?"

Bluntly, the other girl replied, "I'm not supposed to talk about it. I had to sign a NDA."

Doyle nodded, reluctantly conceding that this was only to be expected. "I suppose a non-disclosure agreement is standard procedure. After all, they may be investigatin' someone who's innocent, and you'd not want anyone tainted, by word leakin' out." Frustrated, Doyle wondered how she was going to find out what was going on if she wasn't allowed to find out what was going on.

As they waited for the lift, the other girl frowned slightly. "Do you know anyone, over there at the ACC?"

"I can thankfully say that I do not. Why?"

The doors slid open, and the Spanish girl shrugged, as she stepped within. "They seem a bit strange, is all. Everyone else resents them, so I suppose you'd have to be a bit odd, to want to do that kind of work."

"Well, we need them to ferret out the corrupt cops, Munoz—we've just seen what happens when the system gets corrupted. It's horrendous, and now no one trusts any of us."

The girl glanced into her reflection in the lift doors, and smoothed her hair back. "I know, I know. But it doesn't seem like they are looking at corrupt cops—it's almost MI 5-type stuff."

This seemed a bit ominous, and Doyle offered, "Gabriel's on loan from MI 5; can you ask him about it? Mayhap the units work together, sometimes."

"I can't. I've got the NDA."

Doyle nodded as they walked out into the lobby, and wished Munoz weren't quite so by-the-book. On the other hand, Doyle had been scrutinizing Munoz very carefully, and hadn't picked up even a hint that the girl was being influenced, in some way, by the villains. Perhaps it was just a coincidence that her sister had been seized—however unlikely that seemed. Harding-the-ghost seemed to think it was important, but he also thought she shouldn't trust Acton, for some reason, which only went to show that he was as dim-witted in the afterlife as he'd been in real life.

As they got into the unmarked vehicle, Munoz instructed, "You should read the prelim, to get up-to-speed. Gabriel spoke to the QC's girlfriend on the phone, and he thinks she's worth an interview."

"Give me the short version," suggested Doyle. "I'll get sick, if I read in the car."

Munoz gave her a look that indicated she was well-aware this was a lame excuse for laziness. "The girlfriend says they were newly engaged—she's a flight attendant, and met the QC on a flight."

Doyle raised a skeptical brow. "I wonder if she's sportin' a ring?" It was a strange truism of detective work that the girlfriends of dead men tended to elevate their status to fiancée, now that there was no longer anyone around to refute it.

"I don't know, one way or another, but Gabriel thought she was sincerely upset."

Doyle made no comment, being as how she may be a weak link, but she was also a fine discerner of who was sincerely upset, and who wasn't.

They met the woman at her flat, and introduced themselves as they were seated at the kitchen table. The witness was in her thirties, and a bit rough around the edges—blowsy, Doyle's mother would have said. She was a slightly plump, had a generous bosom, and wore a bit too much make-up, considering the situation.

Not one of those posh flight attendants, then, thought Doyle; and it was not a surprise to see that there was no engagement ring in evidence. However, the woman emanated a profound sadness—apparently, she was sincerely grieving the dead man.

She explained to the detectives that she'd come home for a four-day layover, and had grown alarmed when she couldn't contact her boyfriend. "He's busy, being a barrister and all, but I thought it was strange. He always called me back as soon as he had the chance."

Munoz checked her notes, and offered in a neutral tone, "I understand that his wife made the ID at the morgue."

But the woman didn't seem shaken by this revelation, and nodded. "Yes. They were getting a divorce, so's he could marry me. They hadn't lived together in quite some time, even though they stayed married."

I'll bet my teeth he'd no intention of going through with a divorce, thought Doyle, who'd seen this situation many a time. Divorces cost money, and why go to the trouble, if your estranged wife doesn't care whether you're consorting with women of this stripe?

But Munoz had seen the hint of a motive. "Do you know how his wife felt about you? Or about his philandering?"

Good one, thought Doyle, and resolved to pay closer attention.

But the woman seemed genuinely surprised by the suggestion. "You mean was she behind the murder? Oh, no—I'm certain. She was tired of him, too, and ready for the divorce. She knew all about me, and the other girlfriend before me. It was all very civilized."

Yet again, Doyle reflected upon the foolishness of a woman who'd believe protestations of love from such a man, and then asked, to show Munoz that she could also spot a motive, "Who was the other girlfriend, before you?"

For the first time, the witness' spirits plucked up. "Oh—she was someone from his work. She didn't know he was dating me on the sly, but she was suspicious, and called my number from his mobile."

"That's brass," said Munoz, and Doyle noted that her compatriot couldn't keep a tinge of admiration from her tone.

"Oh, she was brassy, all right. He liked me better, and so he dropped her and decided he wanted to get married." She paused, and her lip trembled. "He said he was sick to death of the deceitful people he had to deal with, and that I made him feel comfortable—like an old slipper."

Munoz passed the woman a handkerchief, and they waited for a sympathetic moment before getting back to business. "And the old girlfriend's name, if you know?"

"Morgan something," the woman said, her brow knit with the effort of remembering. "She worked at his chambers."

9

It had been a foolish mistake, but he could feel some sympathy; he'd made a foolish mistake himself, once.

On the way back in the car, Munoz was musing aloud over what they'd learned, whilst Doyle was sincerely regretting that she'd asked to come along.

"We should follow up, just as a matter of form, but I think we can rule her out—the wife too; unlikely she'd want to kill him, if this situation has been going on for some time. I suppose we could check the mobile records to see if there were any suspicious calls, but it almost seems unnecessary—this looks more and more like a stranger-robbery."

"Yes," Doyle agreed glumly. "It does seem unnecessary." Mainly, this was because Doyle was certain that the spurned girl-friend was Morgan Percy, the junior barrister on Williams' case, and Morgan Percy was the type of person who was willing to kill people—or at least arrange to have them killed, as it seemed un-likely that Percy would deign to swing a truncheon in her mani-cured hands. In point of fact, Doyle knew that Percy had killed her old boss—the head of her chambers—to protect his repu-tation. Unfortunately, no one else knew this—save Acton—and so now Doyle was squarely skewered on the horns of a dilemma, which always seemed to be her natural state, post-marriage.

Doyle had been semi-friendly with Percy, and Williams had been—she suspected—more than semi-friendly. A kettle of snakes, it was—if she raised her suspicion of Percy's involvement in the QC's case, then the murder of the old boss might come to light, and Acton had already decided that particular sleeping dog should be allowed to lie.

On the other hand, if Percy killed the QC out of jealous spite, Doyle should not cover it up—the girl was dangerous, and should be brought to justice. Not to mention if this was indeed a spite murder, it also meant that the other murder—Blakney, the shoe-less pawnbroker—was completely unrelated.

Doyle frowned, because her trusty instinct had been telling her otherwise. There was always the possibility that her trusty instinct was wrong—unless Percy was dating the pawnbroker, too? This seemed highly unlikely, but the fair Doyle should probably shake her stumps and find out.

And there was yet another dilemma, in what seemed like an unending list; should she tell Acton what she'd discovered? Did Acton know, already? After all, she'd had the sense that he was trying to keep her away from something, so perhaps she should follow Williams' advice to stay away and trust her husband, despite advice to the contrary by an irksome ghost.

On the other hand, there was the continuing problem of Acton's taking-justice-into-his-own-hands tendencies; she shouldn't just stand idly by, and put blinders on. She was fairly certain that she was supposed to try to save Acton from himself—or at least, that was the general impression she'd gleaned, based on her strange and eventful marriage to the man.

But on yet another hand, perhaps she was jumping the gun, thinking that the QC's murder could be laid at Percy's door. The girl had killed her old boss out of admiration and respect, and this murder—if indeed it was a spite murder—would not fit her m.o. With a twinge of guilt, Doyle tried to decide if she was leaping upon any excuse not to make a decision, but was thankfully interrupted when Munoz's voice broke into her thoughts.

"You're quiet. Are you worried that Holmes is seeing someone like her, on the side?"

"Holmes" was Acton's nickname amongst the lesser detectives, and Doyle chose to be amused, rather than annoyed. "I think I can safely assume that Holmes is not seein' anyone on the side."

"Don't be so sure; you *are* pregnant."

"Give over, Munoz." Interestingly enough, pregnancy did not seem to abate her husband's ardent desire to jump her bones on a daily basis, but this was not a piece of information she wished to share with Munoz. "So, what's next?"

"I'll write up a report, and tell Williams we don't think the wife or girlfriend is a suspect. I'll let him decide about allocating resources for a recent-records search; that's above my pay grade."

Doyle looked out the window for a moment. "Should we take a gander at the QC's caseload? He was criminal defense, so he may have been killed by a vengeful client, or somethin'."

Munoz quirked her mouth. "Maybe the Santero put a curse on him."

Doyle turned to her in surprise. "Why—that's right; the QC was workin' in the same chambers as the defense for the Santero case."

With a pitying look, the other girl forestalled any conclusions-leaping. "I was kidding, Doyle—there's no connection. The QC wasn't working on that case, and even if he were, the Santero's not going to put a curse on a member of his own defense team."

But Doyle's scalp was prickling like a live thing, and she was trying to understand why it would—there must be a connection, somewhere. "What if—what if the QC stumbled across somethin' dicey about the Santero in the course of his own work, and the Santero decided he should be eliminated. I think we should try to rule it out, at least."

But Munoz was not having it, and shrugged an irritated shoulder. "Of all the stupid theories you've ever had, I think this one is the stupidest. How would we investigate around attorney-client privilege? There's absolutely nothing to go on, and we haven't enough resources, as it is."

Since Doyle couldn't tell Munoz why she was so certain that there was indeed a connection, she was forced to fall back on persuasion, which was not exactly her strong suit. "Well, hear me out, Munoz; I was just tellin' Williams that I think no one is willin' to grass on the Santero because they're all afraid, and the reason that they're all afraid is because he's havin' people killed, pretending that it's bein' done by evil spirits under his command." She paused, considering this. "It's a crackin' good plan, because whilst we might find a few brave souls who are willin' to grass on a mere mortal, we'll not find anyone who's willin' to grass on murderin'-evil-spirits. No one's that brave."

Munoz rolled her eyes in the manner of someone who knows she is exhibiting stoic patience. "But there *isn't* a connection, Doyle, and even if there were, I don't know how we'd find it."

Stubbornly, Doyle insisted, "It's a hunch, I guess. But we've no other suspects, so may as well rule it out."

Munoz was fast losing interest, as she turned into the parking structure. "It's not a decent working theory, Doyle. Even if the QC stumbled across incriminating information, that wouldn't be sufficient motivation for his murder. If that was the case, the Santero would have to kill everyone on his defense team for good measure."

Doyle frowned, finding it hard to argue with this logic, and casting about for a better working theory. "Mayhap he wanted to keep his own defense counsel in line—scare them, by killin' the QC."

Munoz grimaced. "Well, that would definitely do the trick— I'd turn in my horsehair wig, and start studying up on archeology, or something a lot less dangerous."

As it seemed clear that Munoz was not taking her seriously, Doyle persisted, "We should try to come up with an investigative protocol, just to rule it out."

"Sounds like waste of resources to me," Munoz opined bluntly, as she turned off the car. "But you're welcome to pitch it to Williams. I've got an assignment this afternoon, so thankfully I will be nowhere near, when you do."

Suddenly alert, Doyle asked in a casual tone, "Oh? What sort of assignment?"

"I'm not allowed to say," was the only response.

10

Carefully, he crept out of bed, so as not to awaken her. He'd work to do.

"I t's not about love," Harding was explaining to Doyle. "It never is. It's about externalization. That, and impulse control disorders."

Struggling to focus as the wind swirled around them, Doyle scowled. "That's a pint full o' ridiculous, is what that is. I think that you can't see beneath the surface, and can't see the good that's underneath it all. You're one of those cyntics."

With all appearance of long-suffering patience, the ghost crossed his arms, and bent his head. "Cynics, I think you mean. Good God; to think I've got to try and thread this needle."

But Doyle was not going to stand by and be insulted by someone who should be begging her pardon, fasting. "I never asked for your help, you know—take your sorry self off, and be gone."

The psychiatrist was seen to sigh. "Let's start again, shall we?"

Reluctantly, Doyle calmed herself, and tried to remember what she was supposed to be remembering. "All right, all right—I'm workin' on the Munoz angle, but I don't know how I'm goin' to find anythin' out. There's an NDA."

He looked upon her with mild incredulity. "Well then, find out without making her disclose anything. You're a detective, aren't you?"

"Faith, I'm too busy worryin' about the stupid shoes," she groused.

"I don't have shoes," he pointed out.

She could see that this was true, and she stared at his stockinged feet for a moment.

"You can't trust him, you know. Not this time."

Raising her head, she stared at him. "Who? Acton? Williams?"

"Yes," he said.

She subsided into silence for a moment. "There's somethin' I wanted to ask you—whether you know—"

"Don't ask me, ask him," the ghost interrupted. "You're both avoiding the subject."

But she slowly shook her head. "We're not good at bein' honest, Acton and me—we've already tried it."

"Ask him. Abreaction is often helpful, when it comes to pathological memories."

Doyle blew out a breath. "Haven't a *clue*, what you just said."

He turned his palms up, and shrugged. "Sometimes it helps to talk it out."

Brightening, she nodded. "Oh? Well that's not a hardship. Faith, I can gabble with the best of 'em."

"Indeed."

There was a small silence, and reluctantly she admitted, "I don't know if I'm that brave. Everyone thinks I am, but it's all puffery, and sleight-of-hand."

"Classic avoidant," he agreed.

Annoyed by his smug certainty, she retorted, "You don't understand the people who live beneath your fancy labels. Percy killed her old boss out of love."

He shook his head, and repeated with weary patience, "It's never about love. It's about externalization."

She puzzled over this, as the wind blew, and the man before her stood, unmoving. "Are we talkin' about why Acton murders people, or why Percy does?"

"Both are dissociative."

Because she didn't like Acton's being lumped in with Percy, she made a childish attempt to take the psychiatrist down a peg. "You needn't feel so superior, you know. We got your goat, between Williams and me."

His raised his brows in pleased surprise, as though a child had suddenly made a brilliant observation. "Exactly. Now, do it again."

She woke with a start, and tried to stay quiet, only to discover that Acton was not in bed with her. Brushing her hair back from her face, she could see a dim light from his desk, where he sat at his computer in the next room.

As she gathered the comforter around her, she called out, "What's the point of havin' a husband, if there's no one here to cosset me when I wake up in the middle of the night?"

He looked up with a smile as she padded over to the desk, dragging the comforter behind her. "I beg your pardon. Are you in need of cosseting?"

"I am indeed. What are you workin' on, that's more important?"

"I am setting a trap," he said easily, and it was the truth.

A bit taken aback, she rallied him, "Not for me, I hope?"

"No point; I've already trapped you."

Fondly, she ran a hand along the top of his head. "I was a willin' mark—I don't think that counts as any sort of victory, husband."

"My finest hour," he teased, and leaned his head back for her kiss. "How is Edward?"

She placed a fond hand on her belly. "Edward is excellent—never finer. He's goin' to be hugely disappointed, though, if Savoie gets to have Trestles, and he's left hangin' on the gate, lookin' in."

He took her hand, and playfully placed his fingertips against hers, spreading her hand. "I imagine you are well-aware that Savoie will inherit neither Trestles, nor the title."

"Yes, well—you definitely pushed the other side off their pins, at the hearin'." She leaned against him thoughtfully, and wound her arms around his neck. "I think I've figured somethin' out, though. Remember when we were at Trestles, and I told you that the ghost-knight was all afret about Savoie? I bet he doesn't understand that it's all a trick, and he thinks you're truly goin' to hand the place over to him. He's that angry about it, on account of havin' fought the French, and all."

Acton received this revelation with commendable calm. "I see. Do you think he is dangerous?"

She considered this doubtfully. "I don't think so, but everybody else is afraid of him. I don't know if he can do anythin' other than rant, but I'd rather not be the one testin' him." She thought about it, and sighed. "I suppose I'll have to go to Trestles, and explain it all to him."

Acton tilted his head. "Now? It may not be the best time to make a visit."

She couldn't help but smile. "Whist, Michael; it would be a rare treat—we could show up, bold as brass, and serve up a screechin' fistfight in the portrait gallery, just to confirm everyone's bad opinion of me." She paused. "But we should make the visit, I think. Best take no chances—there's somethin' brewin', and it makes me uneasy. Wouldn't want the knight to burn the place down, out of spite."

"All right," he agreed, as though this were an ordinary topic of conversation. "I will make arrangements."

She brushed his hair the wrong way, so that it stood up on end. "And speakin' of fistfights, when's the next go-round with the committee? I'll wager the chairman would like to do some cossetin' of his own, if you catch my meanin'."

"The next hearing is early next week. Promise me you won't elope with the chairman; at least wait until we obtain a ruling."

She laughed, and leaned her head down, so that she pressed her cheek against his. "I don't know, Michael; if I practiced my wiles, it could tip the case in your favor."

He placed a fond hand on her arm. "Just the opposite; he'll rule that we aren't married, so as to have you to himself."

"A point in his favor, then. He'd definitely be a dotin' suitor."

"More doting than me?" he teased.

She laughed again, because Acton rarely referred to his neurosis and this seemed a good sign, what with the stupid psychiatrist lecturing her. "No—you take the palm, my friend. Although the chairman probably doesn't have bloodthirsty ghosts tucked away in his keep, which is a point in his favor, all in all."

There was a slight pause, whilst her husband ran a gentle hand along her arm. "What's bothering you, Kathleen?"

She blew out a breath, and bent her head against his, for a moment. "You know that I hate it when we're honest with each other—it gives me the willies. Some things are better left unsaid."

"I cannot disagree." He was silent, waiting.

"Only—well, if you want to tell me about this first-wife person—the girl your father killed—I'm willin' to listen."

She sensed his surprise, and his withdrawal. "Why do you think my father killed her?"

"I just do, Michael."

Absently, he ducked his chin, and caressed the arms around his neck. "It is an ugly story, Kathleen."

Shrugging a shoulder, she observed, "We've seen our share of ugly stories in this line of work, you and me."

She could sense he was taken aback, and that she'd get nowhere with this tonight—or perhaps any other night. He said only, "Thank you."

She straightened up. "Good; now that we're done with our dose of honesty, I can garner your opinion, instead. I was goin' to mention to Williams that I think there's a connection betwixt my QC case and the Santero case, but Munoz thinks he'll laugh in my face and throw me out of his office."

"What is the connection?" Acton turned in his chair to face her, and she had the immediate impression that he was suddenly wary, although his outward appearance didn't reflect it.

"The QC is from the same chambers—the one that's representin' the Santero," she replied, and knew—in the way that she knew things—that Acton was already aware of this. "It could be just a coincidence, but I've a feelin' that it's important." With a hint of reluctance, she added, "And there's a Morgan Percy connection, too."

Acton's gaze rested on hers. "How so?"

"She's a former girlfriend—or perhaps not so former—but in any event, the victim threw her over."

"He would not be the first," Acton pointed out, and pulled her onto his lap.

Willingly, Doyle nestled into his arms. "Truer words, never spoken. Faith, if that's the motive then we'd have a pile of corpses, one would think. But even if Percy were a suspect, it wouldn't be the same m.o. as her other murder—that one had an altrutistic motive."

"Altruistic," he corrected gently. "Although I am not certain Percy ever serves anyone but herself."

"Yes—well, she's got some sort of dissociative personality disorder, I think. It just—it just makes me uneasy, for some reason. Would you mind if I told Williams that you'd already given me the green light to look into possible connections? Although I'm not sure what it is I'm lookin' for."

"Certainly," Acton replied smoothly, but Doyle knew with complete certainty that he was not happy about this line of inquiry. He continued, "In fact, I would like to interview the Santero myself, with you to listen in. Williams should be present also, as he is the CSM."

Oh-oh, thought Doyle, with a blink; I believe Williams is in some sort of trouble with my husband.

11

There was no reason to believe she'd ever find out, so in the end, there was no harm done. It had to be carefully handled, of course; interesting—that he hadn't just come to him, and confessed the whole.

D oyle, Acton and Williams were conferring in the gallery before the interrogation of the Santero, who sat at the interview table on the other side of the one-way glass. Doyle wasn't overly familiar with the case, but knew the suspect was a bad actor from the Lambeth borough, and used his position of power within the immigrant community to silence his critics and enrich his coffers. Lambeth was also where the QC had met his fate, and even though this might seem to be significant, in truth, it wasn't much of a coincidence since the borough had the dubious distinction of having the Met's highest murder rate.

Thus far, they had the Santero on charges of practicing medicine without a license, along with benefit fraud and tax evasion, but they were hoping to nail him on several murders that could in all probability be laid at his loathsome door.

A bigger creep never put his arm through a coat, thought Doyle, as she watched him through the glass; the Met had been after him for quite some time, and were hoping to put him away permanently—hence the frustration with the superstitious witnesses.

As she listened to Acton confer with Williams, Doyle sized up the suspect, who was seated alongside his solicitor, waiting for the interrogation. He was a rather bony, older man—hard to gauge exactly how old—wearing tribal dress, and emanating a bitter anger, although he concealed it behind a fine show of disdain. He's like a spider, she thought; all evil, and gangly.

For a moment, the suspect's gaze wandered over to the glass panel that hid the gallery, and Doyle was a bit surprised; he knows that we're back here, watching, she thought, and it makes him uneasy, for some reason.

Acton was saying to Williams, "We should scrutinize all other local murders that share the same m.o.; if we can find other victims to lay at his door, it may give us a means to work around the reluctant witnesses. It may also convince defense counsel to be a bit more cooperative in hammering out a concession."

Williams nodded. "Yes, sir."

Acton's level gaze rested on the younger detective. "Has his shop been searched?"

Of course, it has, thought Doyle in surprise. We're talking about Williams, here.

"Yes, sir."

The suspect suddenly gestured toward the glass partition, and asked his solicitor in an agitated voice, "Who is there? Who is hiding there?"

In alarm, the solicitor leaned forward and spoke to the suspect quietly, his hand gestures indicating that his client should calm down, and think before he speaks.

I'd be the worst client ever, in that department, Doyle thought; I'd be gabbling like a jackdaw, and confessing to crimes I hadn't committed.

In any event, counsel's admonition didn't seem to carry much weight because yet again, the suspect's gaze slid sidelong over toward the glass partition, the whites of his eyes showing in stark contrast to his dark skin.

Mayhap he's aware that DCI Acton has taken an interest, and he's nervous about what Acton knows, Doyle surmised. I can relate; I know the feeling well.

"Shall we begin?" said Acton to Williams. "Sergeant, if you will please remain here, and observe?"

"Yes sir," Doyle responded, and settled in to listen as the two men left the gallery. Hopefully, Acton could make some headway; they'd only two more days to charge the suspect with murder—otherwise, he'd be free to go home on bail, since his other crimes weren't major ones.

Acton and Williams entered the interview room, and took their seats across the table from the suspect and his solicitor. Acton made the preliminary statements for the recording, whilst the Santero sat with a clenched jaw, staring at the opposite corner of the room, away from the glass panel. He's anxious, and trying to hide it, thought Doyle; he can't be much of an underworld-spirit-summoner, if he can barely hold it together before questioning begins.

Acton watched him for a long moment, and then said, "I understand you have been selling illegal supplements in Lambeth and Southwark."

With a recalcitrant witness, a favored interrogation technique was to come in hot, so to speak, so as to shake up the interviewee and make him think that law enforcement knew all his secrets.

Counsel sat up a little straighter. "I am aware of no charge—"

The suspect, for his own part, kept his rigid gaze fixed on the far corner of the room. "You speak of that which you do not understand."

His solicitor leaned forward. "Answer the question—yes or no."

The suspect nodded, once. "Yes."

"And in these supplements, you pass off opiates as herbs."

Swallowing, the witness nodded. "Yes."

Faith; he doesn't much seem like a ruthless Santeria kingpin, thought Doyle, watching him with surprise. Seems more like a thoroughly nervous Neddy.

Acton produced a photograph of the QC's body, lying in the Lambeth alley. "Do you know this man?"

Reluctantly, the man glanced at the photograph, then returned his gaze to the opposite wall. A sheen of perspiration had appeared on his balding forehead. "No."

"Do you know who killed him?"

"No." Unfortunately, this was true—so much for Doyle's theory that there was some sort of connection.

Acton paused for a moment, his gaze fixed on the suspect. This was also an interrogation technique, as nervous people tended to fill in any prolonged silences by talking too much. Acton must have seen that the suspect was a bundle of nerves, and so he was hoping for a lapse in composure. However, the suspect remained silent, so Acton continued, his finger tapping the photograph. "It is believed he was last seen leaving your shop."

Doyle sat up, as this was an interesting wrinkle, mainly because it seemed to her that Acton didn't think it was true. Perhaps he was trying to shake the witness somehow—he'd definitely surprised Williams, if she could gauge by the jolt of emotion that emanated from the calmly-sitting detective inspector.

The Santero bared his teeth for a moment, and then shook his head from side to side, as he recited in a high-pitched voice, "I had nothing to do with—with this man's death. Nothing."

This was not exactly true and not exactly false, and Doyle frowned, leaning forward to concentrate.

Acton glanced at his watch. "May we have five minutes?"

Doyle blinked, as this was unexpected. Quickly, she texted, "Mixed signals, but NTK"—not the killer. Usually, Acton didn't want her sending him any messages during an interrogation, so that no one would wonder why the illustrious DCI was taking cues from his better half. Perhaps he was needing to touch base with her, for some reason.

The solicitor glanced at his own watch. "So long as we wrap it up before noon."

His fists clenched, the suspect lowered his gaze to the table, and Doyle idly watched him, as she waited for Acton to make his way into the gallery.

Her husband came in, closed the door behind him, then pulled up a chair, lowering his head to hers. "What do you think of the solicitor?"

Staring at him, she repeated blankly, "The solicitor?"

Acton turned his gaze toward the tableau before them, where the solicitor was checking his mobile for messages whilst his client sat, rigid and unmoving. "He isn't doing a very good job, is he?"

The penny dropped, and Doyle nodded. "Faith, you're right; he's top-drawer, after all, and he should have been instructin' his client not to respond to you, with all your fishin' for uncharged crimes."

Acton added thoughtfully, "He seems a bit nervous, to me."

"Oh—oh, I haven't noticed, Michael; I'm too caught up in our strange-fish suspect. I'll pay closer attention."

"If you would," asked her husband in a mild tone. "And what do you think of our suspect?"

Unfortunately, Doyle couldn't take this opportunity to redeem herself. "It was true that he didn't kill the QC, but when he said he had no connection to the crime, that wasn't true, so there's somethin' there. It's a bit hard to get a read on him—he's—" she knit her brow, trying to explain. "He's all over the place. He's having trouble concentratin', which makes it hard for me to concentrate."

Acton thought about this for a moment. "Could it be that the killer is an associate of his?"

"I don't know." Slowly, she added, "I don't think so, but it's possible."

Acton raised his head to review the two men seated at the table, and said nothing further.

She respected the silence for a small space, and then offered, "I'm that sorry I'm not much help, Michael, but now that I'm alerted, I'll pay closer attention to the solicitor."

He brought his gaze to hers. "Would it help to be in the room, perhaps? I can say I asked for a list of known associates, and once you bring it in, I can ask him about each one, to see if you can catch a sense. We would very much like to charge him with a homicide, even if it's conspiracy."

She nodded. "All right. Do you have such a list?"

"Here's one." He handed her a print-out, from his folder of notes.

Williams came through the door, holding two cups of coffee. "What do we think?"

"Creepy," declared Doyle.

"Definitely," Williams agreed, as he handed a cup to Acton.

"What d'you think of the solicitor?" asked Doyle. "D'you think he's nervous?"

Williams shrugged. "Didn't seem so, to me."

This, interestingly enough, was not true, which meant that dim-bulb Doyle was the only person who hadn't noticed, and so she resolved to focus, and be a helpmeet to her poor husband who was apparently wary about something above and beyond a creepy Santeria suspect. In her best reliable-detective-sergeant voice, she asked him, "How long shall I wait before I come in, sir?"

"Give it a few minutes," Acton instructed, and with a nod to Williams, the two men left.

Doyle watched as they re-commenced the interview, and began stating the preliminaries again for the record. Then she hoisted herself to her feet, printout in hand, and noted that the suspect glanced up at the glass panel—almost as if he could see her moving. Creepy, she thought again, suppressing a shudder. Like a nasty spider.

She explained to the guard who was manning the door that Acton needed the list, and then entered the room quietly, pretending as though she was looking for an opportunity to hand it to Acton, but actually focused like a laser beam on the solicitor, who had looked up, briefly, upon her entry into the room.

But his reaction was nothing compared to that of his client, who knocked over his chair as he leapt to his feet, and backed against the far wall, his horrified gaze fixed on Doyle.

"Away! Away! Ah-no! *Osorbo!*

Acton had risen to stand before Doyle and call out, "Guard!" although it was hardly necessary, as the PC had already burst through the door at the first shout.

"It's the red hair," Williams declared loudly. "He believes redheads are cursed."

"Good heavens; I beg your pardon, officer." The astonished solicitor stood aside as the Santero was bundled away, the suspect frantically making the sign against the evil eye even though his hands were cuffed.

12

So; Williams knows. She must have told him.

"I t was just so—so *creepy*, Reynolds. Sellin' potions, and grindin' up bones. Acton thinks even the man's solicitor is afraid of him." After having raised such a ruckus, Acton sent his red-headed sergeant home early, and she was now reciting the morning's events to the servant, who was reacting with predictable distaste, which was half the reason that she liked to tell him things.

"Deplorable, madam. A reign of terror."

She propped her elbows on the table. "Well, the terror didn't rain down on me—I wasn't afraid of him. Instead I think—I think I felt a bit sorry for him, which doesn't make much sense, but there it is." Her scalp prickled.

Reynolds pressed his lips together "I'm afraid I have no sympathy, madam. A good riddance, I say."

She teased, "Well, now where's everyone goin' to buy their ground-up kitten bones?"

"I'd rather not think about such things, madam. I am amazed such practices still persist."

With a wry mouth, she advised, "Whist, Reynolds; this may not be a news flash, but there're a lot of people out there who are desperate to fix their problems, any way they can." She then paused, because her instinct had given her such a jolt that she had to hold on to the table edge for a moment, to steady herself. What? Who was desperate to fix their problems? The solicitor? He didn't seem very significant to her, at all. Trying to grasp hold of the elusive thought, she closed her eyes tightly, and concentrated.

"Are you unwell, madam?" The servant hovered, worried mainly because he knew that if any ill befell her on his watch, there would be swift and terrible repercussions.

Opening her eyes, Doyle sighed. "No; I was just tryin' to think of somethin', and away it went."

The servant nodded. "A will o' the wisp."

"A willow what?"

"A will o' the wisp, madam—an elusive thought."

"Like a phantom," she offered.

"No, madam, I'm afraid a phantom is not quite the same."

She sighed again. "And a leopard doesn't have spots."

"Leopards have rosettes, madam."

Doyle regarded him, all admiration. "Faith, Reynolds; we should pair you up with Munoz. She could hardly do worse."

The servant paused beside the sink. "It is hard to imagine that the detective sergeant suffers from a lack of suitors, madam."

Doyle hid a smile. Munoz had come over to their flat to sketch a suspect, once, and apparently Reynolds was as susceptible as the rest of the male population. "It's not about quantity so much as it's about quality, my friend." Which reminded her that she should find out about stupid Munoz's ACC assignment, so that stupid Harding wouldn't plague her dreams any more. Not to mention she had to trot up to Trestles, and soothe the stupid knight— faith; the dead were causing her more trouble than the living, which was truly a sorry state of affairs. Although the Santero wasn't dead, he was still alive—but not for long. She lifted her head at this thought, and wondered why she was so certain that the Santero's days on earth were numbered.

"Will Lord Acton be arriving soon, madam? Shall I prepare dinner?"

Resting her chin in her hands, Doyle considered this request thoughtfully. There was little doubt that Acton would be all on end, after today's battle of the witch doctors, and the last needful thing was to force him to make idle chit-chat beneath the servant's watchful eye. "Just ice cream, Reynolds. And then you should probably make yourself scarce."

The servant adopted a wooden expression, and bowed slightly. "Certainly, madam."

He probably thinks I'm planning something kinky, she thought with amusement; although that's not such a bad idea—after all, Acton may be second-thoughting his whole marriage-to-a-diviner-of-ghosts.

And so, as Acton came through the door, his wife was lying naked on the sofa, eating a bowl of ice cream that was balanced on her pregnant belly.

He paused at the threshold. "Reynolds has left?"

"He has. I tried to talk him into naked ice cream, but he said that was a bridge too far."

Her husband smiled, and loosened his tie as he approached to lean down and kiss her. "I would pay good money."

"Well, I wouldn't. D'you want ice cream first, or a dramatic reenactment of this morning's events?"

"Neither," he replied, and bestowed a lingering kiss on her neck.

"I see where this is goin'," she sighed, and lifted her chin so as to grant him greater access. "I am such a sexy thing."

"Magnificent," he murmured into her throat, a hand on a breast.

Laughing, she placed her hand over his. "Remember when you could cover this one completely with one hand?"

"I can. I can't decide which size I like better."

"Liar." She giggled, and pulled his head down for another kiss. "It's lush, I am; like that Indian goddess, with all the arms."

"Durga."

"Faith, you're worse than Reynolds; is there *anythin'* you don't know?"

His mouth moved along her collarbone, as he shrugged out of his shirt. "I don't know how to get you to stop talking."

She giggled again. "Oh, yes, you do."

As his mouth moved southward, she sighed with bliss and sank down into the sofa. "Cover your ears, Edward; your mother's about to stop talkin'."

A very satisfying space of time later, they were lying on the rug, sharing the melted ice cream and watching Doyle's abdomen shift and move. "That's got to be an elbow. Or a knee."

Acton ran a finger over the protruding lump. "I woke him up. Sorry."

"You're not sorry a'tall, husband."

He met her eyes. "Can we discuss it now, or would you rather not discuss it at all?"

She sighed in mock-resignation. "I see how it is, you were tryin' to soften me up, before hittin' me with an interrogation."

With a small smile, he drew a finger down her belly. "I beg to differ; I think I was the one being softened up."

"Caught me out," she confessed without a trace of shame. "I have to use whatever arrows I have in my quiver, my friend—can't have you throwin' me out, this late in the game."

Acton leaned back on the rug, an arm bent back to cradle his head, and regarded her with an unreadable expression. "It appears that the Santero is not a fraud, after all."

She tilted her head in agreement, as she sucked on the spoon. "You could've knocked me over with a feather, Michael."

He lifted a tendril of her hair and watched it fall. "You terrified him."

"Well—I am terrifyin'." She reached across him for another bite of ice cream. "Mayhap he'll turn over a new leaf, and start evangelizin', once he gets to prison." This, in reference to the former detective chief superintendent of the CID, who'd been convicted on corruption charges and was now participating in prison ministry.

But Acton was not distracted by her breezy manner, and continued to gently probe. "Why was he so frightened? Do you know?"

"I think—" she paused, and steeled herself, because it was always difficult for her to speak of her perceptive abilities. "I think he was worried that his chickens were comin' home to roost—that all his misdeeds had caught up with him."

Acton thought about this. "So—we've the wrong goddess; instead of Durga, you are Nemesis."

She smiled, and fed him a spoonful. "Not a *clue* what that means, Michael."

He pulled gently on another tendril of hair. "Nemesis is implacable justice."

Leaning over him, she helped herself to another bite. "Still no clue."

"She follows wrongdoers around, and makes them pay for their sins."

Doyle paused, much struck. "Faith, wouldn't that be grand? I could shake my chains, and right all wrongs."

He offered up a half-smile, but she could see that he was worried, behind his calm façade. "Can you give me any other insights? Or would you rather not speak about it?"

Lowering her hands, she blew out a breath. "No—no insights, I'm afraid. I was as gob-smacked as everyone else."

There was a small pause. "I believe that not everyone was gob-smacked."

She bent her head to finger the spoon. "I'm sorry, Michael, but I had to tell Williams about—about it. It was important, at the time, but I'd rather not say why."

He was not happy with her, was Acton, and he placed a finger under her chin to lift her face. "No one should know of it, Kathleen; no one at all. Surely you can see this?"

But she met his eyes a bit stubbornly. "I had to, Michael; it was important. And I think we can trust Williams."

He made no reply, and in the sudden silence, she stared at him in startled dismay. "Mother a' mercy, Michael; never say—never say that's not true? What's he done?"

"I'd rather not tell you, I'm afraid."

Astonished, she remembered the fleeting feeling that she'd had—that Williams was trying to hide something, and that Acton was unhappy with him. "He—he respects you so, Michael. He'd never move against you—it's not in his nature."

"On the whole, I would agree."

Thoroughly alarmed by this equivocal response, she straightened up. "Shall I speak with him? Does he—does he need help?"

Acton brought her fingers to his mouth, to kiss them. "You may handle it as you wish, although I doubt you will discover anything of interest."

"I'm pretty good at discoverin' things I oughtn't," she reminded him in all modesty.

"I cannot argue."

Mustering up her courage, she asked in an even tone, "Is Williams in danger, Michael?" Unspoken were the additional words, "from you."

"No," he said immediately, and it was true. "But I wish you hadn't told him."

She traced a finger on his chin, feeling the end-of-the-day stubble. "He never mentions it. If it makes you feel better, he scolded me for tellin' him about it, too."

Gently, he drew her head down, to lay it on his chest. "That does make me feel better."

Unfortunately, this was not true.

13

He would have to be eliminated, of course. No one else could know about her abilities—the risk was too great.

"The Santero thought I was like Nemorcis," Doyle explained. "But I'm not, I'm just a foot soldier. I'm someone who needs direction."

"It's Nemesis, not Nemorcis," Harding corrected. "And you've got it all wrong; it's not you that's the Nemesis. And that's not what's important, anyway; what's important is who is the Até."

"The Ah-tay?" she asked in confusion. Yet again, she was confronted by the dead psychiatrist in his windy setting, and oddly enough, she felt as though she was on the defensive, this time, and so she was trying to be a bit nicer to him. "I'm truly doin' my best, but there's so much to keep straight—as soon as I start in on one thing, another pops up." Frowning, she thought about it. "I think there's a pattern, but I'm too busy puttin' out fires to see it."

"Find the Até," he repeated.

Bewildered, she shook her head in apology. "But I don't know anythin' about goddesses, and such—I'm as thick as a plank. I'm the weak link, in all this."

"No, you aren't," he replied in a firm tone. "You just think you are."

"Faith, you've got me mixed-up with some other brassy shant. I'm not one to assert myself."

With an ironic air, he lifted his brows. "I beg to disagree."

A bit discomfited by this reminder—she didn't know if it was bad manners to remind a ghost of his earthly failings—she stammered, "Oh—oh; well, I suppose your case was an exception. I knew you were tryin' to frame-up Acton, and I couldn't let you do it."

"Exactly," he nodded, very pleased.

There was a pause, whilst the wind blew, and Doyle was reluctant to ask him what he meant, since he seemed to think she was finally catching on and she didn't want to admit that she was as lost as Jonah, adrift on the deep blue sea. Casting about for a new topic, she asked, "Whatever happened to your shoes?"

"That," he said, "is an excellent question."

"You're no help at all," she complained, and wished she could press her hands to her temples. "Can't you just *tell* me plainly? I've too much to think about, just now."

"Thinking is overrated."

She stared in surprise. "Why, that's what *I* always say; you shouldn't be the one who's sayin' it."

But the ghost shrugged. "On the contrary, psychiatry is all about perception. That, and helping patients avoid desperate measures."

Slowly, she repeated what she'd said in her earlier conversation with Reynolds. "There're a lot of people out there who are desperate to fix their problems, any way they can."

"Exactly." He nodded in approval, once again.

Struggling mightily, Doyle tried to pull together her elusive thoughts. "So, I need to find out why the villains seized Elena, why the shoes are missin', and who's desperate to fix their problems."

Harding leaned forward. "Not necessarily in that order."

Doyle woke suddenly, and stared at the darkened bedroom wall. Figure it out, she thought; and with a mighty effort, closed her eyes tightly in an attempt to piece it together. Why would it be Harding—of all people—trying to send a message? Why had he no shoes—was he a victim of the Santero, also? But that made no sense; the Santero didn't kill the QC in the first place. And anyways, Doyle was certain that Acton had killed Harding—or had arranged to have him killed—and you could hardly blame the man, after what Harding had done. So, what was it—did Harding have something else in common with these other, shoeless victims?

And was there some sort of connection, between Munoz's sister and these murders? This seemed very unlikely, but—if her instinct could be trusted—this seemed to be the tale being told to her.

Shifting her bulky body with an effort, she rolled onto her back, and frowned at the ceiling. Was Williams mixed up in any of this? He was hiding something, and Acton had been grave—so whatever it was, it was serious. Not to mention Acton had been setting a trap for someone, when he was burning the midnight oil the other night—could it be for Williams?

No, she thought immediately; Acton wouldn't hurt Williams, and for no other reason than he knew that Williams was dear to her—in Acton's world, that was enough.

It's all too complicated, she thought crossly, as she re-positioned the pillow beneath her head. And I'm not sure whether I should ask Acton about these many and mysterious things, so I suppose I'll have go to another well of knowledge.

Therefore, the next morning she waited until Acton was taking a conference call in the bedroom before asking Reynolds in a casual tone, "D'you know who 'Até' is, Reynolds?"

The servant paused in taking away her plate. "Até, madam?"

"Yes." She frowned, but was certain she had it right. "If someone said, 'Why, that's not Nemesis at all; that's Até', what would they mean?"

The servant attempted to hide his astonishment with only limited success. "I suppose the difference would be that Nemesis seeks to bestow justice, while Até seeks to bestow ruin."

With a knit brow, she tried to puzzle this out. "So, Nemesis has good intentions, but Até does not."

But the servant raised a brow in dignified disagreement. "Not exactly, madam; both goddesses intend to bring harm to their victims, but for different reasons. Nemesis brings justice, while Até brings ruination—usually as a result of the hero's own hubris."

She stared at him, trying to decide if it was even worth asking what "hubris" meant.

"Shakespeare refers to Até quite often, madam."

"Ah," she replied. "Of course, he does."

The servant continued on his way over to the sink. "I didn't realize that you were familiar with the classics, madam."

"No," Doyle agreed glumly. "Neither did I. For the love o' Mike, why can't he just tell me plainly? It's like tryin' to puzzle out the seven scrolls, where everythin' is so deep and mysterious that you just want to be done with it, and take your chances."

"Certainly, madam." The servant said no more on the subject.

With a small frown, Doyle considered the view out the window for a moment, and then scrolled up Williams' number, to buzz him. "Hey."

"Hey, yourself. Everything all right?"

"Never finer; except that I'm scarin' the dickens out of everyone."

"Let's not do that again."

"No argument, here."

There was a slight pause. "Everything else all right?"

Interesting, she thought; he's expecting bad news. "Everything is crackin' excellent, my friend. Although I'm lookin' for an assignment from my CSM, bein' as I'm a good foot soldier, when I'm not busy bein' a weak link."

"Right, then; I was just thinking that we may need another look-in at the Santero's shop, so I'll hand it off to you, if you're willing."

"I'm willin' indeed; I've never been to a witch doctor's shop—mayhap I can pick up a potion or two, on the sly."

"No tampering with the evidence," he joked, and to her surprise, her scalped prickled.

14

*He was very close to pulling the net in on the ACC—
only a few more loose ends. It had to be carefully done,
of course, with an ironclad case lined up against them.
There would be but one opportunity.*

At least now I've got some direction, Doyle mused, as she
and Officer Gabriel knocked on the door of the Santero's
shop. Yesterday, Acton had asked—idly, it had seemed
at the time—whether the shop had been searched, and now
Williams had sent her to do a re-search. It wasn't a coincidence, of
course; lately, it seemed that nothing was.

As they waited on the doorstep, Doyle thought over these
events, and remarked, "Here we are yet again, you and me."

Gabriel smiled. "You aren't going to say it's the blind leading
the blind, again, are you? That one still stings."

But Doyle was unrepentant. "We're not a case-breakin' team,
my friend—we're only the supportin' cast. I wonder what's afoot?"

Any further discussion was curtailed by the door curtain's being twitched aside so that a harassed, older woman could indicate
that the shop was not yet open to the public. Doyle held up her
warrant card, and with an open show of distaste, the woman unlocked the door.

As they crossed the threshold, the woman eyed them with extreme misgiving. "Why are you here? The police have already come and gone."

"Just a follow-up, ma'am; it shouldn't take long." Doyle made the introductions, and discovered that the woman had been minding the shop since the Santero's arrest, but—as was only to be expected—business had slowed to a crawl since Scotland Yard's finest had taken such a keen interest in the place.

As they spoke, Doyle looked around and decided that it was exactly the type of shop that one would anticipate; crowded with questionable religious items, and a bit shabby. The shelves behind the counter were conspicuously empty by contrast, and Doyle surmised that the various potions and artifacts that had been for sale were now awaiting their moment at trial in the Met's evidence locker.

"I have to keep the accounts on a pad of paper," the woman complained. "The police took the register, and the ledgers." Very much put-upon, she held up a flowered bag with a drawstring. "I keep the money in here."

Doyle offered cold comfort. "I imagine the place won't be open much longer."

But Gabriel seemed sympathetic to the woman's plight, and asked, "How long have you known the Santero?"

"No questions, or I will call a lawyer," the woman threatened, shaking a finger at him. "You will not arrest me, too."

Gabriel then said something in another language, his tone soothing, and whilst Doyle watched in surprise, the woman grudgingly responded in kind. They conversed for a few minutes, the woman becoming more talkative as she complained to her sympathetic listener, her agitated hand gestures conveying the depths of her annoyance.

Whilst they spoke, Doyle decided to be useful, and began a discreet search—although she very quickly realized she wouldn't recognize a clue if it reared up and bit her; there was too much clutter, and the objects themselves were unfamiliar to her. She tapped on floorboards with her boot heel, and eyed the walls and shelves to judge whether there was room for a hidden cavity, but finally decided it was a futile endeavor; the SOCOs made their bread and butter doing this sort of thing, and had already come up empty.

Gabriel called out, "She says the Santero's rooms are above-stairs. They've already been searched, but we can take another look, if we'd like."

"Thank you, ma'am," Doyle said in her best respectful-of-foreigners voice, and then as she mounted the stairs with Gabriel, asked in a low tone, "What was that all about?"

"She speaks Farsi; she's Persian. It seemed a little odd to me; I wondered why she'd be affiliated with the Santero. I also wondered how she was being paid for her services, if he's in custody."

Much struck, Doyle could see his point. "Good one; what did she say?"

"She said he'd once done a favor for her and that she was happy to help him out, only she didn't want to do it for much longer. She wanted to know whether I thought he'd be out on bail, soon."

They paused before the Santero's living quarters, and Doyle gave a perfunctory knock on the door. "That's a good question actually. They can't hold him much longer, so they need to charge him with murder but everyone's afraid to grass, due to a dread fear of evil spirits."

Gabriel raised his dark brows. "Are they? I know someone who will grass."

Doyle paused in surprise. "You do? Who?"

With a smile, Gabriel nodded his head down the stairs, where the woman could be seen, idly peering out one of the smudged windows. "She will. The Santero's favor was that he killed her husband for her. The husband wanted to take her back to the old country, she didn't want to go, and so she had him killed."

Agape, Doyle stared at him. "She told you *that*? Without battin' an eyelash?"

He grinned. "She did. People like to talk."

But after a moment's consideration, Doyle shook her head with regret. "I don't think we can use it, Gabriel; she wasn't read the caution."

The young officer shrugged. "Who's to say that she wasn't read the caution?"

This attitude was not surprising, it was rumored that MI 5 people played a bit fast and loose with the protocols, being as—in their minds—the ends justified the means. "I'm to say, I'm afraid."

He accepted this intrusion of the rule of law with good grace, and shrugged. "All right."

It did seem a shame, so she offered, "We can always caution her, and try again."

"If you'd like," he agreed, but she could tell that he didn't think they'd get the confession again, after taking such an alarming and pointed step.

Tentatively, Doyle pushed open the door to the Santero's rooms, and braced herself, expecting the atmosphere within to be very uncomfortable for her, considering the recent contretemps in the interview room. With some relief, however, she realized that there was no such feeling—she'd no sense that the occupant was an evildoer, doing evil deeds. Instead, the place was small, spare and rather tidy, with a kettle on the ancient stove that still showed traces of fingerprint powder.

They stood for a moment, taking in the layout, and then Doyle suggested that Gabriel search the bedroom, whilst she took the kitchen and the small sitting room. It seemed unlikely that the task would take long; the rooms were shabby and small, and there were clear signs that the SOCOs had already done their very thorough job.

They were thus engaged for perhaps fifteen minutes when the shop's bell rang, and the woman downstairs could be heard speaking to a newcomer. Ah, thought Doyle, raising her head to listen. The plot thickens, yet again.

She went over to the doorway and called down, "We're up here, Ms. Percy."

"Who is it?" asked Gabriel, who was going through the drawers in the bedroom.

"Morgan Percy; she's the junior barrister representin' the Santero."

The young woman appeared at the doorway, looking cool, professional, and none too happy. "Have you obtained a warrant for an additional search, Officer Doyle?"

"We had permission," Doyle replied, and belatedly realized that the permission of the temporary volunteer below may not be legally sufficient.

Fortunately, it seemed that Percy was willing to let it go, as she moved on to her next pointed complaint. "Am I not aware of new evidence?" Any material evidence found by the prosecution had to be shared with the defense team, and it was clear that Percy was worried she'd been left out of the loop.

"We're planting evidence," Gabriel explained in a cheerful tone, as he leaned against the door jamb.

Hastily, Doyle intervened. "Officer Gabriel is on loan from MI 5; please forgive him." To Gabriel, she said, "Can't joke around about such things, officer. Our Ms. Percy may look like a kind woman, but she'll have you thrown off this case in a pig's whisker."

Unabashed, he raised his dark brows. "Am I *on* this case?"

"No," Doyle conceded. "For that matter, neither am I."

Yet again, Percy seemed inclined to overlook these various irregularities, and positioned herself against the wall. "I'll observe, if you don't mind."

But Doyle was not quite such a fool, and declined this offer. "I'm afraid I can't have any contamination of the site."

Percy lifted an elegant palm. "What contamination? The site's been searched and released, already."

"Sorry; rules are rules—you'll have to wait outside." This was not exactly true, but Doyle had the niggling suspicion that Percy was worried, for some reason, that Doyle was going to find something useful, which was exactly the impression she'd got from Williams, who also seemed to think she'd find something useful on this otherwise sleeveless errand. If I didn't know better, she thought a bit crossly, I'd think that everyone—including Acton—is standing back and waiting for the fair Doyle to put two and two together.

She and Gabriel continued the search without speaking, finding little of interest amongst the man's personal effects. Doyle was in the washroom and Gabriel was standing in the small closet when he called out, "Not much, I'm afraid—although it looks as though some clothes have been removed."

Straightening up, Doyle replied, "Yes—the poor SOCOs thought they had him dead to rights because they'd found traces of blood on one of his robes, but it turned out to be animal blood."

"Sorry I mentioned it," said Gabriel. "Nasty customer."

Blowing a tendril of hair from her face, Doyle braced her hands against her back and walked over to join him. "I haven't seen anythin' that's even worth baggin' to take back. How about you?"

"Nothing. It looks like the SOCOs were pretty thorough."

Doyle nodded, noting that the offerings in the small closet included a suit of western clothes, which the Santero would probably don when the occasion warranted. Along the floor was a double-row metal shoe rack, which contained a few pairs of western shoes, interspersed amongst some tribal-looking leather sandals.

Looking them over, Doyle suddenly caught her breath. "D'you see those brown shoes? Those are Bruno-somethings; they're Italian, and ridiculously expensive. Acton has a pair like them, at home."

"Oh? Do you think the Santero stole them?"

Slowly, Doyle said, "I don't think they're his. Look at the size."

Gabriel crouched to examine the Italian shoes. "You're right—they're way too big; I'm surprised the SOCOs missed it."

Doyle did not voice her opinion on this subject, but instead unsheathed her mobile. "I think we'll need to ask the evidence officer to bring in all these shoes."

Gabriel looked up at her in surprise. "Some still have print powder; do you think they need a re-test?"

Bluntly, Doyle informed him, "I think the shoes belonged to his murder victims, and I think we've just solved our Lambeth case."

His brows raised in surprise, Gabriel straightened up to stand beside her. "You think the brown shoes belonged to the QC?"

"Yes. And the others belong to other victims." With a nod, Doyle indicated the line of assembled shoes. "It looks like there were four victims—d'you see?"

Gabriel put his hands on his hips, and ran his considering gaze along the shoe rack. "But why would he take the shoes from his victims if they were already dead—what was the point?"

"I don't think he took them to perform a curse," Doyle replied, as she waited for the EO to pick up. "I think the shoes are trophies—that's why he took them."

"Nasty customer," pronounced Gabriel again.

15

It would be interesting to see what was planned, with respect to Blakney's death. He'd monitor the situation and step in, if necessary.

As Gabriel drove them back to the Met, Doyle frowned out the window whilst she thought over the morning's events. She'd supervised the evidence gathering, and fended off Morgan Percy's sharp questions as the forensics team carried the new bags of evidence downstairs. "You'll hear all about it, Ms. Percy, but first let me see what we've got, for heaven's sake—it may be nothin'."

The girl had then proceeded to be outraged on her client's behalf, which was interesting, since any decent criminal attorney would know that the chain of custody had been interrupted—the shoes had sat in the closet for days, and there was no saying who'd been in and out of the flat. Not to mention they didn't have proper permission to search in the first place—both excellent reasons to bring a motion to suppress the new evidence.

Doyle had texted Acton and Williams to inform them of this latest development, and Williams had immediately asked if she'd mind following up—matching potential victims' foot measurements, and asking friends and relatives to identify the footwear.

Slog work, but at least they had a lead, such as it was. Acton had simply asked if she was available for lunch.

As she contemplated the passing scenery, Doyle asked Gabriel, "D'you know what a shadow murder is?"

"I do not," her companion replied. "But I have a feeling that I will soon find out."

"A shadow murder is what they call it when someone seizes the main chance and frames up a murderer for a murder that they didn't actually commit. It's not your normal frame-up, because instead of an innocent person's bein' set-up, it's a murderer who's bein' set-up, with the idea bein' that no one's goin' to look very hard at yet another murder, hidden away amongst the others."

He considered this. "Like an add-on."

Nodding, she turned to look at him. "Yes—like an add-on. In fact, the first murder I worked with Acton was a shadow murder; a wife had seized the opportunity to kill her husband, because he was involved in the corruption rig and all suspicion would be turned elsewhere."

He glanced over at her. "Can I assume you think we're looking at a shadow murder, here?"

Thoughtfully, she nodded, and turned away to contemplate the passing scenery again. "Yes. I wouldn't be a'tall surprised if someone's doin' some shadow murders, and pinnin' them on this fellow. After all, he's a prime candidate for a frame-up, and has indeed killed a victim or two—just not these ones."

He glanced at her again. "Is this going into the report?

She shook her head. "No—I don't want to do anythin' that might let the cat out of the bag. Let me speak with Acton, just to gauge it." She eyed him sidelong. "You don't happen to know anythin' about the QC's murder, do you?"

"I do not," he said, and it was true.

This was a relief; she'd been a bit suspicious, since Gabriel had been with her at the scene and yet again today, when she was practically spoon-fed the new evidence that would implicate the Santero in the QC's murder.

His voice interrupted her thoughts. "Do you think Percy knows about it—knows about the shadow murders?"

Indeed, Doyle did, but she was not about to let Gabriel in on this interesting little fact, and so she feigned amusement. "Unlikely, Gabriel; she's his defense, after all."

Good-naturedly, he shrugged as they turned into the parking structure. "I just wondered. She shouldn't have been there, you know."

Doyle turned to him in surprise. "Why is that?"

He put the gearshift into park, and turned off the vehicle. "You said she was a junior barrister. She's not a solicitor."

This was a very good point, and unfortunately, Doyle—who, truth to tell, was indeed a bit of a dim bulb—had missed its significance. A barrister would not be involved in any doings outside of the courtroom; instead, the suspect's solicitor would handle any concerns about illegal searches and seizures. No doubt Gabriel had put two and two together about Percy's involvement, which served as an excellent example as to why the fair Doyle should keep her thoughts to herself.

As they walked together toward the parking structure's lift, she repeated, "Please don't mention any of this—at least not until I've tested it out with Acton. It may be nothin', but if it's somethin', it's got to be handled carefully."

"No argument here," he agreed, and made no further comment, which only reminded her that he was MI 5, and used to staying mum, when the occasion warranted. I wouldn't last a day as a spy, Doyle conceded; I tend toward panic, and I'm always putting a voice to any spare thought that passes through my poor brain.

Thinking along these lines, she was prompted to ask, "Would MI 5 ever do a joint exercise to help out the ACC?"

This surprised him, and he glanced at her. "I'm afraid I'm not sure what you mean."

"Would the ACC ever work with MI 5 personnel on an MI 5 matter?" She was thinking of what Munoz had said, and of Harding's warnings.

"No," he said bluntly, and he seemed amused by the very idea.

"I'd thought—" she began carefully, "I'd thought that you were asked to come over to the Met so as to take a look into some of our doin's, over here." She hoped this cryptic comment was vague enough; Acton had mentioned that Gabriel had been quietly recruited to monitor DCI Drake, Acton's counterpart, who'd been suspected of participating in the corruption rig.

"Can't speak to that," he replied easily.

"I suppose not," she agreed with resignation, as they waited for the lift. "But I truly, *truly* must learn how to drive myself about."

He glanced at her in surprise. "You can't drive?"

"I can, more or less, but it's a hazard, I am. I may need to recruit you to help me." She thought over her options, and then decided there was nothin' for it. "I'd like you to help me tail someone from the CID."

Admirably, he hid his surprise. "Off the record?"

"Yes—I hope that's all right. I wouldn't ask, but I think it may be important." Stupid Harding the stupid ghost certainly seemed to think so.

They stepped into the lift. "All right, but then I get a favor in return."

"That depends," she said cautiously, "on what sort of favor it is."

"Tell me about Morgan Percy."

Men; honestly, she thought. "Morgan Percy is trouble, my friend."

He smiled as the doors slid closed. "So I gather."

16

It was the season for shadow murders, apparently.

D oyle managed to catch Williams between field visits—
he'd been working a white-collar embezzlement case
that kept getting more and more complicated, which is
what happened, sometimes. It was a shame the villains couldn't
keep things simple for the benefit of law enforcement personnel,
but there it was; the harder it was to figure out what was going on,
the more time there was to destroy the evidence, particularly in
financial crimes.

Williams was going over a spreadsheet with a forensics accounting person, and it sounded to Doyle like they were wondering what had happened to the aforesaid embezzled money. She
positioned herself in his line of sight and adopted a patient posture, so that he'd know it wasn't urgent. After glancing at her, he
held up a finger to signal that he'd be wrapping up shortly. He's
not exactly happy to see me, she thought with a pang of sympathy,
but at least he's not making the sign against the evil eye.

After giving some final instructions to the analyst, Williams
walked over. "Hey, Kath; good catch on the shoes."

In a rush, she blurted out, "You—of all people—know that I'm not any good at subterfuge. I'm slated to have lunch with Acton, and so first I'd like to know what's what."

Startled, he met her gaze. "What do you mean? Are you all right?"

"I am, but you're not. Let's straighten it out, please; I have to figure out how to smooth it all over." She paused, and touched his sleeve. "We're goin' to smooth it over, you know; I just need to know what's happened."

He knit his brows, half-amused. "What's happened to what? Start at the beginning, Kath."

Doyle decided there was no point in beating around the bush, as she was on a deadline. "I think Acton thinks you've done a shadow murder."

He stared at her in surprise, and then lowered his head to hers. "Let's go." With a hand on her back, he steered her out the door, and into the hallway outside.

"I don't have a lot of time," she reminded him. "So, give me the short version."

"Not here," he replied in a terse tone, and seeing the wisdom of this, she allowed him to escort her outside the building and away from potential surveillance coverage.

They walked for a bit at a steady pace, and as he seemed reluctant to broach the subject—and she was fast running out of breath—she ventured, "Why would you want to be killin' the QC?"

He ran a distracted hand through his hair. "It's not what you think, Kath, and—and, it's complicated. What does Acton know?"

"I'll not be grassin' on my own husband, Thomas. But I think it would be safe to always assume that Acton knows everythin'. Leastways, that's always my startin' point."

Williams raised his gaze to the sky for a moment, emanating waves of unhappiness. "Christ."

Such was the depth of her sympathy that she didn't chastise him for blasphemy, but instead halted his progress by laying a gentle hand on his arm, so that they stood face-to-face. "If you'd rather not tell me, you needn't. But Thomas—as strange as it may seem, I think Acton would lay down his life for you."

He ducked his chin. "Not for the reasons you'd think, Kath."

Stubbornly, she persisted. "You're a good man, Thomas Williams. You'll not convince me otherwise."

He made no response, but lifted his head to gaze at the horizon again, deeply unhappy, and avoiding her eyes.

She'd always found him difficult to read—closed up like an oyster, he was—but she made an attempt to relieve his misery. "Is there any chance you could confess your sins, and take your lumps?"

This brought his attention back to her. "Confess? Confess to who?"

"Whom," she corrected. "And my priest is a very understandin' man, who would take any and all secrets to the grave."

With a curt gesture, he shook his head. "No."

This was not a surprise; Williams was not a believer, and he would probably just as soon confess to the Santero. When he offered nothing further, she pleaded, "I want to help, Thomas; please, please tell me how I may."

He finally met her gaze, his own eyes very blue. "I appreciate it, Kath, but it's important that you stay out of it. Promise me."

Her scalp prickled, and she stared in astonishment. "What—what has any of this got to do with *me*?"

But he deftly changed the tenor of the conversation, and offered a small smile. "If I'm in prison, who's going to pick up the pieces when Acton dumps you for Munoz?"

She knew he was attempting to distract her, but she couldn't resist making a derisive sound. "If Acton wanted to dump me for the likes of Munoz, I would only wish them well with the sincere belief that they thoroughly deserve one other. But don't change the subject; you can't plot against Acton."

"Then you can put your mind at rest; I am not plotting against Acton."

Every syllable rang true, and she paused to stare at him in bewilderment. "Then why did you do it?"

Slowly, he repeated, "It's complicated, Kath, and I'd rather not say anything further on the subject."

Trying to puzzle this out, she decided that Williams must have laid down a bit of home-brewed justice, and didn't want her to find out about it. It wasn't much of a surprise, truly, considering that he'd learned such things at the feet of the master. "You can't take justice into your own hands. Thomas. And you can't try to be an Acton; no one can. He's—" she tried to remember the right word. "He's intimtable."

"Inimitable. Yes, I know that."

Delicately, she added, "And you'd not want to walk that path, anyways. He's—he's not exactly a happy soul."

But his intense gaze met hers again. "I disagree; you make him very happy."

Her scalp prickled again, and she wished she knew why. "I'm not sure that 'happy' is the correct adverb."

"Adjective, Kath. And I'll disagree again; he lives to serve you."

He lowered his gaze to the pavement, and again, she got a glimpse of deep unhappiness—but why? Anyone who was paying attention knew that Acton was devoted to her, and Williams paid more attention than most. She wondered, for a moment, if he chafed at his role; he'd carried a torch for the fair Doyle—he still did, truth be told—and perhaps he was struggling with the now-rather-obvious fact that he could never be more than a friend to her. But what connection could this tangle of human emotions have with the shadow-murder of a posh QC? It was bewildering, even though she knew, down to the soles of her shoes, that there was a connection.

He raised his head. "I appreciate that you want to help, Kath, but in the meantime, I should walk you back to headquarters."

"Aye, then—although I'm to meet Acton on the pavement, in front." She fell into step beside him, and offered thoughtfully,

"It's a shame the church can't just torture people to make them convert, like in the old days."

He managed to muster a half-smile. "And why is that?"

She placed a hand in the crook of his arm. "Because religion helps people deal with frustration. You and Acton both; you get frustrated, because you can't believe the world is the way it is, or that people behave the way they do. You've no faith in a higher power, and you don't have the perspective of two thousand years at your back, so you take matters into your own hands out of sheer frustration."

He bent his head for a moment. "I suppose that's a valid point."

She teased, "Don't sound so surprised, that I made a valid point."

He glanced ahead, as the building loomed before them. "Acton is willing to convert, though, so your theory may be a little flawed."

"Acton is convertin' because he lives to serve me," she admitted in a dry tone. "I'm only hopin' that somethin' takes root before half the population of London is laid waste."

He chuckled, and she chuckled in response. They rarely spoke directly about Acton's doings, but she'd decided that she needed to show Williams that she had his back, come what may.

He must have sensed it, and he squeezed her hand against his side. "Are we all right?"

"We are. We always will be, Thomas."

As Acton was waiting in the Range Rover at the curb, she took her leave of Williams and hurried over, so that the duty officer wouldn't be put in the awkward position of having to tell a DCI to move his car.

17

It promised to be an interesting luncheon.

Acton was taking her to Candide's, which was one of her favorite restaurants—mainly because the staff was too busy to be pretentious, and the food was uniformly good.

As he pulled away, she leaned over to kiss him. "Sorry I'm late; I'm that hungry."

He reached to run a fond hand over her belly. "How does Edward?"

"He's been quiet, today. We must've scared the poor boyo, what with all the sex and ice cream." She spoke to her belly. "Get used to it, my friend. More to come."

Acton smiled in response, but she wasn't fooled, and settled back to regard him thoughtfully. "So; I can't decide whether you're worried that I'm catchin' on, or you're worried that I'm not catchin' on fast enough."

He did not pretend to misunderstand, but instead asked, "What did Williams have to say?"

Sighing, she admitted, "Nothin' of the least use. Although I'm poleaxed, because now I'm convinced that the death of the QC has got somethin' to do with *me*, of all people. There's some sort of connection, but he won't say what it is."

Acton watched the road for a moment. "I am aware of no connection."

This was true, but it was also apparent that he wasn't telling her everything that he knew, and so she shifted her weight crossly. "I feel like I did at the committee hearin'—that I'm bein' poked and manipulated, like a puppet on a string. I don't like it, Michael—I get enough of that from the stupid ghost."

He frowned slightly. "The knight is still bothering you?"

"No—no, just ghosts in general," she replied vaguely, and wished she'd held her tongue. The last needful thing was for Acton to find out that his dead psychiatrist was banging about the flat, issuing dire warnings. She paused, surprised by this thought. *Were* they dire warnings? They didn't seem dire, but perhaps they were—after all, she'd the feeling that a clock was ticking down, for some reason. Or was it a spider, weaving a web? And there was that Até person, who sounded like a fistful of trouble, no matter what Shakespeare said. Faith, Shakespeare had a lot to answer for, when you thought about it.

"Speaking of which, I've arranged to make a visit to Trestles, this weekend. How much time do you think you will need, to address the problem?"

She shrugged. "Not a clue. Not long, I'd think." Amused, she leaned forward to look up into his face as he drove. "Confess; you never thought you'd be discussin' how to best cool down the family ghosts with your future wife."

As he watched the road, he leaned to plant a kiss on her forehead. "This is true; you are a constant delight."

Sighing, she leaned to rest her head against his shoulder. "Not for Williams, though; he's unhappy that I'm winklin' out his misdeeds."

"Is Williams a problem?"

The question was asked in a neutral tone, but she was quick to assure him, "No; in fact, it's just the opposite. For some reason, Williams was desperate to fix a problem, but he dealt with it in the wrong way, and now he's that unhappy." She paused, thinking about it. "He's stuck, and thoroughly frustrated. I'd like to help him, if I may, and I'm hopin' that's all right with you."

"By all means."

There was a small silence, and she lifted her head to look at him. "Do you know what he's done, Michael?"

"I can guess."

She blew out an annoyed breath. "Honestly; I'd rather not play twenty questions, husband."

"I'm afraid I'd rather not tell you," he said slowly. "I am sorry, Kathleen."

She warned, "I think it's important that I find out, you know. Usually, when I have this feelin', it turns out I was right."

"I suppose that is a matter of perspective."

She had to laugh at his ironic tone; she'd an excellent record of winkling out Acton's best-laid plans so that she could swoop in at the last minute to save him from himself. "Poor you; I bet you never thought your future wife would be runnin' around, spikin' your guns left and right."

Gallantly, he demurred, "I wouldn't have it any other way."

Laughing, she raised her face for another kiss, and decided not to point out that this last statement was not exactly true.

They found a parking space, and Doyle reviewed the busy lunchtime crowd that was passing by on the pavement. "Are we puttin' ourselves on public display, yet again? Should I weep into my handkerchief?"

"The next committee hearing is tomorrow," he admitted. "And much is at stake."

"Well then; let's give them a good show. I'll try to be a bit grave, and fret about bein' thrown out into the street, bag and baggage. I'll bemoan aloud what a sad state of affairs this has turned out to be for the heroic bridge-jumper."

"If you would."

She smiled fondly as he came around to open the door, and decided it was rather sweet, actually; Acton was the last person who'd want to parade around in public, but he was banking on their mutual fame to turn the trick at the stupid succession hearing, so that he could keep his stupid estate.

No; her instinct told her. That's not what's going on, here.

With some surprise, she examined this thought, as a solicitous maître d' allowed them to jump the line, and escorted them toward the back of the main dining room. What? Acton *wasn't* putting them on display, so as to help his case? Of course, he was; he hated appearing in such a public setting, but needs must, when the devil drives, and there was a hereditary succession to steal.

They passed though the crowded room, Doyle being careful not to accidently bump her belly into anyone, when suddenly her gaze fell upon Morgan Percy, who was striving mightily to keep her own gaze averted from Doyle's. The girl's luncheon companion was Judge Horne, the presiding judicial officer in the Santero case, and they were seated side-by-side, rather than across from each other.

Ah, thought Doyle; I stand corrected. "Why, hallo Ms. Percy; are you still smartin' about the new evidence?"

"I'll recover," the girl replied, not betraying by the flicker of an eyelash that she was seated cheek-to-jowl with a supposedly impartial judge.

"Frederick," said Acton, offering his hand. "How are you?"

"I am well, Michael," the man replied, half-rising to shake. "Would you care to join us? Ms. Percy and I ran into each other, outside."

"Please," said Percy, her limpid gaze fixed on Acton.

Doyle would have rather enjoyed calling their bluff, but Acton demurred in a polite tone, "Some other time, perhaps."

Doyle made to leave, but before she could do so, she was presented with yet another player in this little drama as Williams approached between the tables, only looking up to recognize her at the last moment.

"DI Williams," Doyle said heartily, offering her hand. "How very nice it is, to see you again."

"DS Doyle," he replied steadily, the only clue to his discomfiture being the flush of color rising up his neck. "Sir."

In his aloof, well-bred manner, Acton politely completed the introductions. "Are you acquainted with Judge Horne, DI Williams? And Ms. Percy?"

"I am," said Williams, and nodded to each of them.

"Please join us," Percy asked Williams in a bright tone, as though he'd come purely by chance.

Doyle decided it was time to step away from the almost suffocating aura of dismay and alarm that hovered over the three of them, and so she nodded her goodbyes and turned to follow the waiting maître d' to a quiet, out-of-the-way corner, where no less than two waiters were assigned to fuss over them.

After solicitously placing a napkin on what passed for Doyle's lap, the staff discreetly withdrew, and she was finally given an opportunity to say, "Good one."

Acton didn't pretend to misunderstand. "I thought it necessary, I'm afraid."

She lowered her menu to glance at him over the top. "It was a crackin' fine shot across the bow, Michael—a guiltier trio never lurked in a finer restaurant. Although Percy couldn't help battin' her eyes at you—*such* a brasser, and with her current paramour sittin' right there beside her. Although as I am hugely pregnant, she probably thought you'd be willin'."

"I'm afraid she'll have to spread her favors elsewhere."

Doyle hid her face in the menu again. "I could say somethin' vulgar, but I won't, bein' as we are sittin' in this fine establishment. Faith, what is she thinkin', canoodlin' with the judge in a pendin' case?"

"There is no rule against meeting up with court personnel in a social setting," he pointed out in a mild tone.

She made a derisive sound, and shook her head slightly. "Doin' it too brown, husband. They were clearly up to no good, but now you've put the cat amongst the pigeons—although they're not pigeons, in my book; they're more like sneakin' weasels."

"Indeed," Acton agreed. "My thought exactly."

She glanced at him over her menu again. "I believe it was Judge Horne who ordered Blakney's rushed cremation."

"I believe you are correct," Acton replied, as he signaled to the waiter.

Doyle ordered a fried ham sandwich with extra strawberry jam, and after Acton ordered some fancy salad with a fancy French name, she decided it was time to get down to brass tacks. "So; what are the sneakin' weasels plottin', and how is poor Williams a part? He can't be willingly involved." She eyed her husband, watching his reaction. "I'll bet my teeth there's a shadow murder or two, lurkin' about. The shoes were just too findable; may as well have had a trail of bread crumbs, leadin' up to them."

He paused for a moment, and she sensed he was weighing his words. "I shouldn't be surprised. And I imagine there are more shadow murders to come."

Dismayed, she watched him cut his salad with a knife and fork—Acton was the sort of person who would cut his salad with a knife and fork. She leaned forward slightly, and said with quiet intensity, "If Williams is involved, Michael, we have to put a stop to it—we *have* to."

He reached to place a hand on hers, and met her gaze with his own reassuring one. "Please don't worry. I do not believe Williams was involved in the QC's death."

This was a huge relief, but she warned, "He's involved in the cover-up, though—you'll not convince me otherwise."

"Then I will not make the attempt." He bent his head to re-address his salad.

It was a great comfort, in a way, to realize that Acton had a handle on all these ominous doings. As she'd said to Williams, it was always best to assume that Acton knew everything, and then work from there. Although—although he hadn't known about that other shady judge— that night at Trestles—and the plot to do him in. With a pause, she knit her brow, because she'd the sense—she'd the sense that history was repeating itself, in a strange way—

Her train of thought was interrupted, however, because as it turned out, Acton was cutting his salad so that he could split it with her, and she regarded the proffered pile of greens with a baleful eye. "Holy Mother—is that kale? Who would willingly eat this stuff?"

But before her husband could make a response, Doyle discovered that they were to entertain yet another acquaintance, in the form of the elderly chairman from the committee of lords, who rose from his own nearby table to approach theirs.

Beaming, the courtly gentleman bent over Doyle's hand. "Lady Acton; how wonderful to see you—although I suppose I mustn't refer to you as Lady Acton." He looked about him with guilty good humor.

"Join us, please," said Acton, rising politely.

"Mustn't," the chairman chuckled, and shook a bony finger at him. He then directed his fond attention to Doyle. "I'm tempted, though; I knew you had the look of my late wife, Lady Acton, and I was delighted when your husband informed me that you also hail from the Orkneys."

Without missing a beat, Doyle dutifully smiled a dimpled smile at him, and kicked Acton's foot under the table.

18

It was a delicate matter, and it would take some delicate handling, but in the end, he had every confidence that she'd never discover the truth. There would never be another lapse like this one, certainly.

"Mother a' mercy." Doyle blew out a long breath, as she sat behind the Range Rover's blessedly anonymous tinted windows and watched the restaurant fade from view. "Now, there's a meal I won't be soon forgettin'. It's a shame Savoie himself didn't wander by."

"I did expect him," said Acton, and to Doyle's astonishment, it was true.

She processed this for a moment as they drove back to headquarters. As usual, her husband seemed disinclined to discuss these strange and assorted events, which was no surprise—the last thing he'd ever admit was that he was arranging matters behind-the-scenes, even though it was as plain as day that such was the case. "It's like you've heard the soundin' of the trumpet," she mused, "and now you're only waitin' for the walls to start collapsin' down."

He smiled his half-smile, and took her hand. "Surely not."

"You've got the nerves for this, husband, but I don't. You're lucky I didn't upend the table in a panic, and flee the scene."

He squeezed her hand. "On the contrary, I think you handled yourself very well."

Dropping her head back on the headrest, she couldn't help but smile. "Only because the three of them were as guilty as the mark of Cain, and it was all rather amusin'."

"They did seem rather surprised to see us, didn't they?"

"They did indeed. It makes you wonder what they're cookin' up, although I'd be very much surprised if you didn't already know."

There was a small silence, and because she knew he wasn't going to spill whatever it was, she asked instead, "How d'you find out the things you find out? It's nothin' short of amazin'."

He shrugged a shoulder. "Much of it is guesswork."

Turning her head to regard him, she teased, "Well, that's not true *at all*."

With a smile, he amended, "Much of it is gathering information, and then understanding what is significant; what motivates behavior."

"Yes," she mused, turning to rest her head back again. "You're rather like a psychiatrist—that's all about perceptions, too—but while a psychiatrist is tryin' to put a stop to desperate measures, you're encouraging them."

Amused, Acton glanced her way. "You astonish me, Lady Acton."

She drew down the corner of her mouth. "Just thinkin' out loud."

They sat for a few minutes in silence, as they made their way through the post lunch-time traffic. Since he seemed in a benign mood—and small wonder, after stirring-up the caldron to such good effect—she ventured, "Are you angry with Williams? I can't tell."

"No," he replied slowly. "Instead, I am sorry for Williams."

Watching him, she insisted, "He's not a back-stabber, you know. There's somethin' else at play, here."

"I am inclined to agree."

With a knit brow, she contemplated how to winkle more information out of her sphinx-like husband, who was carefully guarding his words. "I'm worried that he's got himself tangled up with Morgan Percy."

"That would be unfortunate."

She quirked her mouth. "She's another one who needs to be saved from herself."

Tilting his head, he observed, "I'm not certain that she has any desire to be so saved."

"I'll grant you that—she's rather breathtakin' in her brass, when you think about it. Mayhap it's Percy you should have married; she'd be eggin' you on, like that Lady Macbeth person—the one with the bloody knives, and such."

"All in all, I believe it is just as well that I married you, instead."

She turned her head to him. "You think you're teasin', husband, but it's the unbarked truth; at least I'm a check on your heathenish ways. If you were with her, you'd both wind up in prison, and it'd be a sorry end to all your mutual schemin'."

He lifted her hand to kiss her knuckles. "I am indeed fortunate, to have avoided such a fate."

"Keep it to mind, then, next time you're wishin' for a wife who suits you better; I'm a brake on your certain downfall, and all those guns aren't goin' to spike themselves."

"You and I are well-suited," he insisted. "We are both fond of butter pecan ice cream."

She made a derisive sound. "We may be well-suited, but there's no denyin' that we're opposites—like chalk and cheese, or Nemesis and Até."

Acton looked over at her in surprise, and then couldn't help laughing, a rare event for him. "Good God, where did that come from?"

She feigned insult. "What? Are you implyin' that I'm not familiar with the classics?"

"I am." He smiled, still very much amused.

With an answering smile, she admitted, "Reynolds. It's a rare wonder, he is; I only hope he's civil to poor Mary."

Mary was set to be Edward's nanny. She'd been a witness in an earlier case, and Doyle had known immediately that she was the perfect nanny, even though she was not well-educated, and had been living in the projects, at the time. The woman had emanated honesty and kindness, and Doyle was relieved to think that the next addition to the household would be someone who would blend in so effortlessly, rather than the sort of nanny Reynolds envisioned, from one of those hoity-toity services.

"I am certain Reynolds will behave with all due civility."

She froze in surprise, because there was something underlying her husband's words—something that made him suddenly grave. What? Something about Mary? Or about Reynolds? Glancing at him, she ventured, "Has Reynolds done somethin' he oughtn't?"

Her husband turned to her, a teasing light in his eyes, and Doyle's feeling was gone. "He doesn't dare."

She laughed in agreement, and decided that she was just being fanciful, to think there was some sort of undercurrent in the Reynolds-and-Mary-the-new-nanny scenario. Leastways, it reminded her that she should pay a visit to Mary to see how she did, and perhaps warn her not to be too intimidated by Reynolds—which was irony indeed, as Doyle herself was mightily intimidated by Reynolds.

"If your calendar is clear, I would appreciate it if you would attend the committee hearing tomorrow morning."

She teased, "Oh? So, I'm not to be manipulated into bangin' through the doors this time?"

"There can be only one dramatic entrance, I'm afraid."

As they pulled into the premium parking garage, she eyed him a bit dubiously, because he clearly did not repent of all his guileful maneuvering, which only showed you that she wasn't much of a check on his heathenish ways, after all. "I'll say it again; it's amazin'. You figure out how everyone's goin' to react, and then all it takes is a tiny push—here and there—to make it all come out just as you'd like. And I must admit, husband, that it's a bit demoralizin' to think that I'm just as suceip—sutecce—"

"Susceptible."

"Thank you—susceptible as everyone else."

With all sincerity, he squeezed her hand. "I only do what is best for us, Kathleen. I'm afraid I must ask you to trust me."

"*A'course* I trust you." The words were said a bit sharply, because Harding's warnings were utter nonsense. "Although it's no easy thing, what with the walls about to start collapsin' down. Fortunately, I've had a fine fried sandwich, to help steady my nerves."

"Didn't the kale steady your nerves?" he teased.

"Horrific stuff; it should be fed to prisoners."

He parked the car, but instead of opening the door he sat for a moment, and lifted her hand to kiss the knuckles again. "You should trust me to feed you kale, too."

"Never," she declared with spirit. "Kale is the work of the devil. Give me a humble tin of chickpeas, any day."

"Chickpeas," he repeated, lifting his head with an air of immense satisfaction.

"Do you like chickpeas?" she asked in surprise.

"Certainly," he replied, and it was a lie.

19

All was in train, and the situation would be soon resolved in a very satisfactory manner. Perhaps the heir should be born at Trestles; it was only fitting.

"You can't blindly trust him. Not this time."

Yet again, Doyle was having an obscure conversation with Dr. Harding, and struggling to concentrate, as the wind blew in the stony background. "I can't *not* trust him; I wouldn't know how. On the other hand, I'm not so sure I trust *you*." Especially considering Acton had no doubt murdered the man, although it would probably be bad manners to mention it.

"But you do trust me," the ghost pointed out reasonably.

Reluctantly, Doyle conceded this point, and went on to the next. "I'll admit that there was somethin'—there was somethin' about Morgan Percy; about how Acton spoke about her. It made me uneasy."

Her companion nodded. "Yes. Follow your instinct."

Dubiously, she eyed him. "That doesn't sound like somethin' a psychiatrist should say."

"On the contrary, much of psychiatry is bringing into consciousness those matters which are circulating in the unconscious."

"Well, I've got a basketful of things circulatin'," she complained. "I'm pig-sick of all of it."

"Unravel it—follow your instinct," he repeated. "Unmask the Até, before it's too late."

She sighed. "It's a shame—about Percy, I mean. I rather like her, although I don't know why I do; I've nothin' in common with her."

"On the contrary. She has classic father-abandonment issues; practically a textbook case."

Doyle regarded him a bit dubiously. "Oh? I don't know the fancy names for things; I just know people." She paused, thinking about it. "For instance, I know that Acton wants to tell me about his father, but he's afraid to."

"Excellent diagnosis," the psychiatrist proclaimed, with heavy irony.

Defensively, she explained, "Well, I can't go bangin' in like a busker at a weddin'—Acton trusts me, too. He trusts me not to hurt him, and so I've got to be careful, bein' as I'm the only one who can." She paused, thinking about it. "This feelin's business is all very complicated, and I'm doin' my best."

This remark, however, seemed to garner the ghost's immediate attention, and he leaned forward to say with emphasis, "No—it is far better to assert yourself. You've forgotten entirely about the other one."

She stared at him, not following. "The other one what?"

"The other shadow murder."

"Oh—oh, the pawnbroker." After a slight pause, she confessed, "There's actually lots of reasons for a pawnbroker to be gettin' himself killed. It would be a rare tangle, to try to sort it out."

"No, it wouldn't. It's 'that feelings business,' as you would say."

With some surprise, she repeated, "The pawnbroker is dead because of feelin's?"

"Yes."

Whilst she considered this in confused silence, he repeated, "Unmask the Até."

Still at sea, Doyle slowly shook her head. "But I'm not Lady Macbeth, I'm the opposite—whatever that is. I'm not the one who goads him—I'm the one who spikes his guns."

Very pleased, Harding nodded. "Exactly."

Doyle woke with a start, and instinctively reached for Acton, but once again he'd crept out of bed and was seated at his desk, the dim light from the laptop visible through the bedroom's open doorway.

Doyle blew out a soft breath, and rolled out of bed, wrapping her robe around her expanded girth as she padded over toward the kitchen, crossing in front of him in the process.

"Couldn't you sleep?" he asked, watching her. "I think there is some ice cream, left."

She opened the liquor cabinet, and squinted in the dim light, reviewing the bottles within. "How goes the trap-settin'?"

Although he was wary, he spoke to her in a level tone. "It is too soon to tell, I'm afraid."

A bottle of scotch in hand, she straightened up, and regarded him. "Is the trap for Williams?"

"No," he replied immediately, and it was the truth.

As he watched her with an unreadable expression, she approached to set the bottle on the desk with a small clink. "I'd like to hear about your father. We'll do it once-through, and then we'll never have to speak of it again."

There was a small pause, whilst he kept his gaze focused on the bottle. "I'll need a glass."

"Ice?"

"Not necessary."

She fetched a glass, and then settled into the corner of the sofa as he poured himself a healthy tot. For a while they sat in the darkness, whilst he drank and she held her tongue, waiting—no small feat, as she was not one who tolerated silences well.

Into the darkened stillness, he began, "She was a protégé of my father's. She was a brilliant pianist—first rate."

The faint light coming in from the streetlights below illuminated his profile, and he kept his gaze fixed on the glass in his hand. "I was in university at the time, and a callow fellow. I was infatuated with her; she was older, and—" he paused, thinking about it. "She was rather wild, and passionate; everything that I was not."

Doyle nodded, knowing all there was to know about his infatuations.

"I suppose there can be little surprise that she tried to seize the main chance; the heir to the house was clearly besotted, and of age. She need only convince me to elope, and she'd be a baroness." He paused. "There was also an element of revenge involved. I didn't realize it at the time, but she was also sleeping with my father, and trying to convince him to leave my mother."

Doyle was shocked into remarking, "Holy Mother, Michael; a brasser, through-and-through."

At this, he looked up at her with a small smile. "Yes. But a brilliant pianist. I think—I think her wildness was part and parcel of her brilliance."

As Doyle—having lived amongst some very wild Irishmen—was more inclined to think that wildness was only self-destruction in disguise, she made no comment.

He lowered the glass, and cradled it in his hands. "I would—I would tryst with her in the old kennels, since no one ever went there."

He'd paused, and so she prompted, "And where are the old kennels? Are they by the stables?" She hadn't really been paying attention, on her one tour of the place.

"The building is no longer there. It used to house the hunting pack, in days gone by."

She nodded, and noted that his language was reverting to House-of-Lords, which tended to happen when he was drunk, and only served to show you how much he toned it down when he was talking to the bride who he'd plucked from the raw ranks of the peasantry.

"On the night in question we'd determined to elope, but a vehicle would have raised the alarm, so instead we were to hike overland, to the nearest transport station."

Doyle was skeptical, and offered, "She doesn't sound like much of a hiker, to me."

"No," he agreed. "Looking back, I should not have been surprised when I discovered that it was all an attempt to force my father's hand."

Again, there was a silence, whilst he contemplated his glass. "Your father doesn't sound like someone who'd let his hand be forced," she prompted.

He made no response, and so she inquired gently, "Was there an ugly confrontation, there in the kennels?"

He nodded, his fingers pressed tightly against the glass. "Indeed, there was. When I came in, my father—" he drew a breath. "My father was waiting for me. He'd tied her up, and took great delight in her frustrated fury, and my pleas for her release."

"Holy *Mother*," Doyle repeated, thoroughly shocked. "A monster, he was."

"Yes. He'd taken hold of a clearing axe, and threatened to cut off her fingers, one at a time, so that she could never play again."

"Oh—oh, Michael, that's *horrid*. To think that he'd threaten such a thing—"

"But she would not be cowed—foolhardy, under the circumstances. Instead she cursed him, and spit in his face. In a fit of rage, he swung the blade, and severed one of her arms."

For a few seconds, she could only gape at him. "He—he cut off her arm? Oh; oh, Michael—" Swiftly, she rose and went to kneel before her husband, taking his hands in hers. "How truly awful—"

His head bent, he ran a distracted thumb over the small hand that clasped his. "It was very hard to bear."

Nearly flinching from the toxic combination of bleak misery and black anger, she gazed up into his face. "Then we won't think about it—ever again. We'll put it in a balloon, and let it float away, forever."

He took a breath, his chest rising and falling. "My father then left me alone with her. I was—I was distraught, but she was still alive; when a limb is amputated, the blood vessels constrict immediately, so as to prevent a bleed-out. I enlisted Hudson to stay with her, while I ran to ring up Timothy. When I returned, though, Hudson informed me that she'd died."

As he paused to pour another glass, Doyle gave voice to the unspoken thought. "A shadow murder, I imagine. Hudson is nothing if not loyal to the House of Acton, and this little episode was a problem in more ways than one."

"I would assume." He took another healthy swallow.

"So," she ventured. "The girl—along with the building—disappeared."

"The building burned down," he replied, and offered nothing more.

She kissed his hands, one at a time. "I am unsurprised, my friend. And then your father was made to pay the price for his many misdeeds."

He nodded. "Hudson informed me there was a loosely-organized group of men in the area who could procure black-market guns, for a price."

"Ah," she said neutrally. She was too much the police officer to express admiration for this wholesale breaking of the law, but it now seemed clear from whence her husband's illegal gun-smuggling urges had sprung. "Our Hudson is a trump. Poor Reynolds hasn't got a prayer; he'll have to settle for bein' the under-steward, or somethin'."

Acton struggled to focus, and met her eyes. "I can't be sorry."

Gently, she reminded him, "But you should try, Michael—it's in the rules. And redemption is always miles better than retribution—you're supposed to try to keep your eyes on eternity, rather than what gives you relief in the here-and-now."

But he was past philosophizing, as he lifted his hand to lay a palm against her cheek. "I love you."

She turned her head to kiss the palm. "You don't have to say; not to me. Now, let's get you to bed."

This was not as easy as it would seem; Acton was unsteady on his feet, and she was off-balance in trying to support him, but she managed to navigate him into the bed, and pull the comforter over him, as he settled in. She straightened up, her hands on the small of her back, and watched him for a moment as his breathing became more regular. Small wonder Acton was compelled to do his masterminding—he never wanted to be that helpless again. And now she knew why he always stroked her arms—creepy, it was, but she couldn't very well ask him to stop.

One of his hands groped across the bed and he murmured in his sleep, clearly seeking her out. "I'm comin', husband," she soothed, and carefully crawled in beside him.

20

Today's proceeding should set the hook.

D oyle had decided to wear her best black knit maternity dress—despite the fact it was getting a bit too tight—to the committee hearing, being as she thought it made her look as though she respected the gravity of the committee's work, and didn't think it all a pack of nonsense. She'd pulled her hair behind a black headband and did her best to appear composed, like a worthy baroness, and not like some skimble-skamble pretender who'd married a fellow pretender who was certainly much better at pretending than she was.

She'd half-expected Harding to make a re-appearance in her dreams last night after she'd heard Acton's horrifying story, but she'd no ghostly visitors, and had slept as well as could be hoped for when one was half the size of a baleen whale, and expected to play a starring role in Parliament the next morning.

Neither she nor Acton made reference to the prior night's recital—which was to be expected, after all—but she'd sensed that his mood this morning was upbeat. Looking forward to matching wits with Sir Stephen's team, he was, and more power to him; it would be a nice change not to have to constantly suspicion that Acton's stupid heir was trying to kill her.

At present, she was seated in her armchair against the wall whilst the committee was discussing some point of order with the chairman, their heads all huddled together. Acton's counsel had made a motion to preclude any further argument that Acton had been previously married, being as Acton had unequivocally testified that he hadn't been, and the only evidence offered by Sir Stephen were documents that were not supported by any live testimony—not even that of a records-keeper. In general, documents didn't make their way into evidence without someone swearing to them under penalty of perjury, and Doyle decided that she probably shouldn't mention that the reason there were no records-keepers for these particular documents was because Philippe Savoie had managed to murder both of them.

Sir Stephen's counsel had argued that the birth records were official in nature, and therefore should be admitted outright into evidence; any questions about their authenticity should be directed toward how much weight to give them, rather than whether they were admissible in the first place. Counsel focused on the significant fact that there were two separate documents from unrelated places that referenced a marriage—the Holy Trinity Clinic record, where the supposed first wife had supposedly given birth, and the copy of the same record found in Lord Aldwych's archives.

Acton was seated at the respondent's table with his counsel, and appeared serenely unconcerned with this point of law, but Doyle knew he was keenly interested in the outcome of the discussion. Therefore, it was with some surprise that she could sense his flare of satisfaction when the chairman—rather regretfully—informed the committee that the records could indeed be admitted into evidence, and the argument about the first marriage could continue to be made.

Acton's counsel, however, pretended to be very unhappy with this turn of events and reluctantly rose to his feet. "If that is the case, my lord, would it be possible to have the two documents examined by a forensic specialist? As there is no evidentiary foundation for them, the committee should be assured by an expert that they have not been falsified in any respect."

"We cannot have anyone from the Met examine them, my lord," Sir Stephen's counsel protested. "It would be a clear conflict of interest."

Acton's counsel offered, "We would have no objection to an independent specialist, my lord, appointed by this committee."

"Duly noted," said the chairman, who made a note. "That will necessarily delay the introduction of the documents themselves, though. Is there any other live testimony, with respect to the alleged first wife?" He then rested his forehead briefly against his hand, so that he could cast an apologetic glance at Doyle, who was actually somewhat relieved by this gesture, as his contrite attitude suggested that he was not looking to navigate her out of her marriage. She'd entertained the alarming possibility that he was hoping to lay romantic siege to the next Orkney Islander in line, regardless of her whale-size.

Sir Stephen's counsel stood. "As it was a secret marriage, we could find no witnesses, per se, but we do have a witness who will testify about the relationship between the principals during the time frame in question."

"Objection, my lord," said Acton's counsel. "Unduly speculative."

"I will allow," the chairman decided. "As is the case with the records, the committee can sort out how much weight to give the testimony."

"Then the petitioner would like to call Mrs. Wright."

Doyle sat up in alarmed surprise. Mrs. Wright had been the treacherous cook at Trestles, who'd been conspiring to ruin Acton. Needless to say, once the plot was exposed Mrs. Wright had been unceremoniously given the sack. Her presence here could only be considered ominous, and Doyle resisted the urge to send a panicked glance in the direction of her husband.

After having been called by the clerk, the former cook made her way down the aisle with her hands clasped tightly before her, apparently so nervous that she did not dare raise her gaze. Despite the woman's meek mien, Doyle's level of alarm rose because she was not fooled; Mrs. Wright was enjoying herself hugely.

After the witness had been sworn, Sir Stephen's counsel began his questioning. "You were employed at Trestles as a cook, during the time period in question?"

"I was," the woman agreed, her double chins bobbing. With some dismay, Doyle noted that Mrs. Wright exuded plump and plain English honesty in the best tradition—which was why she'd deceived Doyle, back when she was colluding with the villains. This did not bode well, as it seemed evident that no one was going to believe that such a pattern-card of traditions-gone-by would be anything but honest and believable.

"Do you recall observing a romantic relationship between the respondent and the young lady in question?"

The woman nodded earnestly. "Oh yes; I do remember it well. She was always about, and very fond of the young master."

"You are not aware whether there was, in fact, a marriage between the two, however."

"That is correct." She nodded again, her cheeks a bit pink.

"But—" and here the man paused, so as to create an emphasis, "but you were made aware that an elopement was planned."

"Oh, yes," Mrs. Wright testified, as a rustling of movement amongst the committee members could be observed. "The young lady did confide in me, once."

This was not true, and Doyle could only close her eyes, and prepare for the worst.

"And what, Mrs. Wright, did she confide?"

"Objection, my lord." Acton's counsel stood, and a thread of outrage could be heard in his voice. "It would be the rankest hearsay."

"I'll allow." The chairman gestured vaguely with his hand. "Proceed."

Mrs. Wright leaned forward, and lowered her voice. "She said she was going to talk him into going up to Gretna, or mayhap Dunby, and that she'd already researched it, to make certain the marriage would be binding."

This response was apparently not according to script, and counsel was seen to hesitate for the barest instant, before he asked in a more forceful tone, "But the plan went forward, as far as you know, and the respondent went away with her, of his own free will?"

"I don't know as he did," the witness admitted, with a slight frown. "He never mentioned it to me, even though he would come to seek out my fresh-baked scones, and we'd have a good chat, now and again." She turned to smile upon Acton with all appearance of fondness. "He was such a sweet boy."

Doyle was forced to sink her face into her hands, and hope that anyone observing her might think that she was overcome with emotion, rather than desperately trying not to laugh out loud.

Counsel was striving mightily to hide his extreme dismay at the unexpected turn that the witness's testimony had taken, and seemed to be trying to decide whether this line of questioning was even worth pursuing. The decision was taken out of his hands, however, as Mrs. Wright could be seen to flush, and lower her gaze. "The young master did tell me that his cousin, here, was very angry about his—his relationship with the young woman." Here she paused to slip a fearful peep at Sir Stephen. "And the next thing you knew, she'd disappeared, and was never seen again."

And there you go, thought Doyle, reaching down to collect her things. When all was said and done, you could always trust Acton to turn the tables.

21

She looked very well in black.

"Nicely done," Doyle said to Acton, when they finally had a moment alone. They were yet again seated at the corner table in the Parliament cafeteria, so as to be put on display before their assorted well-wishers, who watched them with unabated good will and a great deal of whispering behind hands.

"It did appear to go well," her husband remarked mildly, as he considered the offerings listed. "I see that the soup today is lentil. May I fetch you a bowl?"

Doyle grimaced in distaste. "May as well be gruel. A shame they've no deep-fried sandwiches, like the ones at Candide's."

"We could share a beefsteak."

She raised her brows in surprise. "You're wantin' a beefsteak?" Acton was not a hearty-beefsteak-for-lunch sort of person.

"Let's." Without waiting for her say-so, he rose to walk over to the counter, and signal to the chef.

Saints, she thought, watching him in bemusement. He must feel the need for fortification, and small blame to him, after the latest round of guileful maneuvering—it was amazing the man got any sleep at all. She resolved to humor him, even though she wasn't a hearty-beefsteak sort of person herself, being as hearty-beefsteaks had been as rare as hen's teeth in her life, thus far.

After he'd returned to the table, Doyle took the occasion to observe, "Well, to sum up this continuin' holy show, we're left with the impression that—in his zeal to acquire the title—Sir Stephen not only murdered your father, but also murdered your potential bride. Although on his behalf, she's been portrayed as a flamfoo who was tryin' to trick you into marriage."

Acton offered a half-smile. "I am reluctant to agree until I first discover what a 'flamfoo' is."

She gave him a look. "You know very well what I mean, my friend—you're the one paintin' the picture, after all. And although Mrs. Wright's turned up a trump, she's still a crackin' blackheart, and she's not foolin' me one whit."

Tilting his head, he reminded her, "But she will fool everyone else. Impressions, in a case such as this one, are more important than the evidence."

Doyle could only agree, as she tried to cross her legs but had to be content with crossing her ankles, instead. "Aye that; there's not a soul alive who wouldn't believe her. Mrs. Wright looks like someone who would sell apple-butter for the parish, and Sir Stephen looks like someone who would steal from the offerin' plate."

"Precisely."

They'd had this conversation before; humankind put a priority on instinctive reactions—reactions that could be exploited, depending on the desired outcome. Instinct often took precedence over facts—even facts that were inarguable, in the cold light of day. It was the way the juries ferreted out the liars, and in a broader sense, it was the way the species survived. All the evidence in the world was not going to convince anyone that the smarmy Sir Stephen was in the right—even though he was—and Acton was not above exploiting that impression. It all went back, of course, to Acton's belief that the ends justified the means, and that the justice system needed the occasional push in the right direction.

With Mrs. Wright's fairy-tale fresh in her mind, Doyle observed, "I was that surprised, Michael; I didn't think I'd ever see Mrs. Wright again." This was an understatement; it was a miracle that Acton hadn't added the former cook to his long list of retribution murders.

Lifting the carafe from the table, he topped off her water glass with a careful hand. "It was fortunate that she was persuaded to come forward."

Doyle guessed, "You offered filthy lucre, and plenty of it. Well done, you; she's one who's always had her eye on the prize. I hope you didn't empty the vault."

"No such thing; she was all too pleased to offer her assistance."

Doyle gave him a skeptical look as their lunch was served, and they ate for a few minutes in companionable silence. He wasn't going to tell her the particulars, and—truth to tell—she'd rather not know the particulars, as it would no doubt involve the suborning of perjury.

Acton offered her the rarer portion of the beefsteak, which was duly appreciated—the English had a tendency to cook the flavor out of everything—and she devoured it with gusto. "So; I suppose there's to be a third act to the holy show, what with the two documents havin' to be checked out. Are we worried about what the specialist might say?"

"Not particularly," he replied, and it was the truth.

Eying him shrewdly, she ventured, "It does seem to be an extraordinary coincidence; that two documents referencin' this supposed-marriage were unearthed, and from two completely different places."

"Extraordinary," he agreed in a mild tone, without raising his gaze.

"Sir Stephen must have felt like it was Christmas and his birthday, all rolled into one."

"I shouldn't be surprised."

She'd get nowhere with this, of course, and so she re-addressed her meal, but couldn't resist remarking, "That counsel of yours does a fine job of pretendin' to be dismayed. I think a good barrister is nothin' more than a good actor."

"I will agree. You should finish up your beefsteak, as we'll be reconvening soon."

She glanced up at him, and decided to take the bull by the horns. "Should I expect more drama from your counsel, this fine day? You're cock o' hoop about somethin', husband."

Thus confronted, he hesitated, and then equivocated, "In due course."

Annoyed, she stabbed at the last bite. "I'm not goin' to be your pregnant courtroom prop unless you treat me better. Honestly, Michael."

He reached to take her hand. "You are not very good at subterfuge, I'm afraid."

This was inarguable, and she sighed in wistful acknowledgment. "No, which is why I won't be testifyin' any time soon—I'd blurt out all the wrong things, and the clerk would have to hit me with a mindin'-staff."

"You must trust me, I'm afraid."

"I do trust you," she declared firmly. And it was true; she'd always trusted him, and from the first moment they'd met. It was inconceivable that Acton would betray her, so Harding must have got it by the wrong leg, for some reason.

After lunch, she headed back through the muted hallways alongside her husband, listening to the discreet, excited buzz that could be heard in their wake. "Who will testify, next? They're goin' to have to re-trench, poor things, and I can't imagine they'll want to call you back." It seemed unlikely; the last needful thing Sir Stephen's counsel would want would be for Acton to get up and verify everything Mrs. Wright had said.

"We shall see," was the only response she got, and again, she had the impression that he was looking forward to something.

"Is your mother comin' back?" This asked with a trace of dread.

"I doubt it." He held the entry door open for her.

Doyle glanced up at him as she passed through. "Talk about your Lady Macbeths, she'd fill the bill."

"An apt comparison," he agreed. "Down to the vengeful ghosts."

"The ghosts don't much like her," she informed him, and carefully settled into her seat.

22

There was no question that her iron count would be in a better range, next visit.

Doyle was soon to discover the other side's counter-move, because Sir Stephen himself was called forward to testify. Under questioning by his counsel, he spoke of the two different points of contention: Acton's alleged first marriage, and the rumors of an imposter heir when Acton's grandfather held the title.

The chairman himself leaned in to note, "You were not living at Trestles, though, when either of these supposed events went forward, and cannot testify, either way."

"No, I was not." Sir Stephen had taken pains to come across as a reasonable truth-teller, and Doyle grudgingly noted that he did indeed tell the truth—or the truth as far as he knew it, anyways.

The chairman reviewed his notes. "With respect to the marriage, we must await the findings on the two documents." He looked up again at Sir Stephen's counsel. "In the meantime, have you a corroborating witness, with respect to either the alleged marriage, or the alleged substitution of heirs?"

Counsel replied with regret, "Unfortunately, my lord, it was difficult to find any direct evidence, and anyone who was a witness to the post-war events is now deceased. But we have circumstantial evidence that shows a pattern of secretive behavior."

Oh-oh, thought Doyle with a pang of alarm. Don't like the sounds of that—Acton has a basketful of secrets that should never see the light of day. Please God, amen.

"Utter speculation, my lord," Acton's counsel protested. "The petitioner has no admissible evidence, and so wishes to use this opportunity to defame my client with unrelated matters." As the man paused, his gaze rested on Doyle for the barest instant, and the significance of this action was not lost on anyone—the implication being that the longstanding bachelor had some secrets best not discussed before his wedded wife.

The chairman rested his own sympathetic gaze on Doyle and nodded in agreement. "Sir Stephen, it is your obligation, as the petitioner, to bear the burden of proving your claim. I'll not allow innuendo or calumny in an attempt to prejudice this committee. Instead, let us proceed with the matters at issue."

Under the skillful questioning of his counsel, Sir Stephen then described the longstanding family rumor about the imposter heir.

At its conclusion, Acton's counsel stood and roundly proclaimed, "The tale is a preposterous one, my lord—to disparage an ancient and illustrious title in such a way is nothing short of appalling."

"Is there a question pending?" asked the chairman, his chin resting upon his hand.

"I beg your pardon, my lord." Acton's counsel appeared to tamp down his outrage, and then slowly approached Sir Stephen, asking in a level tone, "You believe that a switch was made generations ago—a switch that no one noticed, apparently—and as a result, you were deprived of a present-day barony."

"Yes, I do."

"Yet you've made no claim before now? Why is this, sir?"

It was clear Sir Stephen was prepared for this rather obvious question, and answered steadily. "I was the heir to my cousin, and I was content to be given a role in running the estate—living there, day to day. But now—now that the information about the first marriage has come to light, it seems clear that there is a pattern of deception that can no longer be ignored."

"Not to mention you are about to be replaced as heir, and will no longer live at Trestles."

"That was also a consideration," Sir Stephen admitted. "So long as I was the heir, the true line would eventually be re-established, and no harm done. Now, that is not the case."

Counsel paused, and faced the committee. "Do you forget that there is another claimant?"

But Sir Stephen could not contain his scorn. "That's the claim that is preposterous—there is no long-lost heir. After all, if such an heir could have been identified, there would have been no reason to substitute an imposter in the first place."

Counsel raised his brows. "You have no knowledge of Mr. Savoie's claim?"

"No, of course not."

"Have you ever met with Mr. Savoie?"

"No, I have not."

There was a slight pause, as though to give emphasis to the last answer, but Doyle frowned a bit, because it was the truth. Nevertheless, it appeared that Acton's counsel was implying mightily that some chicanery was afoot, here.

But whatever impression the barrister sought to make was not pursued, as he suddenly changed tack. "Sir Stephen, can we be assured that Sir Peter was indeed your father? I understand your birth record is missing, and has been missing for many years."

"Objection, my lord." Sir Stephen's counsel rose to his feet in outrage, as the committee members murmured amongst themselves.

The chairman, however, seemed to be discreetly enjoying himself, what with the twists and turns that the matter had taken, and shook his head. "Overruled; the committee must determine the petitioner's standing to inherit, along with the respondent's."

Sir Stephen's face became a bit mottled, and it was only with an effort that he was seen to control his temper. "A scurrilous rumor. No truth to it at all, and I cannot be held responsible if the hospital has lost the record."

The chairman asked, "Would anyone have firsthand knowledge of the circumstances of your birth?"

"Of course—the entire claim is nothing short of preposterous."

Acton's counsel spread his hands, and addressed the chairman. "Perhaps this is another issue that can be resolved at the next hearing—we have only to subpoena those hospital personnel who were witnesses."

"Duly noted," said the chairman, who then bent his head to listen to a whispered message from the clerk. At its conclusion, the elderly man clasped his hands before him in pleased anticipation, and announced, "The additional claimant, Mr. Savoie, is without. I do not believe he is represented by counsel, but let us hear what he has to say."

Mother a' mercy, thought Doyle, closing her eyes briefly. It wants only this—I hope Acton knows what he's doing.

The clerk opened the door, and Savoie sauntered into the room, dressed in a sleek black turtleneck instead of a coat and tie, and looking as disdainful as only a Frenchman can, when confronted with a room full of superior-minded Englishmen. He was asked to be seated, and as he was sworn in, he pulled a cigarette from a silver case, and lit it up.

With a severe expression, the clerk advised, "You cannot smoke here, sir."

"*Non?*" Savoie blew out a breath of smoke in the general direction of the clerk, and then stubbed out the cigarette.

"You must swear that you will tell the truth, sir," the clerk prompted.

Savoie leaned back, at his ease, and looked amused. "*Bien sûr.*"

"I'm afraid we must ask you to respond in English, unless you wish to request a translator."

Still amused, Savoie rendered his thin smile. "Yes. I will tell the truth." Doyle duly noted that this was a lie, which was not much of a surprise, all in all.

"Petitioner's counsel may proceed to examine," said the chairman.

Sir Stephen's counsel rose, and addressed Savoie. "I understand, sir, that you claim to trace your ancestry back to the House of Acton, by way of the ninth baron."

Savioe nodded in a condescending fashion, and smirked a bit. "*De vrai.*"

The chairman leaned in. "You must respond in English, sir."

"Yes." The Frenchman nodded in mock solemnity.

The chairman continued to address Savoie, apparently having decided that the Frenchman needed matters plainly explained. "You will have to present your case before the committee, Mr. Savoie, or waive all claims. You may wish to seek out counsel, to help you."

"I do not wish the English counsel," the witness replied, his malicious glance resting for a moment on the two barristers present. "*Salauds.*"

The chairman hurriedly decided not to seek a translation, and instead plowed ahead. "What is your evidence, then?"

"I have the—how do you say? The *généologie.* The chart of the family."

"I see." The chairman leaned back, frowning. "We will need to see this chart, sir."

"And this man—" Savoie tilted his head negligently toward Acton. "His mother; she can tell you. She speaks with my *grande-tante, en Normandie.*"

There was a surprised silence. "Your great-aunt, you say?" The chairman looked up, and conceded, "If this is the case, we may have to re-call the dowager Lady Acton."

This suggestion was met with palpable dismay, and Acton's counsel stood. "May I, my lord?"

"Please."

Counsel regarded Savoie with an expression of grave concern, which only prompted another amused smile from the witness. "Mr. Savoie, why has no claim to the title been made before now?"

Savoie slid his malevolent gaze toward Acton. "Me, I did not know this Lord Acton is—how do you say it? Cahoots. A fraud."

There was a rustling of movement amongst the committee, expressing their well-bred disapproval of such plain speaking against one of their own.

Acton's counsel continued, "I believe, sir, that you have rather a lengthy history of run-ins with law enforcement. Indeed, you are currently featured on Interpol's Watch List in connection with black market arms-dealing, and government corruption."

Several of the committee members were heard to murmur to each other in alarm, but in response, Savoie shrugged. "It is the English policemen who are in prison for corruption, not me, *n'est pas?*"

"Thanks to Lord Acton," retorted one of the committee members, with barely-suppressed outrage.

"*De vrai,*" Savoie agreed mildly, and was seen to reach for his cigarette case before he thought the better of it.

Doyle watched these events with deep admiration, and thought, it's like that Agatha Christie story; the one where the witness is so unlikeable that no one wants to believe her—the film with that famous German actress. Acton is right—perception will trump the evidence; at the rate things are going, Savoie will be lucky if he gets out of here with a whole skin.

Acton's counsel then asked, a thread of incredulity in his voice, "Do you seek to take up residence at Trestles, sir?"

But Savoie could be seen to curl his lip at the very idea. "*Non*; I could not live in England. Instead, I will build a resort—how do you say it? A spa."

There was a horrified silence. Sir Stephen's counsel leapt to his feet, and protested, "My lord, we must have a chance to examine the family documents, and verify this man's story. We've been given no foreknowledge of this witness's testimony—"

"Silence," ordered the chairman, much shaken. "We will reconvene a week hence, and try to lay this matter to rest."

23

She would know, of course, that he'd put Savoie up to it,
but with any luck, she'd never discover their arrangement.
She'd not approve, and he hated to see the disappointment
in her eyes.

Doyle had noticed that Munoz's ACC undercover work always seemed to happen in the afternoons, and so after she returned to headquarters she went to seek out the other girl, to see if an opportunity to spy might present itself.

Mentally, she reminded herself not to mention anything about the committee proceedings to Munoz, who was apparently unaware that her beau was posing as the true pretender in this ridiculous morality play. If nothing else, it showed that Savoie was good at keeping a secret— but Doyle already knew this, since he'd never told anyone about their own little adventure together, and he seemed to have his own code of honor, despite the questionable means by which he earned his living.

As a case-in-point, Doyle knew that Savoie had worked with Acton in bringing down the corruption rig, and now it seemed clear that they were allied, yet again. There must be some aim in putting the Frenchman up as the heir, but she didn't know what the plan was, which was probably just as well. All in all, it seemed very unlikely that Acton was going to cede his title to the likes of Philippe Savoie—although one never knew, with her wily husband. It would almost be worth it, to see Savoie turn the dowager out, bag and baggage.

Doyle found Munoz seated at her cubicle, typing up a report with a small frown between her brows. "Ho, Munoz. How's our Elena?" Munoz's sister had recently married their supervisor, and was expecting her own child. The sister was the one who'd been abducted into the sex slavery ring, and Doyle focused carefully to see if Munoz showed any consciousness of the reason the evildoers had decided to abduct Elena.

Munoz did not deign to stop typing, and replied, "She's gone to meet Habib's family, in Pakistan."

"Holy Mother," breathed Doyle, distracted by this revelation. "That's goin' to be a nine-day's wonder."

Apparently resigned to the fact that Doyle was not going to be ignored away, the other girl swiveled around in her chair. "Maybe not. She says his mother is so happy he's finally got married that nothing else matters."

Doyle considered this. "I suppose that's the way it's always been, and always will be. Mothers get a little less picky, as time goes by."

"I don't know; my parents would *freak*, if they knew about me and Philippe."

This was of interest, and Doyle ventured, "About his bein' French, or about his bein' a criminal kingpin?" It was unclear which would be the worst transgression.

"French. Since he's rich, they wouldn't mind the other so much."

"Well, there's that, of course. My mother used to say that money can plaster over the deepest cracks."

The beauty frowned at her. "He talks about you a lot."

This, of course, was a topic fraught with peril, and so Doyle teased, "Well, it's very allurin' to the opposite sex, I am. Especially in my present condition."

Thus reminded, Munoz eyed Doyle's pregnant belly. "I don't think he's the type to settle down."

Fairly, Doyle pointed out, "I would have agreed with you, except that he's devoted to that little boy, which doesn't seem in keepin'. So, I've given up guessin'."

Absently, Munoz considered this, as she fingered her keyboard. "I might be good for him—I could keep him on the straight and narrow."

Good luck with that, thought Doyle, who'd been treated to a hearty helping of Savoie underhandedness this very day. Aloud, she ventured, "I don't know if he's someone who'd want to change, Munoz."

Sighing, Munoz wistfully observed, "He's got that accent."

"*Everyone's* got an accent," Doyle countered crossly. "It's annoyin', is what it is."

"And it's so unfair; everything worked out perfectly for you, and you didn't even *try*."

You don't know the half of it, thought Doyle; my husband's one step ahead of a Class-A prison sentence, and his ancestral home may very well become a Euro-spa. That, and brassers like Morgan Percy were always doing their level best to steal him away. Suddenly reminded, Doyle asked, "Didn't you say that Officer Gabriel has a live-in girlfriend?"

"He does. Why?"

"Nothin'. I just thought he was showin' an interest in someone else, is all."

Munoz did not find this surprising in the least, and gave her companion a look of superior scorn. "News flash, Doyle; men are men."

"Well, then mayhap he'll be susceptible to your fine eyes, Munoz—he seems rather nice. Has a sense of humor, which is always a good sign."

But the beauty shook her head with real regret. "I'm not ready, yet. I've got to have my heart broken, first."

Doyle offered, "This feelings business is way too complicated."

"Amen to that." Munoz looked up. "Speaking of which, what's with Williams?"

Williams is miserable, Doyle thought; but he doesn't want to tell me why. "I don't know. Maybe he's under a lot of stress—we're still so shorthanded."

"Join the club." Pointedly, Munoz turned back to her laptop and re-commenced typing.

I need to follow-up on why Williams is miserable, and whether there's a shadow murder tied up in it, somewhere, Doyle reminded herself; but I've a feeling that I'm not going to like what I discover. Mentally girding her loins, she checked the time on her mobile, and then belatedly remembered the whole reason that she'd stopped in to speak with Munoz. "Are you busy this afternoon? I could use a bit of help on the Santero case."

This caused the other girl to pause, as the Santero case was high-profile, and a good way for an ambitious detective to bring glory upon herself. "Sorry," she said with real regret. "How about tomorrow?"

"Oh—oh, are you doin' your ACC work today, then?"

"Yes, but I'll be free tomorrow, I promise."

"Right-o," said Doyle, as she scrolled for Gabriel's number. "See you then."

24

He should broach the subject of maternity leave, soon. She was avoiding it, of course.

To his credit, Gabriel willingly abandoned whatever it was he was doing to drive Doyle on her Munoz-shadowing operation, and she thanked him profusely as they waited in an unmarked vehicle outside the parking garage.

"I hope it won't take too long," Doyle said. "I truly appreciate it."

With an easy gesture, Gabriel shrugged. "What's the protocol?"

Doyle knit her brow. "I just want to see where she goes, and what's she's doin'."

He glanced over at her. "Is this the ACC assignment that you mentioned? What's your concern?"

She debated what to tell him, since she couldn't very well say that the ghost of a dead psychiatrist was haunting her. "I'm just a bit worried, is all. She may be bein' duped."

Interestingly, he didn't ask the next obvious question as to who was doing the duping. Instead, he observed, "She doesn't strike me as someone who's easy to dupe."

"No, she's as shrewd as can stare, that one."

"Does this involve Morgan Percy?"

Surprised, she turned to look at him. "No, but that seems like an odd thing for you to be askin'. Unsnabble, if you will."

Again, he shrugged. "I don't know as I'd trust Morgan Percy."

But Doyle offered a half-hearted defense of the girl, as she returned her gaze to the parking structure's exit. "I don't think she's a bad sort, truly. She's got textbook abandonment issues."

Amused, he lifted a brow. "Does she? Someone was paying attention, in forensic psychology."

"Not really," Doyle admitted. "I hated that class." It was true; there were too many labels and presumptions for someone like her, who could unerringly cut to the nub, all on her own. Not to mention that she had to pretend for the entire class that she couldn't cut to the nub, all on her own.

"All right, then. We'll agree to disagree, with respect to Morgan Percy."

There was a nuance in his tone that prompted her to eye him, sidelong. "Never say you're doin' a line with her?"

He smiled. "I can't; I don't know what that means."

Hastily, she took hold of her nosy self. "Never you mind—it's none of my business, after all."

"I suppose not," he agreed, his smile taking the sting out of the snub.

Doyle stared at the parking structure, frozen with surprise. This last comment was a lie. But why on earth would Gabriel's interest in Morgan Percy be any of her business? And why would *he* think so? What—whatever could it possibly mean?

"That's Munoz, isn't it?" He nodded toward an unmarked vehicle, going through the gate at the garage's exit.

Pulling herself together, Doyle nodded. "Yes—let's stay back, and tail her as best we can. I'd rather we lose her than we get twigged."

He pulled into traffic, keeping an eye on their target. "We could always say we were just out on a date. A perfectly innocent explanation."

She laughed, and shook her head. "Not a soul would believe it, my friend. I'm a million months pregnant, and I'm married to your CO."

"All right; instead we can say you think you're in labor, and I'm driving you to the hospital."

"Even though we're goin' in the wrong direction. You'd have to say the GPS went out, and for some reason you didn't contact Acton immediately. All in all, that excuse would only make the goin'-out-on-a-date excuse more believable, and I'd wind up in the soup."

With a smile, he conceded, "Then I'll just have to make sure we don't get twigged. She's heading south, it looks like."

"Yes," Doyle mused. "Stay well back, since there'll be less traffic, soon." She was still distracted, struggling mightily to figure out how to raise the Morgan Percy topic again, so as to probe why Gabriel thought whatever-it-was that he thought. She hit upon a potential tack to take, and ventured, "Did Percy say anythin' about gettin' the Santero's shoes into evidence?"

Ah—he was suddenly wary, although his relaxed attitude didn't change. "Not to me."

"They're subject to a suppression motion, you know—unless Percy doesn't care that shadow murders seem to be lyin' thick on the ground. You'd think she'd care, though—it's her client that's gettin' framed-up for them."

There was a small silence, and she could tell he was choosing his words carefully, despite his negligent manner. "I suppose we'll have to wait and see."

She sank back in the seat, aware that he didn't like this topic of conversation. "I haven't had a chance to check—did forensics get anythin' off the shoes?"

"They were clean; no prints." He gave her a glance.

She quirked her mouth in acknowledgment. "Naturally; the last place you'd expect prints is on your leather shoes, after usin' your fingers to pull them on and off, every day."

They sat for a few moments in silence, processing this very interesting fact as they followed Munoz's vehicle. Doyle asked, "Remind me; how many of the shoes were odd sizes?"

It was clear that Gabriel had already gone down this path, and he answered readily. "Four. We can presume the expensive Italian ones belonged to the QC; they're his size."

"And another pair can be matched to Blakney-the-pawnbroker, I imagine."

"No doubt," he replied evenly.

"What is it?" she turned to ask him, alarmed.

He glanced at her in surprise. "What is what?"

"Oh—oh; I just thought—I just thought you knew somethin' about Blakney, and his shoes."

He raised his brows. "Do *you* know something about Blakney and his shoes?"

"No," she admitted. "But I think I should." Harding had certainly been banging on about the stupid pawnbroker, but honestly, Doyle didn't know where to start, and besides, all her spare time had been taken up at Parliament, watching a passel of ridiculous people who were still stuck in the eighteenth century.

On the other hand, she couldn't shake the nagging conviction that Gabriel knew something that she should make it her business to find out—after all, she'd enlisted him to help shadow Munoz, even though Williams was usually her go-to, in situations such as this. There's something here, just below the surface, she acknowledged with a touch of bewilderment; but I'm lost, and I don't know how to lead him into a useful conversation without bringing up stupid Morgan Percy again, which would sound completely daft.

Instead, she decided that she would be as subtle as a serpent. "You aren't involved in the corruption rig, are you?"

He looked over at her in amused surprise. "No. Are you?"

"No. I just thought I'd make sure."

Still grinning, he pointed out, "If I were, it's very unlikely I'd admit to it, Detective Sergeant."

She smiled in response. "Now, that's true."

"If I may say so, sometimes I think you are a little too trusting."

Again, there was a nuance behind the words, and she exclaimed in exasperation, "Faith, Gabriel; if you're tryin' to warn me about someone, you've got to say it, straight out—it's thick as a plank, I am."

At this, he laughed aloud. "No, no—instead, it's my turn to apologize, for intruding where I shouldn't."

"We're even, then. I tried to nose my way into your business, first."

"Then let's tip our caps and say no more."

They drove for a few more minutes in silence as they headed toward Surrey, and Doyle wondered aloud, "Where's she goin'? You wouldn't think the ACC would be investigatin' somethin' so far afield—they're supposed to worry about corrupt cops at the Met."

"Well, the whole set-up seems a little bizarre—that the ACC recruited a CID for undercover work. She's fairly recognizable, after all."

Doyle immediately perked up. "Oh? D'you think she's pretty?"

He laughed again. "Wait—I thought I was doing a line with Morgan Percy."

"Never you mind," Doyle demurred hastily. "I'm oversteppin', again."

But now that he'd mentioned it, Doyle realized this was one of the things that had been bothering her. "You're right, though; it's a little strange that they are usin' someone like her for this—she's too recognizable. She's like me; I'm as recognizable as Big Ben, and roughly the same size."

"I'll make no comment, other than to agree that your undercover days are probably over."

She smiled in acknowledgement of this sad fact. "And it's just as well; it occurs to me that I sound like a fool, tellin' someone like you how to tail someone."

"Nonsense; you have a knack for it."

This, of course, was not true, but Doyle very much appreciated this attempt to make her feel less a fool. "Except for the sad fact that I can't drive, and this accent of mine gives the game away."

"Not necessarily a mark against you; they have to use native Gaelic-speakers in counter-terrorism, because non-native speakers are always caught out. There are too many idioms and regional differences."

Doyle decided not to ask what "idioms" meant, and instead disclaimed, "I don't speak it very well anymore—I'm rusty." Absently, she gazed out the windscreen at the car ahead of them. "I wish I spoke French—everyone speaks French but me." Surprised at herself, Doyle stilled for a moment, her scalp prickling.

Gabriel was understandably at sea. "Who speaks French?"

Button your lip, my girl, Doyle cautioned herself. The last needful thing was to blurt out to Gabriel that she'd overheard Acton and Savoie having a low-voiced discussion in French at Trestles, and that one of the ghosts had warned her that it was just as well she didn't know what it was they were talking about.

She turned to smile at him. "Nothin'; I was just wishin' I had the patience to learn another language." But it wasn't nothing; she knew—in the way that she knew things—that it was important, for some reason. At the time, she'd assumed that the two men were negotiating a suspect's surrender to the authorities, but why would Savoie be in on it, then? And why speak in French?

Gabriel interrupted her thoughts. "There—Munoz is turning in. Looks like she's heading to the racecourse."

With a small frown, Doyle watched the other car. "I suppose it's all makin' a bit more sense, then—she wouldn't be as recognizable, at such a place, and there's always a basketful of black-legs hangin' about a racecourse. That's how we caught the mighty Solonik, Williams and me."

He turned to regard her with interest. "The Russian? What was someone like him doing at a racecourse?"

143

Doyle was suddenly aware that she should be careful about what she said. "Solonik was tryin' to cut in on someone else's smugglin' rig, but he got a bit careless. Mainly, we were lucky, Williams and me; there was a witness who could place Solonik at the course with an illegal weapon, and the rest of the case just fell into place." Best not to mention that "the rest" involved some Acton-style strong-arming.

Gabriel contemplated the road ahead, as they followed the other vehicle toward the racecourse. "Maybe some bent coppers were involved in Solonik's rig—that could be the reason for the ACC's interest."

Doyle slowly replied, "Perhaps, but it seems unlikely—that there's a connection to crooked cops, I mean. The Solonik situation was all about rival gangs, and now the gangs have conveniently wiped each other out."

"And Solonik is dead."

"Indeed, he is." She frowned again, bewildered, because her instinct was doing the equivalent of beating her about the head and shoulders. What? she thought, exasperated; no question that the Russian kingpin's evil schemes were dust and ashes. The man died in prison, and the vile sister who took his place was now incapacitated—

"Solonik still incites a lot of interest, for someone who's dead."

She turned to him, having the impression that this time, it was Gabriel who was fishing for information. "What d'you mean?"

He shrugged, his manner off-hand. "I just think there are a lot of loose ends that are still under review."

Giving him a look, she replied in a dry tone, "Meanin' you're doin' somethin' mysterious, and you can't tell me about it." It was on the tip of her tongue to mention Chief Inspector Drake, but she held back, not sure whether she was supposed to know that Gabriel was investigating Drake, on the sly.

Smiling, he agreed, "More or less."

"Holy Mother of God," she said suddenly, so startled that she braced her hands against the dashboard. "We've got to turn back."

Gabriel glanced at her in concern. "Are you all right?"

Her mouth dry, Doyle tried to decide how to put her instinct into words, and could only stammer, "I think—I think we're headed into a trap."

After staring at her in surprise for a moment, Gabriel checked the traffic, and began moving over. "A trap? Do you think Munoz is in danger?"

"No." She was unable to resist blurting out the truth. "I think you are."

25

He decided to head home early. Perhaps she'd planned another ice cream surprise.

As they drove away from the racecourse, Doyle tried to cobble together a semi-coherent explanation for Gabriel, but truth to tell, she wasn't certain what it was that she was thinking in the first place—she only knew that they needed to abort the mission, and that Gabriel needed to avoid the racecourse like the plague. She decided to tell him that she needed to check something out with Acton before she explained her concerns, which he took in good part, being as Gabriel was nobody's fool, and had kept an Acton-secret or two in the past.

"Should I be worried?" he asked, as he dropped her in front of her building. The question was casual, but she could sense an underlying thread of concern.

"I don't know," she replied honestly. "Let me speak to Acton, first. It wouldn't hurt to be extra-cautious."

"Right, then." He waited in the car, and watched as she entered the revolving doors of her building, no doubt thinking her a madwoman.

Small wonder I'm a madwoman, Doyle thought crossly as she traversed the marble-floored lobby. No one ever tells me anything, and even when I get a glimpse, it's too complicated for my poor brain. I'll speak to Acton, and see if he can make heads-or-tails of any of this.

Once in the lift, however, she braced her back against the wall and began to entertain second thoughts about this plan. Solonik—the crackin' black-heart—was well and truly dead, but for some reason, alarm bells had gone off in her head whilst they were approaching the racecourse when Gabriel had mentioned his name. Of course, Solonik had been trying to muscle in on Savoie's smuggling rig, so it was not as though there wasn't a connection. From what she'd gleaned from Acton, Savoie had masterminded a huge network that used race horse trailers for black market smuggling—an ingenious plan, considering such horse trailers traveled freely around the country, and incited little scrutiny.

Solonik had wound up dead and in prison—although not necessarily in that order—after tangling with Acton. The self-same Acton, who was now aligned, somehow, with Savoie.

The conclusions that could easily be drawn from connecting these particular dots gave Doyle pause. It could well be that Acton was involved, somehow, and she'd best be cautious; she could be hot on the trail of her own wily husband—yet again—and although she couldn't approve of his dark dealings, she'd rather not be the one to pack him off to prison.

As she made her way to her flat's front door, she regretfully admitted that it was entirely possible that her instinct had sounded the alarm today because she and Gabriel were about to discover Acton's involvement in yet another breathtaking dose of law-breaking on a grand scale, and Gabriel should not be a witness to such a discovery. Therefore, as Reynolds took her rucksack, she decided that she wouldn't raise this afternoon's alarming development with her better half—at least not right away, until she'd sounded him out as best she could. After all, the ghostly Hastings kept going on about how she mustn't trust Acton, and he was also very keen that the fair Doyle find out whatever it was that Munoz was doing.

"It's too complicated," she said aloud. "Nothin' is ever what it seems, and it's a simple creature, I am."

"What is complicated, madam?" Reynolds—who probably thought nothing was ever complicated—seemed understandably confused by her comment.

She blew a tendril of hair off her face. "Everythin'. For two pins, I'd jump right back into the Thames."

"Surely not," the servant replied with a hint of rebuke, and steered her toward the sofa. "If you will put your feet up, madam, I will brew chamomile tea."

Sourly, she sank into the cushions and watched him bustle about, wishing she knew what she was going to say to Acton, and what she was going to say to Gabriel—and what she was going to say to Munoz, too, for that matter. And may as well add Williams, who was miserable for shrouded reasons that needed to be unshrouded, if there was such a word.

I'm under the gun, she realized in bewilderment. The clock is ticking, but I don't know why, or what will happen when the bell goes off. Harding knows—but he's precious little help. Mainly, he keeps saying that I mustn't trust Acton, which is complete and utter nonsense.

"Miss Mary left a message today, madam, and asked that you telephone her when it is convenient."

Doyle blinked, because Mary was her dead mother's name. She then remembered that Edward's future nanny was also a Mary, and took hold of herself—although she wouldn't have been overly-surprised if her deceased mother was telephoning; it was that sort of a day. "What did she want, Reynolds?"

"She didn't say, madam, but only asked that you telephone."

"I should go visit her," Doyle mused aloud, as she rested her head back against the cushions, so as to contemplate the ceiling. "She's a very restful sort of person."

"Your tea, madam."

The cup was offered with a certain precision that did not go unnoticed by Doyle, who soothed, "You're a restful one, too, Reynolds, mainly because you are so efficient." This said because Doyle knew it was the compliment that would be most pleasing.

Mollified, the servant bowed slightly. "Thank you, madam. And I believe that if you are planning to visit Miss Mary, Lord Acton would expect me to accompany you."

Doyle smiled into her cup, as she pretended to sip the tea. "I thank you for the kind offer, Reynolds, but she doesn't live in the housin' projects, anymore. She and her husband now have a nice little place in Fulham." She slid her gaze to his in a meaningful way—no doubt Mary's sudden turn in fortune could be laid at Acton's door, who wouldn't want the Honorable Edward's nanny to be commuting in from the projects.

"Nevertheless, I would be pleased to accompany you, madam."

"We'll see," she equivocated as she blew on the tepid tea, pretending it was too hot to drink. The last needful thing was for Mary to take a gander at Reynolds, who was no doubt itching to whip the poor woman into shape.

A short time later, Acton pinged her mobile to say that he was on his way up—this advance notice possibly given in the fond hope that he was slated for another dose of naked ice cream, but she dashed any such hope by replying that Reynolds was making dinner.

Within the minute, he came through the door and bent to kiss her, whilst deftly removing the teacup from her hand. "How are you feeling?"

She leaned her head back and regarded him, upside-down. "I'm abidin'. The spirit is willin', but the flesh is whale-like."

With a smile, he surreptitiously ditched the teacup on the side-table. "Surely not; Rubensesque, merely."

Laughing, she admitted, "I've no clue what that means, Michael, but I'll take it as a compliment. I've been meanin' to ask you, how's our witch doctor?"

"He's being arraigned tomorrow, I believe."

She watched him walk over to the fridge. "I'm convinced that someone is pinnin' shadow murders on him, and that the QC's murder is only one of them."

"Oh?" Orange juice bottle in hand, Acton sank down next to her, loosening his tie. "Is there anything I should know?"

She made a wry face. "I wish I had somethin' concrete to offer, Michael—but I hate the idea that someone's gettin' away with murder."

As he was a fine example of someone who regularly got away with murder, he made no reply, but instead put a sympathetic arm around her, and pulled her head down, to rest against his chest.

She spoke into his shirtfront. "It's all very smoky—Gabriel said there were no prints on any of the shoes."

Acton nodded in acknowledgment. "No. And we can't prove the shoes belonged to the victims without prints. Instead, we're left with circumstantial evidence, at best."

"Well, the suspect's a crackin' horror-show, so I think a jury will have no problem drawin' a conclusion or two, with or without hard evidence." She watched the fire for a moment, then asked, "How many murders will they try to put forward for the indictment?"

"Two, unless more evidence turns up between now and then."

Doyle frowned. "Is that countin' the shop-minder's husband?"

Acton cocked his head. "Tell me, if you will, about the shop-minder's husband."

Guiltily, Doyle sat up to face him. "I meant to tell you, Michael—truly, I did. Gabriel was chattin' her up in Farsi, and she told him all about how the Santero had murdered her husband, as a favor."

Thinking about it, Doyle sank back down beside him. "She hadn't been read the caution, though, and it seems unlikely she'd be willin' to tell her tale again." She decided to omit the fact that Gabriel wanted to say that the witness had been read the caution, even though it wasn't true—Doyle had a sneaking suspicion that Acton wouldn't necessarily disapprove of such a plan. "He's good at talkin' to people—Gabriel is, I mean. He's all 'hail-fellow-well-met', and stands all cheerful-like whilst he's winklin' out everyone's secrets. Is he still keepin' an eye on Drake, for the ACC?"

"Gabriel was not given that assignment by the ACC."

This was of interest, and she lifted her head to gaze at him. "Because we're worried the ACC is bent, along with Drake? Mother a' mercy, Michael, who's to be left standin'?"

"The corruption rig was a wide-ranging operation," was his only response. Absently, he watched the fire, and rubbed her hand between his fingers. "I'd rather you said nothing about these matters, if you please."

She dropped her head back down against the cushions with a small thump. "Not a problem, my friend; the very idea is horrifyin'— that the watchdogs are abusin' the system. Is Howard involved?" Howard was a Home Office official who'd been originally investigating the corruption rig, on the sly. To spike his guns, the blacklegs had unsuccessfully tried to frame and disgrace him, but he'd been vindicated, and now was an up-and-coming MP. Doyle would not be at all surprised to discover that Howard was the one bringing down the hammer on the crooked ACC.

"I'm afraid I cannot comment."

She reached for his orange juice bottle. "All right then; can you comment about Gabriel?"

Acton bent his head to hers. "Has he said anything that has raised an alarm?"

He was asking whether her perceptive abilities had given her any insights, and she shook her head, slightly. "No—not really. And he's not involved in the corruption rig—I know that much. But he rather reminds me of you, in that it's only after you walk away that you realize he's told you absolutely nothin'."

With a smile, he leaned in to press his lips against the top of her head.

"I think he's very sharp—Gabriel, I mean."

"I would not disagree with that assessment."

She paused for a moment. "D'you think you can trust him, Michael?"

"Do you?" This was, of course, the more pertinent question.

But Doyle could only frown at the fire. "I can't truly say, one way or the other. He seems a good sort—very willin' to help out."

"Then we shall see, I suppose."

Her head resting against his chest, she fiddled with one of his buttons. "Have I mentioned that I haven't the nerves for this, my friend? You do—in spades—but I don't. I'm half-inclined to go to bed, and pull the covers over my head."

"Speaking of which, I believe you were rather far afield, this afternoon."

She teetered on the edge of telling him what she'd been about, but drew back, not yet certain that she should tell him. "I was indeed—I was with Gabriel, in fact. We were followin' up on a lead, but it went nowhere."

He took her hand in his. "If you would let me know, next time."

With a pang of remorse, she could sense his anxiety, and the restraint it had taken for him to wait this long into the conversation to ask her about it. Leaning up to kiss his neck, she promised, "I will. I'm sorry, Michael; I'm truly bein' careful."

His gaze rested on the hand that he held in his. "Perhaps it will soon be time to take maternity leave."

"Oh—oh, I can't," she said immediately, and leaned forward to look up at him in alarm. "There's somethin' I'm supposed to find out, first. It's important, for some reason."

As could be expected, this pronouncement drew his puzzled amusement. "What sort of something?"

"I haven't a clue," she confessed, leaning back into him again. "Or more properly, I've a basketful of clues, and I'm too thick to sort them all out."

"Then I stand ready to help. Which case?"

Again, she decided to step warily, because she wasn't sure if she should let Acton know about her misgivings—faith, she wasn't even certain what her misgivings were, in the first place. "I'm not that far along. I just know—I just know I'm supposed to figure out somethin', and I think it has to do with the Santero, and the shadow murders."

There was a small pause. "It may be for the best," he offered diplomatically, "if you stay away from the Santero case. The two of you are not on speaking terms."

Doyle shuddered. "A nastier creep never contemplated a prison cell, and a good riddance, I say. But there's somethin'—" she paused, trying to put her instinct into words. "He's bitter, and—and *angry*, beneath his creepiness."

"I would ask," he repeated gently, "that you do not attempt to speak with him again."

"Faith, no," she agreed. "That *would* be like openin' the seventh seal. No, thanks."

He idly played with her hand, but brought the conversation back to his objective because he was Acton, and never lost sight of his objective. "Henceforth, could you do your detecting from headquarters, perhaps?"

She teased, "If you say 'henceforth', does that make it an order, Michael?"

He ran a thumb across the back of her hand. "I do not have the ordering of you, Kathleen."

Fondly, she squeezed his arm. "Of course, you do, foolish man. Unless it involves kale—that's where I draw the line."

"Or chamomile tea," he added.

"Or chamomile tea," she agreed, with a conspiratorial glance toward the cup, hidden on the sideboard.

"Dinner is served," Reynolds announced from the kitchen. "Salmon filet, with chickpeas."

26

She must have caught wind about the other shadow mur-
der, although it appeared she was not conversant with the
facts. This was troubling, as she tended to piece things
together. It was extraordinary, really.

That night, Harding seemed frustrated with her—or at
least, more frustrated than his usual—as he stood, shoe-
less, at his windy outpost.

"Hubris is what brings the Até," he explained, as though
speaking to a simpleton. Don't lose sight of the objective—you
are too easily distracted."

Unhappy with being on the defensive, she groused, "Well,
why can't you be a bit clearer? Mother a' mercy, but you're not
the right person for this, with all your goddesses, and fancy
words."

"I'm *exactly* the right person," he replied.

"Oh," she said, much struck. "That's never occurred to me. I
should find out why."

Nodding, he seemed relieved. "Please."

She frowned, and made a mighty effort to concentrate. "I
think Acton knows about whatever it is, but he doesn't want me to
find out. He wants me well-away from it."

"No." Harding spoke with heavy emphasis. "He doesn't know, and that's why you can't trust him. That's how Até works—hubris will be your husband's downfall."

"I don't think I'm acquainted with hubris," Doyle ventured. "Which one's he?"

"It's not a 'him', it's an 'it', and I wish you had more of it. You've got the upper hand, so use it."

She stared at him in surprise. "Upper hand over who?"

"Whom," he corrected.

Holding onto her temper with both hands, she tried again. "I don't have the upper hand over anyone—everyone thinks I'm a hero, but its only puffery, and sleight-of-hand."

"Classic public projection, and hero-worship," he agreed. "But the effect is the same, whether its merited or not; you need only assert yourself. Psychological manipulation through covert intimidation."

There was a small pause, whilst Doyle tried to make sense of these particular words, in this particular order. "Not a clue," she finally confessed.

Exasperated, the ghost demanded, "Didn't they teach you psyops?"

Doyle raised her brows. "Oh—well, yes; that was in forensic psychology, but I didn't pay much attention. I remember the good cop-bad cop stuff, for interrogations."

"Psyops," he repeated firmly. "In this instance, you are the bad cop."

"*Me?*" she asked, with unfeigned astonishment. "There's not a soul alive who'd believe I'm the bad cop. I hate to assert myself—whether it's for cyclops, or not." She paused, thinking about it. "It's just not in my nature."

"Hubris," he repeated wearily. "Find some, and be quick about it."

Suddenly struck, she ventured, "The ghost at Trestles is warnin' me about somethin', too—now, there's a bad cop, if I ever saw one. Are you acquainted with him?"

Surprised, the psychiatrist uncrossed his arms. "You should pay attention to him; the man's a warlord."

With some surprise, she asked, "Am I at war?"

With a gasp, Doyle woke, and instinctively tried to sit up, only to discover that it was no easy thing to sit up in one's third trimester, and so she propped herself up on her elbows, instead.

"Kathleen?" Acton murmured, and reached to turn on the lamp. "Everything all right?"

"I had a bad dream." Then, after a moment's hesitation, she added, "It was about Dr. Harding."

Her sleepy husband stared at her for a moment, and then ran a hand over his eyes. "Dr. *Harding*?"

She shifted so that she faced him, and decided there was nothin' for it; she had to ask. "Who killed him, Michael—Dr. Harding, I mean. Did you? I think it's important, for some reason."

He watched her for a moment, a frown between his brows. "You are mistaken, Kathleen. Harding is not dead."

Now it was Doyle's turn to stare at him. "Oh, yes he is, Michael—my hand on my heart." She paused, and pushed her hair away from her face. "I think he's a shadow murder of some sort."

There was a small silence, whilst she could feel Acton's extreme surprise. Candidly, she offered, "We've a lot of secrets from each another—you and me—and that's as it should be, of course; but I think it's important that I find out what's happened to Dr. Harding. He certainly seems to think so." With a small sigh, she fell back into the pillows, and gazed up at the pool of light that was reflected on the ceiling. "What do you know of it? Harding's disappeared from sight, so *somethin'* must have happened to him."

Acton spoke in a level tone. "Harding is a key witness to the corruption rig, and so he had little choice but to be put into protective custody, and to be given a different identity."

Surprised, she turned her head to face him. "Oh—that's right; he was in cahoots with the nasty DSC."

"Indeed."

Frowning, she turned to contemplate the ceiling again. "So—I suppose if he's had a change of identity, it may not be easy to find out who's killed him."

"Are you completely certain he is dead, Kathleen? I have been informed otherwise."

This was a surprise, and she turned to face him again. "You have? Recently?"

"Yes, recently."

With an effort, she propped herself up, yet again. "Then there's your culprit, Michael; someone's lyin' to you, and Harding wants you to know about it."

He made no response, and she could sense that he was deeply distracted, thinking. After a moment, she ventured, "I suppose you wouldn't be interested in tellin' me who it is—who's lyin' to you about Harding?"

"Williams," her husband replied.

27

Why hadn't the prosecutors told him that Harding was dead? Could it be that they didn't know?

"We're havin' lunch, you and me," Doyle announced to Williams' recorded message on the phone. "No bunkin' it, my friend; I'll meet you at our fish and chips stand—the one on the embankment."

She rang off. Williams hadn't picked up, and although he very well might be busy with field work, she suspicioned that he was avoiding her. Last night, she'd obtained Acton's promise that he'd let her take a throw at Williams first, and he'd agreed—rather readily, which in turn raised a suspicion that Acton would proceed with his own plan, will-she or nil-she, so she'd best fix the problem, and fix it soon. If Williams was lying to Acton, it was something serious.

And truth to tell, that was not the only surprise she'd sustained from the late-night discussion; the fact that Acton hadn't haled off and murdered Hastings himself was nothing short of amazing. Her vengeance-minded husband must have decided that the psychiatrist was too valuable as a witness, and had therefore allowed him to live.

She paused with this thought, much struck. Faith, it was the same situation with Solonik's nasty sister; Acton hadn't strangled her outright, which was an enormous surprise, considering she was another one who was neck-deep in evil schemes.

Knitting her brow, Doyle stared at her computer screen without really seeing it. So, Acton's not killing people, willy-nilly; mayhap this could be interpreted as a good thing—mayhap religious instruction was making a dent, and he was truly trying to be a better person.

No, her instinct said immediately. That's not it.

Fine; she responded a bit crossly. I'll just add another to the long list of things I've got to figure out; Mother a' mercy—it's enough to make a saint swear. And for reasons that are unclear, I'll bet my teeth that all of this is tangled up together, somehow; the shadow murders, and Acton's unexpected inclination toward mercy.

Mindful of Acton's request that she stay close to headquarters, Doyle decided that she'd visit Mary-the-nanny this morning, to see what it was she wanted to talk about, and since the route took her more-or-less near the Santero's shop—if you weren't overly-worried about taking the most direct path—she'd have another look-in, there. She'd been distracted, last time, what with Gabriel and Morgan Percy hanging about, and the shop-minder watching them like Athaliah-at-the-gate. Harding was prodding her about loose ends, and since the Santero seemed to be at the center of this shadow-murder puzzle, it would be best to stop by, and see if she could root out a lead.

The door's overhead bell rang as Doyle entered the Santero's shop, and she noted that little had changed since her last visit; the shop-minder was seated in her chair in the corner and doing some sort of tatting-work, her attitude one of grim boredom. She looked up as Doyle came through the door, and then craned her head to see if Doyle had anyone with her. "Where is the young man, today?"

"He'll be along," Doyle replied vaguely. "He enjoyed speakin' with you—said you reminded him of home."

The woman eyed her dubiously. "He told me he was born here."

"Oh—oh, is that so? Mayhap instead he said you reminded him of his mother, then, and I am mixin' it up."

This attempt at a recovery seemed to be successful, and the shop-minder smoothed her tatting with a benign hand. "He was respectful. Many of the young men today are not."

Doyle sauntered over to a dusty shelf, and fingered a dubious-looking wooden idol. "All too true. I'm a bit worried that he's bein' led astray, though. By the young woman who came that day." Raising her brows, she shot a significant glance at the seated woman.

The minder's hands stilled for a moment, and her dark eyes narrowed. "No; with that kind of woman, it means nothing—he amuses himself."

"I'd hate it, if he came into the trouble, though." Doyle lowered her voice. "She may draw him into the trouble, without his knowin'—she's that kind of girl." Truer words, never spoken. With a vague gesture toward the stairs, Doyle lowered her head and stage-whispered, "The shoes."

The woman sat, stone-faced, and regarded Doyle for a long moment under heavy-lidded eyes. "You have him come speak to me."

Doyle nodded quickly, and then looked conscious, as she re-arranged the idol on the shelf. "Right. Best not to say anythin' more about it—there's trouble enough."

But the woman would not be further drawn, and picked up her tatting again. "Why do you come, this morning?"

Doyle decided there was no point in being subtle with this particular witness, and so she said bluntly, "I wanted to ask you if you've seen anyone goin' upstairs into the Santero's rooms since he was arrested, and if you can give me any descriptions."

The woman glanced up, as she snipped a skein. "The police were here," she observed in a flat tone. "Two days, they were here—many of them."

"I meant after the police left," Doyle clarified, although she didn't think for an instant that the woman needed clarification. "After you started mindin' the shop."

"I saw no one," she replied calmly, and it was a lie.

I suppose I can't blame her for being wary in dealing with the police, Doyle thought; she's a murderess, after all. "Well, if you do see anythin' odd, perhaps you could give Officer Gabriel a call. I'll write his number, here on my card."

The woman took the proffered card, and studied it for a moment. "What will happen to the Santero?"

"Oh—he's bein' set for trial today, I think."

"It will be good when all this is finished." Making a moue of distaste, the woman sank back in her chair and gazed around the shabby little room. "I am tired of this shop."

Doyle decided there was no need to break it to her gently. "I think he's goin' to prison for a long time—may as well lock the place up."

"I will wait to hear." The woman bent her head to resume her tatting. "I made a promise."

Once outside, Doyle ducked into a doorway to ring up the driving service, and think about what she'd learned. The shop-minder knew a thing or two, but she wasn't about to spill it out to the likes of Doyle. It seemed obvious that the shoes had been planted after the fact, to stage the shadow murders that someone was trying to pin on the Santero—the QC and Blakney, thus far, although there might be others—Harding himself serving as a good possibility. It was an excellent scheme, when you thought about it; if they already had a cut-and-dried case against a murderer, law enforcement would be all-too-eager to lay as many cold cases as they could manage at his door—it helped convince the public that the CID never gave up, and any decent piece of evidence would do.

Doyle paused. Except—except this case truly wasn't lining up very well, for the shadow-murderer. The shoes would be easily excluded from evidence on a suppression motion—since the flat was left unsecured for days—and the re-search could easily be deemed illegal as well; the shop-minder's permission wouldn't hold water.

And there were no prints, either. Little point in planting evidence, one would think, if there were no prints to tie them to the victims. All in all, it was a sorry excuse for a smoking gun.

Thinking over these many and puzzling contradictions, Doyle teetered on the edge of calling Gabriel, and asking him to sweet-talk the shop-minder into confessing whatever it was that was going on, but she decided to wait, and think about it a bit. When Gabriel had said that he wasn't involved in the corruption rig it was the truth, but he was one of those emingnas, or however you said it; a puzzle. Best be cautious.

The next person on the agenda was not puzzling in the least, and Doyle smiled with genuine pleasure upon greeting Mary, who invited Doyle in to her neat little flat, and poured out tea. As the two women spoke of Doyle's pregnancy, Doyle noted with a twinge of alarm that Mary was troubled, beneath her serene exterior. Now what? she thought with resignation, as she dutifully sipped the insipid brew. I hope Reynolds hasn't scared her silly.

Mary carefully set down her tea cup. "I wanted to let you know that I'm having to look for work, due to the situation. It will be temporary, of course—until Edward is born—but I thought you should be made aware."

Doyle examined her memory, and decided that she was truly at sea, and not just forgetting things as was her wont, nowadays. "Remind me what the situation is."

Mary stared in surprise. "Oh—oh I'm so sorry; I thought you knew. I'm afraid—well, I'm afraid that my husband has disappeared."

Doyle's mouth went dry, because her scalp was suddenly prickling like a live thing, and her instinct was doing the equivalent of flashing red lights in her face. "Are you—is your husband a QC?"

With a puzzled smile, Mary confessed, "I'm afraid I don't know what that means."

"No—of course not," Doyle breathed in relief, and then castigated her stupid instinct for leaping to absurd conclusions. Honestly; everything was not always connected to everything else, and she needed to stop thinking that it was.

"But no one seems to know where he's gone to."

"Was there—" Doyle asked delicately, "—was there someone else, that he might have been seein'?" It didn't take long, in detective work, to discover that wives tended to be deaf, blind and dumb when it came to their husband's misdeeds.

The other woman frowned slightly. "I don't think so, but I suppose you can never be certain." She paused, and then added candidly, "He did have money problems, and he was worried about some of the people he dealt with."

Gently, Doyle asked, "D'you think he's taken a bunk, then?" For a moment, Doyle tried to imagine Acton ditching her fair self, but this mental exercise proved too incredible even to contemplate, and so she gave it up.

"I don't think so—he is truly fond of little Gemma."

Doyle thought about it for a moment. Whilst Mary was indeed concerned, it didn't seem as though she felt her husband had met a bad end—Doyle had encountered many a desperate, distraught wife, and Mary wasn't one of them. "I can run a missin' person's search, Mary; unless you'd like to keep it private for a bit longer, to give him time to come back."

Mary shook her head. "Thank you, but Officer Williams has already run the check for me. He's been very kind—"

But Doyle was no longer listening, because she was barely able to think, over the roaring sound in her ears. Williams had been—inexplicitly—keeping in touch with Mary, even though there was no reason to, and Doyle had entertained the uneasy suspicion that he was attracted to the married woman. *Holy Mother of God.* She shut her eyes tightly, and could feel herself sway. *Holy, holy Mother of God.*

Mary leaned to touch her knee, concerned. "Are you all right, Lady Acton?"

"Yes—yes, sorry." Doyle pressed her hands to her temples and tried to right herself. Suddenly, all the puzzling loose ends were getting themselves catastrophically tied together, and she fought a feeling of nausea. "I believe—I believe your husband was—is—a pawnbroker."

"Yes, William Blakney is his name—I kept my own name, after we married. I'm so sorry you weren't aware that he'd disappeared; I thought Officer Williams would have told you, but I suppose he was trying to spare my feelings." She paused, and brightened a bit. "He seemed to think it was a good sign that the search came up empty, and so I'm trying to not worry too much." A faint trace of color appeared in her cheeks. "Officer Williams told me that there is a police fund to help families in my situation, and that he could arrange for a stipend, but I'll be all right, once Edward is born—I just need to make ends meet, in the meantime."

"He is a good man," Doyle said aloud, trying to argue against her growing sense of horror.

"Yes." Again, a tinge of delicate color rose in her companion's cheeks.

28

He'd made some discreet inquiries, and it did seem that Harding had not been seen, lately. Surely, the ACC wasn't so desperate? The case was rock-solid against them, even without Harding.

D oyle sat on the shaded bench, and found that she was having trouble putting two thoughts together. She was waiting for Williams near the fish and chips stand on the embankment, and idly watching the passersby—it must be nice, to go about one's daily routine without having the feeling that one had better get to solving one's problems or the world was going to come crashing down on one's head. Harding is poking at me because the clock is ticking, she thought; I wish I knew whose clock, and what it was counting down.

She spotted Williams approaching from the pavement; he seemed a bit grave, with his hands thrust in his pockets, and his head bent. I'll not believe it, she thought stoutly. Not for a minute—unless, of course, I'm forced to, which means I'll have to figure out how to help him, somehow. She mustered up a smile. "Hey."

"Hey, yourself."

He sat next to her, and they were both silent for a few moments. Not good, she thought. He's wary, and he doesn't want to meet my eyes.

"What did you want to talk about, Kath?"

She considered, and then decided that she was never very good at roundaboutation, and besides, there was a clock ticking, somewhere. "I'm worried that you're a David, Thomas."

He dropped his head, and examined his hands, clasped between his knees. "I'm afraid I don't know what that means."

"King David arranged to have one of his generals killed because he coveted the man's wife. Coveting is not good thing, Thomas—there are rules about it." She paused, and then added, "There are rules about murder, too."

He took a long breath. "I didn't murder Blakney, Kath."

This was true, and she stared at him with equal parts surprise and relief. "You *didn't?* Then why haven't you told Mary that he's dead? Faith, Thomas, explain to me what's goin' on, here."

He considered the pavement for a moment. "How much do you know?"

But she shook her head. "I'll not play that game, my friend. Come clean."

Slowly, he replied, "I don't know if I can tell you, Kath. It's complicated."

"I know it is," she agreed in all seriousness. There's somethin' going on that I can't quite figure out, but I've got to hurry up and get the web unraveled, before we're all caught up in it. It has to do with the shadow murders, and the ACC, and—and you, and Munoz."

At this, he lifted his head and regarded her with a small frown. "Munoz? Is she on this case?"

"No, but she's the only other person I worry about, aside from you."

"Why are you worried about Munoz?"

But Doyle had caught herself—truly, she was as loose-lipped as they come—and so she replied in a tart tone, "It occurs to me that I shouldn't be gabblin' to you until I find out a bit more. For instance, if you didn't kill Blakney, I wouldn't be at all surprised if Morgan Percy did. Or someone connected to Percy, since she was at the Santero's shop, makin' sure I found his shoes."

There was a small silence, whilst he turned his gaze toward the river, watching it roll by. "You know, you're a little spooky."

Immediately, Doyle was on the defensive. "I'm not *creepy*, though, like the Santero. There's a big difference, between spooky and creepy."

"Absolutely," he soothed, and she was annoyed to observe that this wasn't exactly true.

She sank back into the bench to watch the river beside him, and then blew a tendril of hair off her forehead "I almost feel sorry for him, though—for the Santero, I mean. He's bitter, because he knows he's bein' set up for the shadow murders."

At this observation, Williams couldn't resist a small smile. "Of course, he knows, Kath—you're not much of a murderer if you can't keep track of who you actually murdered, and who you didn't."

But Doyle frowned. "It doesn't make much sense, though. If he knows he's bein' set up for some shadow murders, why wouldn't he tell his defense, so that they can argue that he's bein' set up for all of his murders? You'd think it would raise a reasonable doubt." Suddenly struck, she added, "Although his solicitor didn't seem interested in doin' a very good job, remember?"

Williams didn't speak for a moment, his gaze on the river. "I can't say that I care much, either way. The Santero is a bad actor, Kath."

Squinting against the sunlight, she lifted her face to his. "There're a lot of bad actors in this little kettle of snakes, and don't think you've successfully changed the subject. Tell me about bad-actor Morgan Percy."

"I don't know if I can," he admitted frankly. "I—I didn't want you to find out." His gaze still fixed on the river, he pressed his lips into a thin line. "I didn't want you to find out about any of this."

She touched his sleeve. "Well, I have, and you are a gobbin' fool, Thomas Williams, if you think I'd ever let you twist in the wind. For starters, you can tell me about Mary."

As he bowed his head to contemplate the pavement, she caught a flash of profound misery. "I can't really explain it. I just—I just want to help her, I guess." He paused. "She reminds me of you, I think."

As this was delving into matters best not delved into, she cautioned with mock-severity, "Don't you *dare* poach Edward's nanny from me."

At this sally, he turned his head to smile at her—but it took a mighty effort. "Right, then."

"Why won't you tell her Blakney's dead?"

"Because it's my fault he's dead." He lifted his head again, to contemplate the river. "Because it's my fault."

She took his arm, and shook it slightly. "Tell me plainly, please."

He took a breath, but she could see that some of the abject misery was dissipating, slightly. "I told Morgan about Mary."

Doyle stared at him in astonishment. "You told Morgan *Percy?* Faith, Thomas; you're lucky she didn't hale off and kill poor Mary, straightaway. Percy's not the type to suffer a rival."

"It was during a weak moment. We were talking about—about people who we wished weren't off-limits."

Oh-oh, she thought; time to skirt this particular subject, yet again. Adopting a light tone, she curled her hand in the crook of his elbow, and scolded, "This is exactly why you shouldn't be havin' sex with anyone who's willin', Thomas. You can't be givin' away state secrets, durin' pillow talk."

Logically, he countered, "Well, it's against the law to have sex with anyone who's not willing."

"I suppose that's a fair point."

All teasing aside, he turned his head to meet her eyes. "But it was a stupid move on my part—we're on different sides of the same case. I can be brought up before Professional Standards."

"Saints, best avoid such a thing at all costs—we know that they're all a bunch of chousers, over there." With absent fingers, Doyle pleated her scarf, and thought about it. "So, Percy—who doesn't mind killin' people, if the occasion warrants—kills Blakney as a favor to you, and knows you can't grass on her, because you could lose your badge. Not to mention poor Mary would be horrified by such wicked goin's-on, and would never speak to you again. Is that it?"

He nodded. "Something like that."

But Doyle frowned, and shook her head. "That doesn't seem in keepin', my friend. Percy may be willin' to kill people to suit herself, but she's not the doin'-favors type. Mayhap instead, she's a Judith."

He hunched a shoulder. "Does Judith know David?"

"Oh—oh, you're such a *heathen*, Thomas. Judith was a seductress—a honeypot, who was sent to seduce the enemy general." Her scalp prickled, and she knew that she was on the right track, but she couldn't very well tell Williams this, because men didn't appreciate being told that they were idiots when it came to women. "Do me a favor, and try to avoid her until I do a bit more diggin'. But don't let her know that I'm suspicionin' her motives, or that you're wary. I think there's a trap about to be sprung, and since I'm the one who's got the upper hand for some reason, I'm the one who's got to stop it."

Frowning, he met her gaze. "What sort of trap?"

But she could only raise her palms in bewilderment. "If only I knew, my friend. But it's important that I figure it out, and I think I'm one step closer, now." She paused. "What does 'hubris' mean?"

His brows drew together. "Hubris? I think you may have the wrong word, Kath. Hubris is from Greek mythology."

"Oh—yes, that's it, I'm sure. It has to do with some goddess who lurks about—although I'd no idea that goddesses could be so crackin' nasty."

"Hubris isn't a goddess—hubris is when the hero thinks he's invincible, so the gods have to teach him a lesson, and show him that he's not."

She regarded him in surprise. "Oh—is that all? Well, that's nothin' new; 'pride goeth before a fall', after all."

"There you go—same idea." He contemplated his hands, for a moment. "Do you think Acton is the one setting a trap?"

"Oh, indeed he is, but it's not for you—I've already asked him. The trap I'm worried about is not an Acton-trap." She frowned, thinking about it. "There are competing traps, I suppose; it's all a bit bewilderin', truly, and I wish—just once—that someone would give me a simple list of the things I'm supposed to be findin' out."

He bumped her shoulder with his own. "You're a good detective, Kath. You just go about it differently than most."

"I will count that as a compliment, and much appreciated. On the other hand, you're an excellent detective, which means you must be aware that Acton already knows about Blakney—knows about this whole mess."

"Yes," her companion replied in a bleak tone, dropping his head down again. "I'm sure he knows."

"And yet he hasn't said anythin' about it?"

"No." The single syllable hung between them.

She tugged at his arm. "Well—shouldn't you speak with him, and make a clean breast?"

"I'd—I'd rather not."

"It's embarrassin', this mess," she agreed. "But it would be a million times more embarrassin' to be beholden to the likes of Morgan Percy."

"I won't let that happen," he replied in a firm tone, and this appeared to be the truth.

She cautioned, "Well, don't you *dare* do anythin' that would make them yank your badge, Thomas; they'll promote Munoz to take your place, and I'll never hear the end of it."

He sighed, and bent his head to run his hands through his hair. "Acton must think I'm an idiot."

Doyle noted with some satisfaction that his abject misery had nearly disappeared, and sympathetically, she laid a hand on his arm. "No; Acton is very fond of you. I think you remind him of him, in a way—if things hadn't gone a bit awry, earlier in his life."

"So, what's next?"

She knew that he was asking what she'd say to Acton, which—come to think of it—was an excellent question. "Let me think on it—I'll let you know. Meanwhile, I'm supposed to set up a psychological manipulation through covert intimidation, but I've no idea who the target is."

Incredulous, he stared at her. "Psyops? You?"

"Oh, I can bad-cop with the best of them, my friend."

At this, he chuckled aloud, and she was very much relieved to hear the sound.

29

In the end, it didn't really matter whether Harding lived.
It would soon be resolved, just as he'd planned.

I'm that tired of being paranoid, Doyle thought with extreme vexation, as she hurried back to headquarters. Especially since it always seems to be with just cause.

The stray thought that she'd entertained whilst sitting next to Williams suddenly seemed hugely significant, and therefore it was with enormous relief that she spied Munoz, working away in the confines of her cubicle.

"Munoz." Doyle was slightly out of breath, and crossed her arms across the top of the cubicle's wall, so as to address the other girl. "Let's have lunch."

"Too late—I already had lunch," said Munoz, without looking up.

"Well, I haven't, and I need some company. It shouldn't take more than a few minutes—let's go off-campus, to the deli."

"Can't. Busy."

Doyle leaned over, and relayed in a stage whisper, "I have good gossip."

Without moving her head, Munoz slid her dark eyes up toward Doyle. "You don't gossip."

"I do so," Doyle retorted, stung. "It's just that no one ever tells me anythin'."

"Wonder why?" Munoz's gaze dropped back to her work.

"It's about promotions."

This was a sure sign of Doyle's desperation, and Munoz recognized it as such. "Acton doesn't tell you about promotions."

Doyle resorted to pleading. "Please, Munoz—it's a lovely day, and I need to take a walk-about."

With a resigned snap, Munoz closed her laptop. "Fine. But I want a Santero assignment—remember, you promised me."

"Done," Doyle agreed. Williams owed her a favor, surely.

The two girls made their way to the lobby, and out the front doors in silence. As they reached the pavement, Munoz prompted, "So? What has you all worked up?"

Doyle cast a carefree glance at the shop windows, but replied in a low voice, "Wait—I want to make sure we're away from the surveillance cameras on the roof."

To her credit, Munoz took this rather grim revelation in stride, and casually pulled out her compact, pretending to check her make-up as she glanced behind them in the mirror. "Are you worried that we're being followed?"

"I don't know. I don't think so." Doyle had been furiously trying to figure out what she was going to say to the other girl, because she definitely couldn't tell her the truth. Earlier, when she'd mentioned to Williams that he and Munoz were the only people she worried about, suddenly it struck her; not-so-coincidentally, Harding was prodding her to find out what was going on with Munoz and Williams. Between those two, the common denominator would appear to be the fair Doyle.

The corruption rig had blackmailed its victims by threatening their female relatives with sex slavery. Doyle had no sisters—faith, she'd no relatives a'tall—but everyone knew that she was thick with Williams, and everyone thought she and Munoz were devoted friends, due to the stupid bridge-jumping incident. So—perhaps someone was trying to find a means to manipulate her—or more correctly, a means to manipulate Acton, since she was an insignificant player, save for the fact that she was married to the man. It all made sense; Harding was Acton's psychiatrist, and he must have told the evildoers that she was the potential chink in Acton's mighty armor.

Munoz's voice broke into her thoughts. "Do we need to find a POA?"

A position of advantage was a place where an officer had a better chance of defending against an attacker. Doyle noted that Munoz was only half-joking, and tried to reassure her, "I know I'm soundin' paranoid, but I've heard somethin' and I can't say where I heard it, but I'm worried you're gettin' set up for a crime." This was an educated guess; Williams had been set up for a crime, and it would explain why Munoz was positioned at the racecourse, where crimes ran rampant.

Munoz thought about this as they walked along. "Is it Gabriel, who's setting me up?"

Startled, Doyle glanced at her. "No—not Gabriel. Or, at least I don't think so. Why?"

The beauty shrugged. "He was chatting me up this morning, but I think he was really trying to find out about my ACC assignment."

This was of interest, and Doyle seized upon this opportunity to be diverted. "Chatting you up? Really? He's rather handsome, I think."

"Not as handsome as Savoie."

"Oh, I don't know, Munoz—Savoie isn't exactly magazine-handsome."

"Sexy," Munoz corrected. "Gabriel's not as sexy as Savoie."

Doyle considered this, and decided it was probably a fair point—leave it to a sinister Frenchman, to carry off the sexy-flag. "What do we know about Gabriel? Mayhap his family is rich, and even if he's not as rich as Savoie, the odds are good that he's not a criminal kingpin, which would weigh in his favor."

Munoz's sharp gaze reviewed the pedestrians passing around them, but she disclosed a bit bleakly, "Savoie said he may have to go back to the continent and lay low for a while, but he wouldn't tell me why."

Doyle recalled that the third succession hearing was the day after tomorrow, and tried to decide if this bit of news was ominous or encouraging. Then, with some regret, she decided that she could no longer avoid the topic at hand, and reiterated, "I'm worried that you're bein' set up." She knit her brow. "I don't think its Gabriel, who's doin' the settin' up, though. I think—I think it may be someone at the ACC."

Mentally, she cringed, waiting for Munoz to castigate her about spouting such nonsense, but instead the girl nodded, thoughtfully. "Do you mind if we keep walking? There's a juice shop, over two blocks."

"What kind of juice?" Doyle asked suspiciously. "Does it involve kale?"

"The healthy kind of juice, idiot. Try to think about the baby, and how he'd like something not greasy, just once."

"Fine, then," Doyle groused, resigned to her fate. It had occurred to her—gauging from Munoz's reaction—that Munoz harbored her own suspicions, and wanted to stay away from potential eavesdroppers.

They continued their walk, and with a care-free posture, Doyle idly watched the traffic go by. "You don't seem very surprised."

"No," the girl replied briefly. "But I don't think I can talk about it, not with the NDA."

"Mayhap you can give me just a hint," Doyle ventured. "That way, you wouldn't be technically breachin' the non-disclosure agreement." She added as a caution, "But it can't be too hard a hint."

Munoz seemed to find this idea within the bounds of her constraints, and disclosed, "I'm supposed to hang around some blokes and pretend I can't speak English very well, so that I can listen to what they have to say."

Reminded of Gabriel's observation, Doyle asked, "Doesn't that seem a bit odd? You're so recognizable, Munoz—especially after the PR work you've done for the CID. It seems strange that anyone would be wantin' you to work undercover."

Carefully, Munoz disclosed, "The location is one where it would be less likely that I'd be recognized. But I'll agree that it seems a bit odd." They'd come to the juice shop, and as Munoz reviewed the hand-written chalkboard menu, she added in a low voice, "Tell me what you've heard."

Doyle pretended to look over the menu, although all the offerings looked frankly horrifying. "I truly haven't heard much, Munoz, but I'm worried that the ACC is settin' you up for a crime, so as to have somethin' to hold over your head."

Munoz was silent, but Doyle caught a flare of emotion, and exclaimed, "Faith; they've already tried, haven't they? That's why you're so leery."

"Can't say," Munoz replied briefly. "But you're a good guesser."

As the two girls stood aside to wait, Doyle casually pulled her mobile, and pretended to scroll. "Mayhap you can speak to someone in Legal, to see if the NDA can be ignored in this situation."

"Who would I go to?" Munoz replied, crossing her arms and looking about her with a bored expression. "Legal would just send it to Professional Standards, and the whole lot of them could be bent."

"There's always Acton." With a stoic air, Doyle stepped forward to receive her hideously green concoction. "You could speak with Acton." She teetered on the edge of telling Munoz that Acton was on the verge of taking down the ACC, himself, but decided she'd best button up—no telling if Munoz was already compromised, although she didn't have the feeling that the girl was anything but wary.

"I'll think about it."

Doyle pretended to take a sip, and warned, "Be extra-careful, Munoz. Don't give them a hint that you've twigged them."

"I'm not an idiot, Doyle."

As this was said in a tone that discouraged any further discussion, they walked back toward headquarters in silence, until Munoz paused in front of a shoe display. As she pointed toward a pair of sleek black heels, she said, "I think we're being shadowed. A man's followed us from headquarters, and he's still back there. Let's take a deviation on the way back, just to verify."

Doyle resisted the urge to glance over her shoulder, and dutifully admired the shoes. "Is it a white man in his thirties; business attire?"

Munoz eyed her sidelong. "Yes."

"That's only Trenton, Munoz. He follows me about because he's Acton's private security."

Munoz took a causal sip. "Oh? Well, he's one of the blokes I'm monitoring, on my assignment at the racecourse."

30

Perhaps he'd take some time off, also. It would be pleasant to be at home with her, after the hardships of the past few months.

After parting with a pensive Munoz, Doyle lingered in front of the shoe shop and decided she may as well buy a pair of the black heels, just so as to give herself cover, and to stall for time until she decided what to do next. Yet again, she was squarely on the horns of an Acton-inspired dilemma, and she was getting mighty tired of it—not to mention that the last thing she truly needed was a pair of spiky heels.

From the very first, Acton had assigned Trenton to keep a watchful eye over his bride, who—to be fair—had run the poor man ragged, having been the target of many a bloody-minded villain. Therefore—as Acton was already well-aware that the ACC was up to no good—it was entirely possible that Trenton was at the racecourse in his role as Acton's man, sniffing out whatever was going on, and running into Munoz purely as a matter of co-incidence. Or—or it was the unthinkable; Trenton was a turn-coat, and he was part of whatever the scheme was to manipulate the fair Doyle into doing some undisclosed something that would definitely not be to her husband's benefit.

The easiest way to find out, of course, would be for the discerner-of-truth to have a conversation with our Mr. Trenton, and thereby discover what-was-what. However, Doyle did not normally engage in conversation with Trenton, and—if he were indeed a turncoat—he'd surely be tipped that she was on to something. Faith—he may be tipped anyway; no doubt Trenton knew very well who Munoz was, and it seemed unlikely that he would be fooled by her undercover role.

I'm flummoxed, Doyle admitted to herself as she thanked the clerk, and accepted her package. And—based on all events thus far in my short marriage—whenever I'm flummoxed, my better half is usually somewhere close at hand, pulling the levers. With no further ado, she rang him up.

As always, Acton answered immediately. "Kathleen."

"Did Trenton report that I was drinkin' some hideous concoction from the juice shop?"

"He did not. Trenton would never betray you in such a way."

This seemed like a perfect opening, and so she plunged in. "D'you think there's any chance that you're the one Trenton is betrayin'?"

There was a small pause. "Now, there's a comment that requires a follow-up. I am at your disposal."

"That is excellent. I'm a little sharp-set, I have to say—I keep missin' out on lunch opportunities."

"Then let's see to it that you are fed. Candide's?"

She smiled into the phone. "Are we wavin' the heroic-Actons flag, yet again? Who's goin' to be there this time, the Prime Minister?"

He soothed, "Only two more days, and then you won't have to be seen with me ever again."

"Mother a' mercy, but this is brutal, husband; all this smilin', and carryin' on."

"We need to fool everyone for just a bit longer, I'm afraid."

"Ongoing psyops," she declared.

She could feel him smile. "You astonish me, Lady Acton."

"Oh, I'm very well-informed," she declared airily. "Where am I meetin' you? The parkin' garage?"

"I'll come to you—don't move. I'll be there in ten minutes."

It went without saying that he knew exactly where she was. "All right, but I'm warnin' you—I bought a pair of spiky heels, as my cover. They were almost as expensive as your shoes."

"I look forward to seeing them."

"Don't get any ideas."

"Too late."

With a giggle, she rang off.

A short time later, they were once again seated in pride of place at Candide's, the wait staff fluttering around them like so many butterflies. As Acton perused his menu, Doyle noted, "Savoie's goin' to flee back to the continent, apparently."

"You are indeed well-informed," he replied in a mild tone. "I believe the beet salad is excellent, here."

She stared at him in disbelief. "Well, that's an outright lie, husband, and it's nothin' short of amazin' that you think I'd come within a gaffin'-stick of a miserable beet." Doggedly, she continued, "It's just as well, actually—that Savoie is leavin', I mean. I've been workin' like a journeyman to convince Munoz to break it off with him."

"I shouldn't worry about it, Kathleen."

Watching him from under her lashes, she added in a casual tone, "Still and all, I'll be that relieved when she's moved on. It could have been worse, I suppose; if Savoie had taken up with Morgan Percy, they could have conquered the world—and not in a good way."

Ah, she caught a reaction from him, as he folded the menu; it wasn't much of a confirmation that he knew all about Williams's troubles, but it was enough.

"I thought I was the one you'd paired up with Morgan Percy, so as to take over the world."

"No, Michael," she chided in mock-annoyance. "I'm stickin' to you like a burr, and tryin' to save you from yourself, remember? Although I'm not in the best shape to run a counter, if she keeps castin' her lures your way."

"Let's see your new shoes, and then we shall decide."

She laughed, much relieved that Acton was aware of the Percy problem, since she was certain that he'd not allow Williams to come to any harm. Not to mention that she'd hate to have to tattle on the poor man—it was thoroughly embarrassing that he'd been played so easily, and he should repent fasting. Of course, the fact that Acton hadn't rushed to Williams' rescue indicated—to her, at least—that Acton was making certain there'd indeed be some heavyweight repenting; nothing like staring professional and romantic ruin in the face, to make a man swear off scheming trollops.

The waiter interrupted her thoughts, so she ordered her favorite fried sandwich—no need to add to all her sufferings, after all—and after the man had fussed sufficiently, it occurred to her that her husband hadn't yet brought up the reason for this meeting. Therefore, after the waiter withdrew she leaned forward. "May I speak of Trenton?"

"Please." He lifted his gaze to hers, and waited.

"Is it possible—is it *possible* that he's tangled up with the corruption rig, Michael? She struggled with how much to tell him. "I'm a bit worried, based on somethin' Munoz said about her ACC assignment."

He frowned slightly. "Has Trenton lied to you about anything?"

"No, Michael—faith, I never talk to him. It's only—" she hesitated, and tried to decide how much to say. "He was in a place he shouldn't have been, I suppose."

He thought this over for a moment. "The racecourse?"

She stared in astonishment; trust Acton to be two steps ahead of her. "Aye, the racecourse. What's he doin' there?"

"He's keeping an eye on Munoz."

She almost laughed out loud in her relief. "Of course, he is—because Elena was kidnapped, and we still don't know why." She reached to take his hand, and said with all sincerity, "Thank you. I would save myself a lot of frettin' if I just trusted you, my friend. Thank you for keepin' her safe."

But he tilted his head. "My motives are not entirely honorable, I'm afraid. Please keep in mind that she may be compromised."

Doyle nodded, to show that she wasn't such a fool that she hadn't considered this uncomfortable possibility. "I don't think so—I've asked a few questions, and even though she can't tell me much, I can't find the whisper of a guilty conscience."

"Do not let your guard down, nevertheless."

"Right-o." She paused, because there was something niggling at her, something that didn't make sense, but she couldn't grasp what it was—another willow-wisp, as Reynolds would say. Trying to catch the elusive thought, she said slowly, "I'm worried that there's a tickin' clock, somewhere."

Acton's manner became a bit grave. "There is indeed a ticking clock, and I'm afraid the CID is in for some further unpleasantness."

This was not surprising information, based on what she'd already pieced together. "I know you hate to expose the ugly truth, Michael, but this time it can't be helped. If the ACC is bent, the public has a right to know about it. And besides, a hail of fire and brimstone is exactly what these villains deserve, once their misdeeds hit the news. There's nothin' worse than the watchdogs turnin' themselves into wolves, and they should be heartily ashamed of themselves."

A bit belatedly, she realized that the man seated across from her tended to blur the watchdog-and-wolf line, himself, and so she decided to change the subject. "Is Savoie goin' to be a star witness in the corruption case, too? You'll have him busy as a fishwife at Lent, if that's the case. He should demand a parkin' pass."

"We shall see," was all her companion offered, as their meals were served.

Doyle made a wry mouth. "Well, can you at least tell me if we'll get a second helpin' of Savoie, in the committee hearing? I'm half-afraid he'll cross the line, and all those old bag-wits will try to slay him on the spot. I don't know which side I'd root for."

"Unlikely, that anyone will resort to violence," Acton soothed. "Although I suppose the possibility cannot be eliminated."

Their conversation was interrupted when an important-looking man in a very fine suit strolled by, and then made a show of nodding to them in a friendly fashion. Doyle smiled a greeting, then leaned in to Acton. "Who's that?"

"I've no idea."

She sighed in mock-resignation. "Yes, well; we're a bit late for the power-lunch people, so we've got to settle for the second tier."

"Not much longer," he soothed. "Soon, it will all be over."

This was true, and she was given the impression that he felt assured of victory. Considering this, she eyed him a bit suspiciously. "Are you goin' to tell me how the final committee hearin' is goin' to go?"

He made a small, self-deprecatory gesture. "I think you place too much confidence in my abilities, Kathleen."

Amused, she made a derisive sound. "Ach, husband; there are times when all I can do is sit back and marvel. I'm startin' to think there's no such thing as too much confidence in your abilities." Her scalp prickled, and she paused, wondering what it was that she was trying to understand.

"What is it?" Watching her, he reached to touch her fingers.

"Somethin's up," she confessed a bit somberly. "But I can't figure out what it is—there are too many loose ends, and I don't know which ones are the important ones."

"Would it help to make the visit to Trestles, now?"

She stared at him in surprise. "Right now?"

He folded his napkin. "Certainly."

"All right—but think of an excuse, so we won't have to stay very long."

She caught a quick glimpse of frustration from him, and was instantly contrite. "Faith, Michael, I'm that sorry—it's a beautiful place, and I haven't given it a decent chance." In her best supportive-wife manner, she declared, "If you wanted to move in tomorrow, wither thou goest, I would go, you know. I'm just bein' a baby."

"You are uncomfortable there. I understand, and I only wish I could remedy the problem."

"No—it's Edward's home, and his heritage. I'll come around, husband; pay me no mind."

"All will soon be resolved," he soothed. "Wait and see."

With a smile, she squeezed the hand that held hers, even though her scalp was prickling to beat the band.

31

He always felt so rejuvenated, when he was here.

And so, a few hours later, Doyle found herself standing in the ancient archives room at Trestles, listening to the silence and feeling a bit foolish. The round, stone-walled room had been part of the original keep and it was always a bit cool, even on a warm day.

Since she needed to soothe the ghost of the angry knight, Acton had asked if it would be best to make the attempt from the oldest part of the manor house. She'd willingly agreed, and hadn't the heart to tell him that it truly didn't matter; the ghosts were always bangin' about in the rafters and they were a noisy, attention-seeking bunch. She didn't tell him because she was worried that it might sound creepy, and—ever since her confrontation with the Santero—it was important that she never sound creepy.

The house was quiet, because Acton had phoned ahead and had seen to it that everyone was cleared out except for Hudson, who'd met them at the door with an impassive, respectful expression; not at all like someone who'd committed a shadow murder or two, in his day.

"Let me know if you have need of anything," Acton had said to her, as he prepared to wait outside the ancient oaken door. "Take all the time you need."

Yet again, she refrained from telling him that the knight had popped up immediately upon their entry to the house, very unhappy with her and rattling his sword as he was wont to do when he was irritated, which seemed to be most of the time.

A bit annoyed with the ghost's high-handed rudeness, she addressed the silent walls in a low voice. "Listen, you—I know you're unhappy about Savoie's tryin' to claim Trestles, but *believe* me, he's not goin' to take up residence here—faith, you'll never even see him again. It's all a misdirection play—a false flag. In truth, he's helpin' Acton."

She was met with the unwavering conviction that she was a fool of the first order.

Exasperated, she retorted, "Fine, then; don't believe me—and besides, it doesn't matter in the first place; France and England aren't at war—France and England are friendly, now. And Ireland is a sovereign state." She thought she'd throw that in, just to knock him back a bit—he was such an arrogant know-it-all.

But again, she was given to understand that she was the next thing to a simpleton, and for a strange moment she was reminded of Harding, imploring her to pay attention, and nattering on about the stupid Até.

"You know that Acton's no fool," she soothed, in an attempt to lay his ghostly fears to rest. "He's goin' to be extra careful, when it comes to all things Savoie. And he'd never do anythin' to jeopardize Trestles—I *promise* you."

But the knight would not be swayed, and thoughtfully, she withdrew from the tower, holding up her palms in frustration when Acton's gaze met hers. "It's like talkin' to the stones in the wall. He thinks Savoie is goin' to take Trestles from you, and there's nothin' I can say to convince him otherwise."

Acton ducked his chin, thinking over this revelation. "Is he a danger to you?"

Doyle stifled alarming visions of her over-fond husband burning the place to the ground, and assured him, "No—he's not. Mainly, he can't believe I'm such a nodcock. He has little use for women—and the Irish in particular—and everyone's afraid of him; they stay well out of his way."

As they walked down the hallway toward the foyer, her husband cast her a glance. "Are they afraid of you?"

"Like the Santero was?" She paused for a moment, and fought a panicked feeling, because it was always difficult for her to speak of it. "No, they're not afraid of me. In fact, some nice woman told me I should use fennel if Edward gets the colic—have no idea what she's talkin' about, but I will keep it to mind."

He paused for a moment, in the spacious entry way, and regarded her. "You are extraordinary," he said, and meant it.

She emphasized with a touch of anxiety, "But not at all *creepy*, Michael."

"Not in the least," he assured her, and it was true. "Let's go home."

"This is home, too." She stretched her arms over her head, and viewed the timbered ceiling with a resigned eye. "Let's lie in front of the fire, and roast potatoes in the jacket. D'you suppose Hudson has any, in the root cellar?"

"You needn't humor me." With a fond smile, he took her elbow. "We'll go home, and if you wish to roast potatoes, you shall roast them there."

"Let's stay here, instead—we can go home after dinner. I don't mind, Michael, truly. And I'll try on my spiky heels; I was too nervous to try them on in the store."

He was very pleased, she could see. "By all means, then."

And so, a short time later, they were seated on the Aubusson rug before the hearth in the drawing room, a crackling fire casting shadows on the walls whilst two potatoes lay roasting beneath the grate.

"We used to do this, my mother and me," Doyle said absently, watching the flames. "Now I realize that we were probably out of money, but at the time I always thought it such a treat."

Negligently, he leaned over to kiss her. "What happens next?"

She smiled at his ignorance. "We split them open and eat them, Michael. I'll let you pull them out; I always burnt my fingertips."

He reached for the potatoes, and eased them out of the ashes with short, quick movements. "Does this call for butter?"

"Indeed, it does. But let me take these shoes off before you call Hudson—he'll think me a wanton, and I'd rather he didn't think someone in my condition might be havin' sex all over the fancy rug."

Acton leaned over to pull the bell cord. "Nonsense; he'll only assume these are your potato-roasting shoes."

She laughed, as she wiggled the narrow shoes off her swollen feet. "I suppose that's true; if I told him that's how we do it in Ireland, he'd mark it down as just one more oddity amongst the many."

Upon hearing their request, the dignified steward fetched the butter as though the sight of Acton—sprawled on the floor like a derryman, and eating with his hands—was the merest commonplace.

As Hudson discreetly closed the double doors behind him, Doyle smiled and licked her fingers. "He's that pleased that you're so happy."

This earned her another fond kiss, this one a bit more buttery than the last. "I am inordinately pleased, myself."

"It's truly a nice place, Michael. My hand on my heart."

"You need to become accustomed; I understand."

Gazing into the fire, she thought about nothing in particular for a space of time, whilst her husband absently rubbed her back. Although she'd downplayed the knight's concerns, she decided that it wouldn't hurt to speak to Savoie yet again, just to make sure that he wasn't working against Acton. She'd asked him once already, and he'd assured her that he was not. In fact, at the time, Savoie had hinted that he was working with Acton as opposed to against him, and subsequent events and shown that this was true. Nevertheless, she should double-check; the knight's certainty was a bit unsettling, truth to tell.

Reminded, she turned to him. "Did you find out why Williams wasn't tellin' you the truth, about Harding's bein' dead?"

"I believe," he said slowly, "that Williams is under intense pressure, and is trying to extricate himself from his problems all on his own."

This was in keeping with what she knew, and it also reassured her that Acton was keeping an eye on the situation. "Foolish man," she teased. "He should unburden his soul to you, and trust you to make it right."

"He may yet; we shall see."

"Well, I think he's bein' too prideful, Michael, but he's a rare knocker, if he thinks he can outfox you. He should just take his lumps, and let you help him."

Doyle winced, as overhead, the knight slammed the flat of his sword into a hammer beam.

32

Unlikely, that she'd developed a taste for juice; she must be meeting someone there, instead.

I'm being run ragged, Doyle thought a bit crossly, as she buttoned her coat against the early morning cold. And the clock is ticking, but I don't know if I'm getting any closer to whatever it is. And meanwhile—although I'm whale-sized—various ghosts are urging me to go faster. Impatiently, she glanced up the pavement, and decided it was a shame no one had ever mentioned that this marriage business was so very complicated, and if only they had, she might have thought it over for more than twenty minutes.

It was the next morning, and she'd arranged for an early meeting with Savoie because the final committee hearing was fast approaching, and she'd best speak with him before it went forward, just to make certain that he wasn't about to pull the curtains down around their heads.

Since she was supposed to stay close to headquarters, she'd hit on the subterfuge of asking the driving service to drop her off so that she could pick up another order of juice, and then walk in to work. Of course, if he heard about this diversion, Acton would no doubt wonder why his better half was doing something so completely out-of-character, but the stores weren't yet open, and it was the best she could do on short notice.

Hopefully, Acton would be too busy to notice that she was taking the slow route in to work, and just as hopefully Trenton wasn't on the case, as yet. It hardly mattered; it was important that she speak with Savoie face-to-face, and if she was confronted on the subject, she'd just admit to it.

As was his usual, Savoie was a bit late—no doubt because he was casing the place; he was a cautious man, and with good reason. Doyle was reviewing the chalkboard menu and trying to decide if anything sounded remotely appealing when Savoie materialized next to her. "*Bonjour.*"

"Hallo, Philippe." She noted that he held Emile by the hand, and smiled at the boy. "Hallo, Emile."

"Hallo. Papa says you are fat because there is a baby inside your tummy."

"Your papa is correct." Unsure of what one should say, she decided to add, "The baby is a little boy like you. His name is Edward."

Emile thought this over. "I will let him ride my horse, when I get it."

This statement raised a flare of alarm within her breast. "Oh—oh; where will you be keepin' your horse?"

"La Belle France. Papa says."

"Emile," Savoie cautioned. "Less talk."

As this seemed a good sign that Savoie was not truly planning to take over Trestles by force of arms, Doyle hid her relief. "Are you headin' back to France, then?"

"Soon." He squinted at the offerings, and then ordered some complicated concoction. "But Emile, he must begin the school here, so I will come back in the fall. What is it you wish, Emile?"

"That one," said Emile, pointing to another patron's orange-colored beverage. To Doyle, he announced, "I will wear a uniform at my school, and they have rabbits, in a pen."

"That is excellent," Doyle acknowledged.

"It is St. Margaret's," Savoie explained, with a gleam.

As that gleam reminded her that he'd no doubt falsified the admission papers, Doyle hastily changed the subject. "I'm that surprised you're settlin' here, instead of back home where you came from."

"You forget," he informed her with a chiding expression. "I have the business interests, here."

Yet again, Doyle quickly changed the subject, because she couldn't very well discuss his massive smuggling-by-horse-trailers rig without arresting him on the spot. "Yes; well, I hope you will keep Emile to mind, and how I'm unlikely to be givin' him any horses if you wind up in prison." Doyle had made a much-regretted promise that she'd stand in as next-of-kin, if anything happened to Savoie.

"Me, I will be careful." With a gesture toward her belly, he teased, "I will be *le parrain*, yes? When *le bébé* is baptized."

Doyle guessed at what the word meant, and quirked her mouth at the picture thus presented. "I can't imagine Acton would look upon such a plan with a benign eye, Philippe."

Very much amused, Savoie rendered his thin smile. "*Non.* He would not have the nine eyes."

"Definitely not." She swallowed, and decided there was nothin' for it; she was running out of time to discover what she needed to discover. "I wanted to meet with you, Philippe, because I wanted to make sure you aren't double-crossin' Acton."

He glanced at her in surprise, as he stepped forward to take his juice from the attendant. "*Non.* I do not do the double-cross of Acton. Is this what he says?"

"No, I am just a bit anxious, is all." Doyle thought about his response—which was true—and cautiously asked a follow-up. "Are you helpin' Acton, then? You're not causin' him any trouble, are you?"

He frowned at her for a moment, as he handed Emile his cup. "Me, I help Acton. Do not worry, little bird; I do what he asks."

Her scalp prickled, and thus prodded, she asked what seemed like the obvious question. "But why? Why would you help Acton?" Acton had cut an immunity deal with Savoie when he'd enlisted his help in taking down the corruption rig, and she wondered uneasily if perhaps more favors had been promised—which was not something law enforcement should probably be doing, with the likes of Philippe Savoie.

But his answer went a different direction. "We are friends, yes? I think you are the only one."

This was said in a slightly melancholy tone, and it immediately raised her defenses. "Don't pitch me a wheedle, Philippe, I'm not buyin' whatever it is you're sellin'."

Savoie's gaze rested for a moment on Emile, sucking on his straw and jumping with both feet on the pavement cracks. "Your husband, he is not a forgiving man."

This was unexpected, and she answered cautiously, "No—I know. We're workin on it."

He eyed her sidelong. "I think to myself, maybe this Acton, maybe he thinks, 'Savoie knows too much'."

The irony was thick on the ground; apparently Savoie was just as worried as she was about who was double-crossing whom. "Yes, well, I wouldn't worry about that, Philippe. Recall that you've duped me into raisin' Emile if anythin' happens to you—and I don't appreciate bein' an insurance policy against my own husband—but there it is. Just don't cross him, and all will be well." She hesitated, then added, "I think—I think despite my best efforts at hidin' it, Acton knows that we're friends, and that goes a long way with him."

He lowered his head. "*Bien.*"

She decided that she may as well ask. "Do you know of anythin'—is there any reason that would make you think that I shouldn't trust Acton?"

The question surprised him, and he lifted his brows. "There is another woman? Yes?"

He genuinely had no idea what she was talking about, and so she shrugged and said lightly, "Definitely not. Forget that I asked, I was just worried about—about somethin' I can't quite put my finger on."

His pale gaze held hers, and he said nothing for a long moment. "*Eh bien*; if you put the finger, you must come to live with me, and Emile." Pausing, he added, "As long as Acton will have the nine eyes."

Doyle duly noted that poor Munoz did not enter into this equation, and disclaimed with a smile, "Never you mind, my friend; I'm just bein' fanciful."

"Papa, will we go soon?"

"*Moment*, Emile." Savoie regarded her, his expression unreadable. "You will let me know if you have the troubles, yes? I will be the Saint Bernard."

"I will," she agreed, and decided she shouldn't elaborate—she'd told him too much as it was. "Thank you for meetin' me."

With no further ado, he put his hand on the back of Emile's head, and steered the boy away and down the pavement without a backward glance.

With a stoic air, Doyle began the walk to headquarters, after having decided that she couldn't bear to order a juice, even as a cover. I'm still flummoxed, she thought as she trudged along. I've plumbed Savoie as thoroughly as I can, and there doesn't seem to be anything amiss—other than the fact he's a criminal kingpin, of course. But when he said he saw me as his only friend, it was true, and when he said he wasn't going to do any harm to Acton—and that he'd help me, if I was in trouble—that was all true, too.

He's nicer, she decided, absently gazing into the distance with her hands in her coat pockets. Savoie was miles nicer than when first they'd met, under best-be-forgotten circumstances. He seemed very content, and there was no question that he doted on little Emile. Mayhap the knight didn't trust him because he hadn't seen the new, nicer version of Savoie. After all, the knight last saw him at Trestles, on another best-be-forgotten evening, when Acton brought down the corruption rig in spectacular fashion. That terrible night, when the DCS had stormed the gates to arrest Acton; the night when Solonik's sister, Savoie, and Acton were all meeting together at Trestles, and speaking in French.

This gave her pause for a moment, since the knight also spoke French, and presumably knew what it was they'd been speaking about. But she'd checked as best she could, and hadn't found the whisper of a conspiracy by Savoie against Acton. Mayhap the knight misunderstood something—he didn't trust the French, after all, and was always going on and on about some stupid battle with King Hank, as though she had the slightest interest in the stupid English and their stupid battles.

So now I've checked into it, she told herself firmly, and I have one less worry. Almost without conscious volition, she lingered in front of the shoe shop's window, but as it was not yet open, she resolutely pushed on.

33

So; she'd met with Savoie, which made sense. She was un-easy about him, and she was uniquely situated to sound him out. He wasn't worried.

Doyle settled in at her desk with the dogged determination to follow up on the shadow murders—she'd been distracted by this whole knight-rampaging-around situation, and felt as though she'd been led on a wild goose chase—or wild Frenchman chase, as the case may be. It was past time to concentrate on putting some villains in the nick, especially the ones who were trying to get away with shadow murders.

Carefully, she went over her notes from the QC's murder and from Blakney's murder, and almost immediately something leapt out at her. Picking up the desk phone, she decided that this was exactly what she deserved from letting herself get distracted from doing the tedious but necessary legwork in a homicide case such as this one, where the forensics didn't point a bright and shiny arrow at the perpetrator. In those unfortunate cases where the forensics weren't helpful, a detective was instead tasked with putting together evidence that showed motive and opportunity, in the time-honored tradition.

Opportunity was one-half the equation, and at the Crime Academy, they drilled into you that a detective's single most important chore was to set up a timeline, so as to rule out potential suspects who didn't have the opportunity to commit murder, and to likewise bring into focus those suspects who were in the right place at the right time. However, the other half of the equation was motive, which is how one came up with a list of suspects to begin with.

And there was the sticking point: what was the motive for the QC's murder? It was staged as a cosh-and-rob, but now they knew that his was a shadow murder, to be pinned on the evil Santero for reasons which were as yet unclear. They'd ruled out the flight attendant girlfriend, but hadn't looked any further than that. Surely, it was too much a coincidence—that he was a member of the same Inns of Court as the Santero's case-sabotaging counsel? Acton famously didn't believe in coincidences, and indeed, it was looking very much as though the QC had been the victim of a containment murder—he knew something dangerous, and had to be taken out with the blame laid elsewhere. Doyle was left with the certain conviction that if she could figure out the motive behind the QC's death, all the shadow murder cases would unravel in short order.

Doyle's call rang through to the flight attendant's voice mail and so she left a message, asking if she could meet up with the woman for a follow-up interview, here at headquarters.

After ringing off, she slowly replaced the receiver, debating whether she should mention this upcoming interview to Munoz, since she'd promised Munoz an assignment. And she should tell Williams, because Williams was the CSM, after all. Not yet, she decided, fingering the phone buttons. At this particular juncture, the better part of discretion was to keep her mouth shut. Munoz and Williams may be the people she most cared about, but she was paranoid enough from all this business to be very wary; at least until she'd another crack at the witness.

Williams pinged her, and she immediately felt a stab of guilt that she hadn't contacted him to assure him that Acton was handling his problems, and that he should not fret himself to death. "Hey," she answered. "I've been meanin' to report in."

"Hey yourself. Are you free for lunch? I'm in need of a chaperone."

"You need a gooseberry?" She smiled into the mobile. "I must say that I'm amazed you let your handsome self get into these sorts of situations, to begin with."

"It's a bit more complicated; I'm meeting Morgan Percy at the deli."

"Ah," she said, suddenly sober. "Say no more."

"I'd rather it didn't look as though I asked you to be there, though."

"Oh-oh," she warned. "I'm not very good at pretendin' things."

"This I know, Kath. It's important, or I wouldn't ask."

Doyle suddenly saw a way to kill multiple birds with a single sandwich. "Shall I bring Acton, as my cover? Mayhap he could shake up our Ms. Percy a bit, and make her re-think her evil ways."

There was a small pause. "Probably not a good idea—and anyway, no one would believe that Acton would go to the deli for lunch. How about Munoz, is she available?"

"I'll arrange it, Thomas, not to worry. Just tell me when and where."

Thoughtfully, she rang off and wondered what this was all about. Williams had been mysterious and guilt-ridden about Blakney's death, and one would think that the last needful thing he would do was lunch with Morgan Percy, although perhaps he needed to placate the girl.

"Have a mo?"

Doyle looked up to see Officer Gabriel, leaning on her cubicle and causing the fair Doyle to suffer yet another pang of guilt in that she hadn't followed up with him after the racecourse incident, and he no doubt thought her thoroughly unhinged. "Oh—oh hallo, Gabriel. I've been meanin' to phone you, truly."

He smiled, and shrugged. "No matter; shall we discuss the case that we're not worthy of? Any news?"

She was tempted to send him to speak with the shop-minder, but drew back, yet again. Gabriel seemed on the up-and-up, but she'd the uneasy feeling that the ticking clock was getting closer to going off, and she wasn't certain who could be trusted, and who could not. Instead, she replied, "Yes, let's brainstorm—I'm lookin' for a motive, and I can't find the whisper of one." Her forehead suddenly cleared. "Are you available for lunch at the deli? A walk would do me good."

34

Another meeting, it seemed. Little doubt that she'd discovered what Williams had done. He hoped it didn't color her affection for him.

Doyle and Gabriel walked over to the deli just before noon, and since the place was not yet crowded, she easily spotted Williams and the fair Ms. Percy, seated at an outdoor table in plain view of any chance detectives who happened to be passing by.

"Morgan," Doyle called out in her best imitation of surprise. "How goes the pursuit of justice?"

"Overrated," the other girl smiled. "We just lost a motion to keep my client's nasty cult practices out of evidence, and so now we've got to try to soft-pedal the fact that he made potions out of kitten's blood."

"Reason number two thousand twenty that I'm glad I'm on offense, rather than defense," Gabriel offered.

"Yes, you're naturally offensive," Percy teased with an arched brow, and Gabriel laughed out loud, pulling up a chair without waiting for an invitation.

Mother a' mercy, this is awkward, Doyle realized, as Williams found her another chair. Doyle had forgotten that there was apparently some canoodling going on betwixt Gabriel and Percy, and so bringing him along on this little outing was perhaps not the brightest idea she'd ever had. Williams didn't seem thrown, however, and so she decided that he probably appreciated anyone who was willing to take the girl off his hands.

"I was just hearing about Morgan's bad morning in court," Williams continued. "They're getting the pre-trials done, and it's not going their way."

"It was the worst," the girl agreed, with a sigh that showcased her impressive bosom. "The judge was completely unreasonable."

Although it truly wasn't much of a surprise, Doyle duly processed the fact that this was not true—Morgan was secretly very pleased. No doubt the corrupt judge was happy to allow any and all evidence that would paint the blackhearted suspect even blacker, so that the jury would convict him without even having to discuss it.

"Are you going to testify for the prosecution?" Gabriel asked Williams.

"Yes; I will lay the foundation for chain-of-evidence," Williams replied.

Doyle straightened up to eye him, because this was not true. Why would Williams lie about something so mundane? Mayhap he didn't want to give away state secrets to the opposing side— although the evidence list had surely been exchanged, by now. Prosecution wasn't allowed to surprise the defense, so all cards would be already on the table.

Whilst she was puzzling over this, Williams met her eye for the barest moment and then looked away.

Ah, thought Doyle, trying to hide her surprise. I'm not on chaperoning duty at all; Williams wants me to hear the lies that are being told, and—and what? Figure out why his hands are tied? Report to Acton?

"The defendant won't wear a suit of clothes," Percy disclosed with an air of incredulity. "Instead, he wants to wear his tribal dress."

"Maybe he can shake some shrunken skulls," Gabriel suggested. "That would impress them."

They all chuckled, but Doyle warned, "Acton says that the jury's perception often trumps the strongest evidence. If everyone hates him on sight, they won't much care whether there's reasonable doubt."

"Then you've got an uphill battle," Williams said to Percy, and it was not true.

This is going to be a very strange sort of lunch, Doyle decided, and wished she could make some notes on a napkin, or something.

With a sympathetic shrug, Gabriel said to the other girl, "Look on the bright side; if it's so very hopeless, it makes your job easier. No one is expecting a miracle, and it will be good experience, if you're sitting second chair. Will the lead barrister allow you to do any questioning?"

Percy shook her head. "Not much—the case is too high-profile. I'm to do some of the preliminaries; chain-of-custody, that sort of thing."

Gabriel grinned. "Then I hope you grill Williams, here, within an inch of his life."

"Oh, I will," she laughed. "Although I think there's no such thing as a good chain-of-custody grilling. Instead, everyone will be asleep."

"I won't," Williams promised. "If you're going after me, I've got to be on my toes—nothing but the truth."

Another lie, Doyle duly noted. Apparently, Williams was going to lie on the stand—or he wasn't going to testify, or something—truly, he needed to be clearer about what was going on, here.

Struck with a sudden thought, she decided to probe a bit. "It's lucky, we are, that you never had to take the stand against Dr. Harding, remember? You'd be impeached in a pig's whisker."

Bull's-eye; there was a heavy, strained moment of wariness. "What happened?" Percy asked with studied casualness. "Never say that Williams compromised a witness?"

With a small smile, Williams shrugged. "Not my finest hour. No harm done; the witness didn't lose any teeth."

They all laughed, and then Doyle idly leaned back in her chair. "Whatever happened to Dr. Harding, d'you know? I don't think he's practicin' in the city anymore."

"I don't know," Williams replied, and it was a lie.

Morgan Percy pushed out her chair. "Anyone want anything? I'm going to need more coffee, to stay awake for the next round."

"Coffee," breathed Doyle, with a great deal of longing. "Would you mind if I smell it, before you drink it down?"

"I'll get one, and you can smell mine," Williams offered. "Gabriel?"

"I'm good," Gabriel replied. "I'll stay here with the baroness."

Doyle noted that Gabriel watched the other two with a thoughtful expression, as Williams held the door for Percy. "I hope you're not jealous," she ventured. "Sorry, if this is crackin' awkward."

"Oh, I'm fuming jealous. Ready to knife DI Williams, and watch him bleed all over the table."

Needless to say, this was not true, and Doyle had to laugh. "Try to resist the impulse; I'd hate to have to put you in a headlock, in my condition."

He tilted his head, as he continued to watch the other two through the window. "So; will you tell me what's going on, here?"

Startled, Doyle stammered, "Oh—oh, what do you mean?"

He turned his thoughtful gaze to her. "Williams shouldn't be testifying about chain-of-custody; you should. You're the one who found the shoes."

"Oh." This hadn't even occurred to her, which only went to show that Gabriel was a sharp stick. Uncomfortably aware that her companion was doing an excellent job of putting two and two together, she hedged, "Mayhap the prosecution has decided not to use the shoes? I suppose it would only make sense; the shoes would be easily precluded because there is no chain-of-custody, in the first place."

203

"Very true."

He offered nothing more, and unable to resist, she asked, "What—what is it that you're thinkin', Gabriel?"

With a small smile, he crossed his arms and shrugged. "Nothing that's any of my business. I'm just a secondary character, here."

His words triggered a sense of deep foreboding, and Doyle blurted out, "No—no, you're not. You should stay away from it, Gabriel. Please."

He didn't answer immediately, but considered her for a moment. "What is the 'it' I'm staying away from?"

Doyle struggled with what to say since truly, she didn't know herself—it was mostly guesswork, thus far. "I think there are some very desperate people, doin' some very desperate things."

He lifted his gaze to the deli windows, where Percy and Williams could be seen picking up the coffee. "Present company included?"

Aware that she was giving away too much, Doyle equivocated, "I don't want to say more. I'm worried—I'm worried other people have been drawn in against their will, and I don't want it to happen to you."

He turned his thoughtful gaze back to her. "You seem to think I'm in some sort of danger."

After hesitating, she decided that she couldn't really deny it— that horse had already left the barn. "Yes, but I can't tell you why." This, of course, was only the truth; she'd sound as crazy as the Santero if she told him of prickling scalps, and shoeless ghosts.

Shrugging again, he replied, "All right," but it was not true.

Stifling her alarm, Doyle eyed him, and wished she knew what he was thinking. "I'm sorry; I know I sound crazed, with all these dire warnin's. I just can't say more."

"Not to worry," Gabriel smiled, and again, it wasn't true.

35

There; she was eating with the others, and no harm done.
She'd not be happy with his intervention, but he could not
be easy.

It was fortunate for Doyle that she hadn't given in to the mighty temptation to take a swig from Williams' coffee before she spotted Acton, approaching in their direction along the pavement. Worried, he is, she thought, assessing his calm demeanor with a practiced eye. Poor man's got a free-range wife, who leads him a merry chase.

"Hallo, sir," she called out, so as to give the others a warning. "Am I needed, or would you care to join us?"

There was not the slightest chance, of course, that Acton would deign to join them and predictably, he demurred. "I am afraid I must interrupt, and beg your pardon." He nodded to the others, who'd all straightened up and pulled their feet under the table.

And so, Doyle allowed her husband to escort her back toward headquarters—their progress necessarily a bit slow, as she was inclined to dawdle. Into the silence, she ventured, "It's only the deli, Michael."

"I cannot like the company."

This was of interest, and she eyed him sidelong. "Oh? Who's in your black book, aside from Williams?"

He tilted his head. "What makes you think Williams is in my black book?"

She made a wry mouth, and allowed her gaze to wander in the general direction of the shoe store, which was halfway down the nearest cross street. "Because he's frettin' about somethin', but won't tell me outright about whatever it is. That, and he nearly fainted when you showed up, just now." She teetered on the verge of telling him that Williams wanted her to know that he was lying, but hesitated, because she knew Acton would not like to hear that Williams was exploiting her perceptive abilities in such a way. Instead, she offered, "I think he's worried about the Santero trial, and the chain-of-custody testimony."

"He should be," was her husband's only response, and it was true.

As she seemed to be getting nowhere, Doyle thought she'd throw a spanner into Acton's wheel-of-closely-guarded-secrets. "Since it was such a fine day, I thought I'd ask him if he knew whatever had happened to Dr. Harding."

She'd sought to provoke him, and it turned the trick, as Acton paused mid-stride and took her arm with gentle insistence, bending his head to hers. "Kathleen, I must ask you—very seriously—not to follow up on these matters. I will have your promise."

Gazing into his eyes, so intent on hers, she decided there was nothing for it—if she couldn't trust Acton, she may as well lie down in sackcloth and ashes. "I can't give you my promise, Michael. I'm bein' told that I'm not supposed to trust you."

The expression in his eyes turned to one of abject surprise. "What is this?"

She covered the hand on her arm, so as to take the sting from the words. "I know you're tryin' to smooth my way, Michael—and it's much appreciated—but sometimes your methods are a bit—are a bit questionable. I'm gettin' warnin's that I mustn't trust you."

He stared at her, speechless, and she had to laugh at his un-feigned amazement; Acton's devotion to her was almost frighten-ing in its intensity—poor man—and the last blessed thing he'd ever do would be to give her the old double-cross. "I know, I know; but it's—it's a persistent message, and so I think it's best that I tell you—it makes no sense, truly."

He frowned, and she could sense that he was genuinely per-plexed. "Can you elaborate?"

Taking hold of his arm, she sighed, and began walking for-ward again. "I wish I could. I wish it was clearer." She knew—in the way that she knew things—that it was important she not tell him that it was Harding who was the relater-of-dire-warnings, and so she didn't mention it. He'd no doubt argue that Harding was stirring up trouble, and he couldn't know—like she did— that he was beyond that, now.

He guessed, "Could it be the succession hearing? Because I can assure you that the ends justify the means."

She lingered at the intersection, wondering what she could tell him when she wasn't certain what it was that she was talking about, in the first place. "In a strange way, I think everythin' is all bound up in everythin' else—the succession hearin', the Santero trial, Williams bein' all afret." She paused, thinking. "Munoz's assignment."

Ah, she caught a flare of emotion from her husband, and quickly lifted her face to his. "What? What is it?"

Slowly, he revealed, "Munoz has asked to meet with me, off the record. Please don't mention it."

But this news was not alarming, and Doyle nodded in relief as she gently steered him down the cross street. "Good. I think there's somethin' gafty about this whole undercover rig, and I even suggested that she appeal to you, given that the net is closin' in around the ACC, and they're dirty birds in the first place." Glancing up at him with a gleam, she teased, "Mayhap that's what all these warnin's are about—mayhap I shouldn't trust you to be alone with the fair Munoz. Promise me you won't be meetin' her at the stables."

They exchanged a fond smile, because Edward was conceived in the stables at Trestles, on a glorious afternoon that featured hurried sex, and the scent of sweaty horses.

But the moment quickly passed, because Doyle felt a sudden jolt of uneasiness. "You know, there was somethin'—somethin' Munoz said about her assignment that struck me as odd, and I wish I could remember what it was. It's one of those willow-wisks, that Reynolds talks about."

"Has she said anything that didn't ring true?"

This was his delicate way of reminding her that Munoz could be compromised, and she was quick to reassure him, "She doesn't tell me *anythin'*, which is just as well—faith, I can't keep all the fish tales straight as it is." She eyed him sidelong. "Orkney Islands, my eye."

With a small smile, he asked in a diffident tone, "Where are we going?"

Since she'd maneuvered him down the cross street, she was forced to confess, "Well, here's the thing, Michael. There are some very sharp-lookin' black boots in the store window, and I don't think I can even zip them over my calves at this point, but I would truly, truly, like to try."

"Then by all means."

Reading him aright, she giggled. "No one is more surprised than I am—it must be my hormones, runnin' amok. I've never been the least bit interested in frivolous shoes, before."

He held the shop door for her. "I confess that I am very fond of your hormones, and willing to indulge them as a reward for past performance."

She giggled again, and pausing for a moment, he bent his head to hers. "Will you tell me if you have any more insights?"

It was bothering him—as she knew it would—and she felt a bit ashamed for making him worry. "It seems so stupid, Michael; I trust you down to the soles of my shoes, and I'll swear to it on all the holy relics."

But his tone was serious, as they continued into the shop. "On the contrary; it was no easy thing for you to bring yourself to tell me of this. Therefore, I believe it is important."

This was, of course, a valid point, and she nodded, matching his seriousness. "Sometimes, husband, I think you know me better than I know me."

"I could say the same, Kathleen."

"No," she disagreed without rancor. "I don't know you half as well as you know me." This went without saying; talk about emingnas—or however you said it—he took the palm.

Since this was inarguable, he did not demur. "Be that as it may, you can always trust me. My own promise on it."

And of course, it was no surprise that his words rang completely true. I am going to go barking mad, trying to figure this out, she thought; I'm the one that stupid Harding needs to put on the stupid couch.

36

It was all immensely satisfying, and the appropriate ar-
rests would soon be made. All that was left was to—gen-
tly—convince her that she needed to stay home, and rest.

The final hearing on the House of Acton succession was
underway, with Doyle taking up her position as the hand-
wringer-in-chief, seated in her usual chair against the
wall. The chairman had opened by reminding the committee
that there were two different claims brought by the petitioner, Sir
Stephen; the first was that an imposter had been substituted in
the latter part of the twentieth century so that the title rightfully
belonged to him outright. The alternative petition claimed that
the current Lord Acton had secretly married, and that his first
wife had borne him a son, with the whereabouts of either being
currently unknown.

The chairman expressed open skepticism with respect to the
first claim, because it seemed so preposterous, and because after
two hearings, the petitioner couldn't come up with any credible
witnesses who could testify as to the alleged imposter.

In response, Sir Stephen's counsel argued, "The heir was a
recluse for years, supposedly suffering from shell-shock, yet suddenly he emerges to marry an heiress, in grand fashion, and with

no signs of mental or physical infirmity save for having to wear dark glasses in the daylight. It seems clear that a switch was made, so as to save the title and the estate."

But the chairman continued skeptical, and raised his bushy white brows. "It wouldn't be the first time we've seen a May-December match, hastily arranged to perpetuate the honors of a house. The Duke of Kent comes to mind."

"But what of the man's miraculous recovery, my lord?"

"We've no evidence to show there was a medical condition, to begin with," the chairman pointed out in a sour tone. "All you've presented is innuendo, based on old gossip."

Acton's counsel stood. "If it would please this committee, my lord, I will move to dismiss the first claim for lack of evidence."

"I believe the claim should be considered," Sir Stephen's counsel insisted. "Empirical evidence is necessarily difficult to come by, but surely there is enough circumstantial evidence upon which to base a decision favorable to the petitioner."

"Very well, then; the claim may be considered," the chairman decided, but his doubtful tone indicated his own opinion on the matter.

Acton's counsel gave all appearance of being perplexed, and raised his palms. "If that is the case, my lord, we'd like to call as a rebuttal witness the current steward of the estate."

This was of interest, but Doyle was not at all worried; Hudson was a brick, and was not about to relate any mayhem-in-the-kennels stories, or Acton-killed-his-father stories. At least, one would hope.

After being sworn in, Hudson testified, "My father was steward before me. He often spoke of the war, and of the difficult period that followed the war."

Amongst the committee, there was a subtle, sympathetic shifting in seats, as all the members identified with the terrible burdens that had been placed on the aristocracy, so as to counter the cost of the two devastating wars.

Hudson continued, "After the Second World War, the heir to Trestles was indeed an invalid for several years, having to recover from injuries sustained in combat." Hudson fixed his resolute gaze on the committee members. "There have long been rumors that a switch was made at that time, because the heir substantially recovered from his ailments—save for his eyesight problems—and then went on to marry, and live a prosperous life. But my father assured me that such was not the case. Instead, it was the twelfth Lord Acton's indomitable spirit that sustained him."

"He provided aid to our flyboys, during The Battle of Britain," one of the committee members said aloud. "'Never was so much owed by so many to so few'."

"Indeed," Hudson agreed, and paused for a moment to gather himself, with the room completely and sympathetically silent.

Sir Stephen's counsel could not like the way things were going, and noisily leapt to his feet. "This is hearsay, my lord; the rankest hearsay."

"I'll allow," the chairman replied, resting his chin on his hand. "Hearsay's all anyone's got, after all."

Sir Stephen's counsel then made a mighty attempt to cast doubt on the testimony. "Mr. Hudson; you are aware, of course, that your own livelihood may be jeopardized, if Sir Stephen's claim as rightful heir succeeds."

Hudson appeared to consider this aspect, and shook his head, slightly. "No—I think there is little question that the young policeman's claim has more merit than either Sir Stephen's or the Frenchman's, at this point. Fortunately, Sir Stephen's claim has never been put to the test, as the particulars are rather distasteful."

There was a long moment of silence, as everyone tried to process what was meant, and it was clear that Sir Stephen's counsel was suddenly wary about asking for further details. The chairman, however, had no such qualms. "Are you inferring that Sir

Stephen may indeed be illegitimate? And that there is yet another heir in the wings?"

"Objection," voiced counsel in outrage.

Young policeman's claim? thought Doyle, slowly sitting up straight. Young policeman?

"You can't object to me," the chairman reminded counsel with a frown. "I'm the chairman."

"I beg your pardon, my lord." Counsel turned and apologized to the committee. "I forgot myself, but this calumny is nothing short of outrageous. Sir Stephen is an honorable man, trying to right past wrongs."

The chairman reviewed his notes. "There is no formal claim with respect to Sir Stephen's legitimacy, and therefore, we needn't cross that bridge unless it becomes necessary. Instead, let us proceed to the second claim—that the current Lord Acton had a previous marriage, which may or may not have been dissolved, and that further, a son was born as a result of the purported marriage." Nodding to the clerk, he continued, "Our forensic specialist has examined the two documents which support this claim, and he will now testify with respect to his findings."

Here we go, thought Doyle, watching as the rabbity young man seated himself at the table. I wonder what Acton has up his sleeve—that he had something up his sleeve went without saying; after all, he'd set up this document-treasure-hunt to begin with, courtesy of Philippe Savoie.

After reciting his qualifications, the forensics expert adjusted his eyeglasses and rendered his opinion with little fanfare. "The two documents were falsified—photoshopped. They are good fakes, but falsified, nonetheless."

After a moment of stunned silence, the committee began to murmur amongst themselves and the chairman had to call them to order. Sir Stephen's counsel rose to his feet, visibly shaken. "My lord, no one is more surprised by this than my client—"

"Your client will have an opportunity to give the committee his explanation, sir; please be seated."

After clearing his throat, the specialist continued, "It is not the photoshopping alone that raised a concern, my lord. Another troubling aspect was the fact that the birth certificates did not reveal latent fingerprints belonging to any of the signatories. Because the documents were stored in a protected environment, one would think it would be a simple thing to pull a partial fingerprint, or even the fingerprints of the person who'd filed the document away. The fact that the principals left no fingerprints at all only bolstered my conclusion that the documents were falsified."

Pale of lip, Sir Stephen's counsel rose to his feet. "Perhaps gloves were worn, my lord."

The chairman expressed his open skepticism. "Unlikely, in this day and age, that everyone concerned happened to be wearing gloves, whilst signing and filing away a birth certificate."

His face a bit flushed, the specialist continued, "If I may, my lord, I do not wish to leave the impression that no fingerprints were discovered at all. Indeed, I recovered several partial prints from two different persons, on each document."

There was a slight pause, and Doyle knew that despite his nervous demeanor, the dry little man was enjoying his moment of high drama.

"And," prompted the chairman impatiently. "Could you identify these fingerprints?"

"Yes." The man nodded. "One belonged to the petitioner, Sir Stephen—his right forefinger."

There was an ominous silence, into which Sir Stephen's counsel protested, "But—but this is only to be expected, surely. After all, it was Sir Stephen who retrieved the documents, so as to present them to this committee. My client had no idea that the documents were not accurate renditions of what they portrayed."

"Indeed, that is possible," said the chairman, who'd suddenly turned rather grave. Then, to the specialist, "And whose were the other prints?"

"The other set, my lord, belonged to Mr. Philippe Savoie."

After an astonished pause, everyone began talking over each other, their voices raised in outrage. Doyle hoisted her rucksack on her shoulder, and thought, good one, Acton. And—thanks be to God—no more stupid meals at the stupid cafeteria, although the beefsteak wasn't half bad.

37

Game, set, and match.

The committee quickly determined that Acton was indeed the fourteenth baron, and the question of who was next in succession was deemed to be moot, since an heir was extant. The committee also tabled any determinations about secondary succession from the splintered-off branch of the family, until such time as it might be necessary to re-visit the topic.

Before the final determination was read, however, Sir Stephen had left the room, furious and shaken, and making no effort to speak with anyone, even his counsel.

Going to have to find new digs, Doyle thought with satisfaction, as she watched him leave. A good riddance to bad rubbish. And, although she was eager to depart this place with all speed, she was forced to possess her soul in patience as various members of the committee wished to speak with her, and bestow their congratulations.

"Never a doubt," one aged fellow said, as he bent so low over her hand that she feared he'd fall forward on the floor. "You deserve every honor imaginable—the both of you. It is only fitting, after all."

Doyle stared at the top of his head for a shocked moment, unable to respond. For the first time, it occurred to her—as incredible as it seemed—that Acton had brought down the Scotland Yard corruption rig for the express purpose of boosting his stock for this stupid committee hearing. After all, it would be in keeping with his "perception trumps evidence" theory, and it only made sense; Acton was not a reformer—he was the opposite of a reformer, whatever that was. And he wanted to get this succession business settled, once and for all, so that hopefully there would be no further potshots taken at his bride and his heir.

The more she thought about it, the more likely it seemed—after all, nearly every scheme Acton had ever schemed could be ultimately traced back to his outsized devotion to his unlikely bride. Therefore, there seemed little doubt that he'd publicly gone after the CID blacklegs because he wanted to be perceived as a hero—just like she was—so that the scales were heavily weighted in his favor at this succession hearing. Which they were; no question about it.

As she stood—much struck, and turning over this epiphany in her mind—her husband came over to take her arm and make his excuses to their well-wishers; Lady Acton should rest, after such a traumatic day. She was then deftly extracted from the group, and steered out into the hallway after she thanked the chairman one last time, and assured him that his offer of a silver rattle would be very much appreciated.

As they made their way to the car, Doyle realized—with dawning amazement—that this entire false flag operation must have been put into motion when she'd made her comment about the color of Edward's eyes, months ago. Edward's eye color would have added fuel to Sir Stephen's fire-of-wrongful-succession-claims, and therefore, Acton had planted the two false documents, and had run a classic misdirection play that was nothing short of brilliant in its workings. The committee was so sidetracked by the scandalous first wife question—and then outraged by its exposure as a fraud—that they didn't dwell on the *truly* troubling point, which was the imposter-switch. And now Edward could have green eyes all he wanted, and no one was going to give two pins about it.

She glanced up at her silent husband, as he held the Range Rover's door for her, and thought in wonder—he's always ten steps ahead of me; I don't know why I even bother trying to catch up. She was then surprised when her scalp started prickling—what? Acton was miles smarter than she was, and she was the weak link, here, despite what stupid Harding said about asserting herself, and about stupid Greek goddesses, lurking about.

In a flash of understanding, she paused. "It's you. You're the one who's the Nemesis."

Startled, he bent his head to hers. "Pardon?"

But she wasn't listening, because she was much struck by this revelation—which seemed obvious, now that she thought about it. "Of course, it's you—Nemesis sees that justice is done, no matter what. For the love o' Mike; why couldn't the man just say, 'Acton is the Nemesis, you idiot'."

Understandably, her husband was at sea. "Has Reynolds been rude to you?"

"No—no," she disclaimed impatiently, and then lowered her bulky self into the car seat. "I'm just tryin' to figure somethin' out—what's the name of that other goddess?"

"I believe you mentioned Até," he offered with commendable patience.

Slowly, she nodded. "Yes. So, if you're the Nemesis, who is the Até?"

Leaning on the open door, he watched her for a moment. "I'm afraid I'll need some more context."

"Aye," she mused. "So do I." Raising her face to his, she smiled in apology. "Sorry. Let's go—I'm ready to shake the dust of the Palace of Westminster from my shoes, and hope we never darken its wretched doors again."

"Here's hoping." He shut the door behind her.

They drove for a few minutes, and she duly noted that they were not headed to headquarters, and that her husband hadn't offered any comment about the morning's resounding victory. It was only to be expected, of course; it may have been a brilliant scheme, but she couldn't approve of all the dishonesty—which may as well be the motto for her marriage, thus far. "So, where is it we're goin'? And don't say Candide's again, or I will throw myself bodily from the car."

"I thought we'd have a private celebration." He reached to take her hand. "I'll find a quiet place to park."

"I don't know if we can manage sex in the car," she warned. "It would take some doin'."

With a small smile, he turned down a side street in a posh residential district. "While I appreciate the thought, instead I've had Reynolds pack a lunch."

This was unexpected, and rather sweet, since it showed he knew she'd like nothing more than a chance to regain her bearings in private, after all these tedious public displays of marital solidarity.

He stopped the car next to a quiet park, and reached behind the seat to pull out a packed lunch, complete with her favorite Chinese noodle dish, and a sandwich for himself. With great gusto, she lifted the chopsticks and pulled out a long strand of noodles before stopping to examine them suspiciously. "Wait; is this kale, sprinkled atop?"

"Oh? Is it?"

Making a face, she eyed his sandwich. "And what on earth is that, Michael?"

"Eggplant, with beets and bean sprouts."

"Holy saints, Michael; who's idea was it to make a sandwich out of such things? I think someone's havin' a very fine joke."

"Would you like a taste?" he teased, offering it.

"I would, just to show you that I'm braver than most."

She took a bite, and after a moment, concluded, "That's actually not half-bad, if you can get past the colors."

"The colors are distracting," he agreed, and took his own bite.

Since he wasn't bringing up the subject, she decided she'd waited long enough. "Well, Sir Stephen is rolled-up—thank all available holy angels. And I'm never goin' to marry Williams under any circumstances, so you may as well save your mastermindin' for another subject."

He did not disclaim, but instead tilted his head slightly as he contemplated his sandwich. "It would be best, perhaps, to have a contingency plan." He paused. "There is a vault, hidden on the grounds; you have only to ask Hudson about it."

Thoughtfully, she pulled his sandwich out of his hand. "Oh? Are there molderin' corpses, in the hidden vault?" She knew of two potential candidates, after all.

"No," he smiled. "There are not."

She eyed him over the sandwich. "Listen, husband; I'm on to you, and how you steer the subject away from where it's supposed to be goin'. You're not to set Williams up as a husband-in-waitin'—I'm not havin' it." She took another bite. "Instead, I'll retire to Trestles, like a proper dowager. I'll wear a veiled hat, and try my hand at gardenin', or somethin' worthwhile. I could grow kale, and beets, and do some tinnin' for the local church. Do they put kale in tins?"

"I don't believe they do," he admitted.

"Well, I'd be the first, then. I'd put Trestles on the map, with my tinned kale recipes."

"I thought there were too many ghosts at Trestles," he reminded her, and leaned to help himself to her noodles.

"You'd be one of the ghosts," she countered. "Faith—it could be fun, although there are some maidservants who were brassers, in their day, and I'd be tempted to take a flamethrower to them."

"It wouldn't be the same, I'm afraid."

"Then don't be dyin', husband. Easy fix to the problem."

He smiled, and leaned his head back so as to tip a bottle of water to his mouth. Faith, he was a handsome, handsome man, and leaning over, she rested her chin on his shoulder. "Shall we head home, to make it a proper celebration? Or, if there's not enough time, we could try to squeeze into the back seat. We need only to put our minds to it."

To reward this thought, he cupped her head with his hand, and kissed her soundly. "As much as I would like to tempt a public indecency charge, I should head back. There's been another death in the financial district, and I've been asked to make discreet inquiries."

Doyle frowned, trying to remember what she'd heard. "Didn't they think the first one was suicide? That the man was embezzlin' money, or somethin'?"

"This appears to be another suicide, and for the same reasons."

She sneaked another bite of his sandwich. "And if they want you to take a gander, someone must be worried that they're not truly suicides. Do they think someone's doin' misdirection murders, instead?" Misdirection murders were false flags, put up to mislead law enforcement with respect to the murderer's true motives.

"We shall see."

It made sense that the powers-that-be would ask Acton to do a bit of probing, since doors would be opened to him that would not have opened to your average detective, and the financial district people were notoriously tight-lipped about their brethren's misdeeds. Faith; there'd been a rash of white-collar embezzlement crimes, lately, and she wondered if it was all connected, in some way.

Since he'd finished off her noodles, Acton snapped shut the plastic container, and then reached into the lunch-pack to produce a pre-packaged fruit pie, fresh from the corner convenience store.

"Michael," she laughed in delight. "You are a saint."

ANNE CLEELAND

As he began to unwrap it for her, he said with all sincerity, "It is you who are the saint, Kathleen. I am sorry to have put you through it, with these hearings."

Touched, she leaned over to kiss him, and snatch the pie from his hand. "Nonsense; never had a nicer time, I assure you. Now, all that's left is to clean up Munoz's ACC mess, and Williams' Santero mess, and be home in time for dinner."

"Perhaps we should have ice cream, before dinner." This said with a great deal of meaning.

Laughing, she conceded, "I suppose it's only what I deserve, for bringin' up sex-in-the-car. Alright then; I'll see you at quittin' time, my friend. Bring the butter pecan."

"Done," he said, and started up the car.

38

He checked with Reynolds, to make certain they had ice cream.

Once back at headquarters, Doyle received a call-back from the QC's girlfriend, who was back in town and available for her follow-up interview. The woman agreed to come in within the hour, and so Doyle reserved an interview room—often they were booked ahead of time, and it was never a good idea to try to question a witness in a cubicle, which wasn't very private.

Doyle knew she needed to concentrate, because this was going to be a tricky needle to thread—she didn't want to alarm the woman, but she needed to try to find a motive for the QC's murder. That it was connected to the Santero case in some way seemed evident—the dead barrister worked in the same chambers, and someone had gone to great lengths to pin his murder on the Santero. So, what was it—why had he been killed? The judge on the case was bent—Judge Horne, who was canoodling with Morgan Percy, who was also canoodling with Williams. And—lest we forget—who was also canoodling with Gabriel; faith, a roster was needful, just to keep all the canoodling straight. And poor Williams was being coerced into giving false testimony, even though he wanted Doyle to know he wasn't going to go through with it. And meanwhile, there was a clock ticking somewhere, and about to go off.

She cradled her head in her hands and closed her eyes, knowing that she was tantalizingly close to a solution, and wishing stupid Harding had told her straight-out who the stupid Até was. The Santero, perhaps? It all seemed to come back to the spider-like Santero, but in all honesty, she'd the strong sense that he was merely the dupe for all these shadow murders—and was bitterly resentful about it, which was not the attitude one would expect from the nasty Até. And—aside from the undeniable fact that he was a crackin' blackheart—in a strange way she felt a bit sorry for him. Truly, it all made no sense.

Glancing at the time, she decided that she always seemed to do better when she didn't have any particular plan, and so she'd just see what the flight attendant had to say and play it by ear—perhaps the woman had heard something significant without realizing its significance, which was always a possibility, since it seemed to happen to Doyle with alarming regularity.

When interviewing a friendly witness, a detective might spend the first quarter-hour trying to ease the person's nervousness, but in this case, it wasn't at all necessary; the woman looked about her with interest and smiled at Doyle in a friendly fashion. She's a flight attendant, Doyle remembered; she makes other people feel comfortable—and that was why the QC wanted to marry her, after all. He was someone who worked in a very uncomfortable world.

Doyle began, "How're you doin', ma'am? I'm sure it's all been quite a shock."

Nodding, the witness sobered a bit. "It helps to work, of course. If I'm busy, I tend not to think about it, or how much I miss him."

Doyle paused, trying to decide how best to approach the subject she needed to approach. Presumably, the woman didn't know that the QC's death was not a random crime, and so she had to tread carefully. "I just wanted to ask some follow-up questions about your fiancé's caseload—the Crown Court has been left high and dry, and they're scramblin'." Doyle pretended to review her notes. "He was involved in the Santero case, I understand."

The witness raised her brows. "That witch doctor bloke? No—no, he wasn't counsel for that case." Doyle could see that she struggled with whether to offer anything more, but in the end, couldn't resist, and lowered her voice a bit. "But he did say that the judge was bent, in that case. And he found out that his old girlfriend was sleeping with him, to boot. I think that's one of the reasons he broke it off with her—he didn't stand for that sort of thing."

Here was a potential motive, and Doyle leapt on it. "Did he confront the judge with his suspicions? Make any accusations, or threaten to report him to Judicial Standards?"

But the woman quickly disclaimed, "Oh, no—it was a Crown Court judge, after all, and he was a QC; he couldn't be rocking the boat. And he didn't want to look petty or jealous, when it came to the old girlfriend." She paused for a moment, thinking about it. "It bothered him, though. He liked to think that the system was honest."

Doyle nodded in understanding, but it was all adding up—Horne was the judge who'd quickly ordered Blakney's cremation, and who was presiding over the Santero trial. He must have been another, undisclosed player in the massive corruption rig, and was currently working hard to cover his tracks, so as to escape the fate of the others. It all fit; here was the motive for the QC's murder—somehow, he'd twigged on to Judge Horne's involvement, and so his murder was hastily arranged, to be pinned on the hapless Santero, who really couldn't be described as hapless under the usual circumstances, but was truly hapless, in this case.

Except—except that didn't make a lot of sense; the QC did not plan to come forward, according to this woman. Of course, he may have kept quiet about his intention to expose the judge—it was radioactive knowledge, after all, and the fewer who knew about it the better. If nothing else, at least it was a working theory for the shadow murders: the QC was killed because he knew of Judge Horne's involvement in the corruption rig, Blakney was killed to make sure Williams gave false testimony about the QC's shoes, and Dr. Harding was killed because he also knew about Horne's involvement, and was going to testify against him.

Doyle frowned at the table for a moment, still unconvinced. That didn't make much sense, either. It was too hard to believe it was all just a coincidence—that Blakney was a pawnbroker dealing with shady underworld types, and that he just happened to be married to the object of Williams' affection. And another thing; Harding's testimony was no doubt already buttoned down in sworn statements somewhere—after all, he'd already been placed in protective custody, and they'd already convicted the DCS, along with a quiverful of other villains.

Would Harding have left Judge Horne out of his testimony, hoping to blackmail him later? That seemed unlikely; Harding had already sung like a bird, which was why he'd been placed in protective custody in the first place. And besides, Doyle had taken her measure of Dr. Harding, and he was not the sort of person who'd have the brass to blackmail a judge. He was no Acton.

With this thought, Doyle's scalp prickled, and she lifted her gaze to stare at the upper corner of the room. This was important, for some reason. Harding was no Acton—no one was. Talk about having brass, Acton was solid brass, through-and-through. It worried her, sometimes.

"Ma'am?

Recalled to the witness, Doyle gathered her thoughts. "I wanted to ask you—well, I suppose I wanted to ask you if he was worried about anythin', in the days before he was killed."

Her companion knit her brow, understandably confused. "Worried about being robbed?"

With some delicacy, Doyle ventured, "Well, he was killed in an unusual place, so perhaps he went to meet someone, or had somethin' on his mind."

Fortunately, the witness took this question at face value, and didn't see the implication. "Well, he was always worried about his cases—he was very conscientious about his work, and trying to do the best job that he could for his clients. And I know he was worried about meeting with the chief inspector—that famous one, who's in all the papers. I can't recall his name, but you know who I mean."

Doyle stared at her, unable to speak.

The witness continued, "He didn't talk about it much, but I know it weighed on his mind."

Doyle swallowed, and forced herself to say the words. "Is it possible—is it possible that he was meetin' with that—the chief inspector, when he was killed?"

Thinking this over with a doubtful expression, the witness shook her head. "No—no; or at least, I don't think so—I don't know as he'd set it up, as yet. Besides, if the chief inspector had been there, he wouldn't have let him get coshed."

Slowly, Doyle nodded, knowing—in the way that she knew things—that here it was; the crux of the matter, and the solution to all mysteries. "So—he wanted to meet up with the chief inspector, but he was worried about it, and wouldn't tell you why."

Watching her, the witness leaned forward, contrite. "Oh—do you think it important? I wish he'd told me more, and I wish I knew why he'd gone to such a place—it's not what they think, that he was after drugs, or—or prostitutes, or something." A wave a grief emanated from her, as she leaned back in her chair. "Such a shame, that he didn't have his gun with him."

Doyle looked up in surprise. "His gun?"

Self-conscious, the witness quirked her mouth. "Oh—I suppose I shouldn't say, but he's dead and gone, now. He had a gun;

he said he'd got it from one of his clients, under the table, so to speak. A pawnbroker, I think it was."

But Doyle was no longer listening, over the roaring sound in her ears. Blessed and holy Mother of God—the illegal guns. Acton was Nemesis, and Nemesis did justice, but the Áté—the Áté brought ruin. She brought ruin, because of her victim's hubris— because of his overconfidence. "That's it," she whispered through stiff lips. "That's it—he thinks he's closin' the net on them, but instead they're closin' the net on him." In abject horror, she clutched the table's edge, and swayed slightly.

"Oh, my goodness—are you all right?"

But Doyle could hardly think, through the blanket of panic that had seemed to have dropped down over her head. Holy saints and angels, that's what this was all about—the ACC was weaving a very patient web, and the trap was about to be sprung. It was about Acton's gun-smuggling rig; the blackhearts must know all about it, and they were going to expose him, so as to ruin his cred-ibility when he came after them—to create the perception that Acton was a bent copper, and therefore not to be believed. And they'd show that someone was framing the Santero for murders he didn't commit—that's why the shoe evidence wouldn't be sup-pressed, it was all part of the plan to sink Acton. Just like Acton, they were creating a perception that would trump the evidence—

Paralyzed with fear, Doyle closed her eyes, and struggled to think. The ACC was going to turn the tables on their Nemesis, and it wasn't even a frame-up, because there was no need for a frame-up—Acton was guilty. And his partner in crime—Holy *Mother*, his partner in crime was Philippe Savoie.

There was a quiet knock on the conference room door, and— still a bit dazed—Doyle opened her eyes to see Officer Gabriel poke his head in, his casual manner disguising his extreme alarm.

"Sorry to interrupt, DS Doyle, but if you wanted to take this witness to meet the shopkeeper in *catagóir amháin*, he'll only be there another hour or so."

Doyle blinked, because *catagóir amháin* was Gaelic for "category one"—the police term that called for an immediate evacuation. Belatedly, she remembered that the conference rooms were equipped for surveillance, and her mouth went dry—Gabriel wanted to evacuate the witness, and immediately. Could she trust him? It almost didn't matter; she didn't dare take the chance, if the witness was in danger.

With a mighty effort, Doyle turned to the flight attendant and offered a smile. "I'm afraid I don't know how to drive, so Officer Gabriel will take us to meet—to meet another witness, who may be able to shed some light. It won't take long.'"

"Of course," the woman agreed, a bit confused as she gathered up her handbag. "Anything I can do to help."

The three of them walked out together, and with a sinking heart, Doyle noted that Gabriel made no effort to further explain the situation, but instead made small talk with the witness in his easy manner, making her smile as they headed down the hall.

They walked out the front lobby—rather than through the parking garage—and Gabriel kept them at a steady pace, so that it was a bit difficult for Doyle to keep up. He held the door, and as she passed under his arm, he murmured, "I intercepted a communication from the ACC about your meeting with her. Not good."

"I need to speak with Acton," Doyle whispered back, as steadily as she was able. "Straightaway."

"I wouldn't stop moving." His tone was slightly grim as he bestowed a smile on the flight attendant.

If an extraction depended on the fair Doyle's ability to hurry along, they were doomed, and so she decided that rather than participate in a thrilling chase, she'd do the next best thing, and call in clouds of witnesses. Pausing to clutch at her belly, she grimaced. "Ow—oh, that smarts."

"Oh—are you all right?" The witness asked in alarm. "Do you need to sit down? Let's go back inside—"

"Oh—ouch, ouch, ouch. I don't think I can move." Pulling her mobile, she texted her emergency signal to Acton, and then sank down onto the pavement, at the entrance to Scotland Yard.

39

It must be time. He asked his assistant to re-schedule all appointments, and grabbed his jacket on the way out.

In a commendably short space of time, Acton appeared through the lobby doors and spotted her sitting with her back against the wall, the flight attendant holding her hand in a soothing manner, and Gabriel standing, so as to block the sun.

Acton crouched down. "Is it time? Can you walk, or shall I call an ambulance?"

Why, he's a bit nervous, Doyle realized, and was touched, despite the knot of misery in her stomach. "An ambulance," she whispered, clutching his hand, and grimacing in pretend-pain. "But it's a false flag, and the other two have to come along."

Whilst Acton stared at her in surprise, Gabriel leaned in to offer in a low voice, "No—I'll take care of the witness, not to worry."

"What's happened?" asked Acton quietly, his gaze intent on hers.

"In a minute." The small crowd that stood at a discreet distance murmured amongst themselves, their hushed tones brimful of excitement. "Wait til the siren's on."

"Have we a t-call?" This was police code for a dangerous situation.

"I don't know," she confessed. "Possibly."

Acton turned to signal to the desk sergeant, who was hovering in the doorway, torn between manning his post and rendering aid to Doyle, whom he admired hugely. Instantly, the man approached, striding over in a determined fashion. "Sir?"

"Let's keep the crowd back, while I call for an ambulance."

"Yes, sir."

"Be watchful," Acton cautioned, as he held his mobile to his ear. "We may have a Section Seven in the crowd."

"A stalker?" the sergeant responded, aghast. "Good heavens, has she been attacked?"

"It is as yet unclear," Acton replied, and then began speaking to the emergency personnel.

With no further ado, the desk sergeant ordered the crowd back a few steps, and then stood like a bulldog, guarding them with his hands on his hips, and surveying the crowd very carefully.

With warm sympathy, the flight attendant asked Doyle, "How are you, ma'am? Any more contractions?"

"Ouch," said Doyle, reminded. "Stay close, please."

"Of course. Please don't worry, I'm sure it will all go well."

"Here's hopin'," Doyle replied in a grim tone.

In a few minutes, the ambulance pulled up, and Doyle was loaded within as the crowd of well-wishers watched, and the desk sergeant called out, "Good luck!"

Once Doyle's gurney was secured inside, she was unsurprised to note that Gabriel and the flight attendant had disappeared in the general confusion, but she didn't have much time to think about it, because the doors had slammed shut, and Acton was bending his head close to hers, waiting.

There was truly nothin' for it, and here they were, having yet another heart-to-heart discussion in the back of a wretched ambulance, and the fact that she'd never been within hailing distance of an ambulance before she'd met Acton should be counted as yet another black mark to be laid firmly at his door.

In a rush, the words came tumbling out, her voice low so that the medic couldn't hear them. "I'm not truly in labor, Michael; I had to warn you—" Pausing, she tried to gather up her disjointed thoughts. "The Até is the ACC; the villains are weavin' a web to bring you down, and it has to do with your gun-runnin' rig."

There it was. And it was the reason that she couldn't stop thinking about the conversation she'd overheard at Trestles—the one where Acton, Savoie and Solonik's sister were all speaking in French. They'd been cutting a deal on the smuggling operation going forward, and small wonder the knight was beside himself, poor ghost. Lord Acton of Trestles should not be collaborating with the enemy, no matter how lucrative the deal.

Acton was silent, and she could sense his abject surprise.

She swallowed. "I know you didn't want me to know about the smugglin', Michael, but that's the key, here. The ACC is settin' you up, so that when you move against them, you'll be exposed and no one will believe you anymore. They're framin' you for the shadow murders, to boot. And just to seal the deal, Munoz and Williams are slated to give reluctant testimony against you, but they'll be believed, because they're my friends."

There was a beat, whilst Acton was silent, but then he asked, "Do you need to go to the hospital? I must take care of this, and I'd rather you were home."

She blinked, because he didn't seem overly-thrown—faith, she'd be wailing like a banshee and drumming her heels, if she were in his place. "No—home is fine. I only pretended I was in labor because Gabriel was worried about getting the witness away safely—she's the QC's girlfriend, and she told me the QC wanted to set up a meetin' with you. He must have found out about the plot, and wanted to warn you about it, which is why they killed him. Gabriel said the ACC was monitorin' my conversation with the girlfriend, and so he wanted to whisk her away before the same thing happened to her."

Struck with sudden dismay, she clutched at his arm. "Mother a' mercy, Michael—if the girlfriend's in danger, then Munoz and William are, too; they've each been given parts to play in this wretched plot, and the evildoers may not be comfortable about that, if it all comes crashin' down around their heads."

Acton nodded, and pulled his mobile. "I'll send them over to the flat, to stay with you."

He was emanating calm confidence, and she felt immeasurably relieved. "Faith, I *knew* there was somethin' smoky about Munoz's assignment—that's the willow-wisk that I was tryin' to remember; you told me that Trenton was at the racecourse to watch Munoz, but Munoz said that the ACC wanted her to monitor Trenton, which shows you they must have known that he was your man." She contemplated this belated realization with a full measure of self-disgust. "Munoz is right; I'm not a very good detective."

"Nonsense," said Acton, who—even in a crisis—would not allow any disparagement of his better half.

"Sir," ventured the medic, who had been visibly dismayed by the appearance of Acton's mobile phone. "I must request—"

"Police business," they both responded in unison, having done this before.

"Oh. Right, then," the man said doubtfully, and leaned back into his seat.

Just as they were pulling into the emergency entrance at the hospital, Acton opened the communication window, and informed the driver that there'd been a change of plans, and that the patient would instead be delivered to her residence. "If you would pull through the basement, and out the other side, I think that would be the most expedient route."

And so it was that a short while later, Doyle was comfortably arrayed on the sofa in their flat, with Reynolds brewing coffee as he listened to Acton's instructions. Munoz and Williams would be by, but no one else was to leave or enter until he'd returned.

"Very good, sir," said the servant, who gave no indication that he felt the situation was the least bit unusual, or that Doyle should not be drinking coffee.

Acton braced his hands on the sofa's back, and leaned in to give Doyle a long, assessing look. "Tell me the truth; are you all right?"

"I am," she said, because she was. It was so very gratifying, to hand this disaster over to her very capable—albeit law-breaking—husband, and trust him to handle it.

No, her instinct told her. You can't just trust Acton—not this time.

Frowning, she wondered what Harding had meant, and what she was supposed to do—she'd little choice but to trust Acton to set it all to rights. She'd winkled out what the plot was—and hopefully in the nick of time—although there was no telling what the ACC had up its sleeve, and whether even the mighty Acton could temper the damage that had already been done.

Her husband dropped a kiss on her forehead, and as he did, she ventured, "Are we worried that someone will show up with a search warrant?"

"No," he replied, and she could see he was amused. "We are not."

"Well, that's a relief. Can't imagine Reynolds is any good at hand-to-hand."

With a small smile, he straightened up. "Please stay here, and I will be back as soon as I am able."

He walked over to the bedroom, to make a call that he didn't want her to hear—Savoie, she guessed. He had to let the Frenchman know that the rig's up, and it was time to go doggo—mayhap retreat back to the continent, which seemed to be the plan, anyway.

She watched her husband carefully for a moment, as he spoke on the phone whilst pulling a light jacket from the closet. He did seem confident— although truthfully, she'd never seen him when he wasn't confident. He may not have known about the ACC plot, but nevertheless, he seemed well-able to deal with the fallout— no doubt he'd a plan already in place, in the event anyone managed to twig on to the extraordinary idea that the acclaimed Lord Acton was running a massive weapons-smuggling rig.

His assurance in turn re-assured her, and she wondered why she still felt a bit uneasy. He'd turn the tables, somehow—although this time, it would be quite the trick, as he hadn't seen it coming. Apparently, she should have seen it coming, but she hadn't been able to understand the message, which seemed to consist mainly of psychological gobbledygook, and references to Greek fairy tales.

She paused, and her scalp prickled. So; she'd been warned and re-warned—by Harding and by the rampaging knight at Trestles—because they believed it was up to her to somehow spike the ACC's guns.

How? She thought in bewilderment. I'm a million months pregnant, and Acton is miles better at thinking on his feet than I am. Acton's got connections, too—the fact that he was certain no one would issue a search warrant served as an excellent example—and it was apparent that he'd gamed this out; he had a contingency plan, in the event the long arm of the law caught wind of his dark doings. But the plot against him seemed equally gamed-out, and perhaps that was what made her feel uneasy; the villains had laid a careful trap, and had only to pull up the strings—it was as though they were all caught up in a spider's web, helpless, and waiting for the boom to be lowered.

Suddenly, an idea began to take shape in her mind, and she slowly straightened up on the sofa. Yes—they were caught up in a spider's web, but the spider was just as caught up in it as they were. And actually—for once—she was not the weak link. Apparently, it was time for the fair Doyle to perform yet another rescue, only this one would be a tough wicket, because some guileful maneuvering would be necessary, and the fair Doyle did not excel at maneuvering, guileful or otherwise.

Her husband strode over to bid her goodbye, and casually lifted his field kit as he passed. "Don't forget that Trenton is outside, if you need anything."

Trenton, Doyle remembered with extreme annoyance. Forgot about stupid Trenton—which meant that yet another layer of guileful maneuvering would be needful. Stupid Trenton.

At the door, Acton paused to remind her, "I should return soon; don't go anywhere, please."

For the first time that she could remember, Doyle told her husband an out-and-out lie. "I won't, Michael."

40

Interesting, that she'd known about his enterprise, all along. She was immensely clever.

Reynold's loyalty was immediately tested, as the concierge buzzed to let them know that there was an Officer Gabriel in the lobby, and that he was looking to come up.

"I'm afraid we are not at home to Officer Gabriel," said Reynolds into the intercom. "Thank you all the same."

"He's all right," Doyle insisted in the background, but Reynolds had already turned off the device.

"I have my orders, madam."

Disappointed, Doyle sank back into the sofa. "Acton wouldn't have minded, Reynolds, and I wanted to hear what he had to say."

"Perhaps the officer could telephone, madam."

"No—he's worried that he's being surveilled by the higher-ups at the Yard."

"Ah. I see," Reynolds replied, which wasn't necessarily the truth, but small blame to him, for not wanting to know the details.

They settled into a silence that was broken a few moments later, when there was a soft knock at the door. "Anyone within? It's the unwelcome guest."

Ably trying to hide his alarm, the servant slid a hand into his coat pocket, but Doyle cautioned him as she struggled to her feet. "Don't shoot him, Reynolds; I *promise* Acton won't be angry if you let him in."

Uncertain, the servant looked from Doyle to the door. "I cannot like it, madam. How did he get past the concierge?"

"He's MI 5," Doyle explained, as she lumbered toward the entry. "They're wily, like that."

Reynolds could be seen to take a deep breath, but remained resolute. "I have my orders, madam."

"Well, you may shoot Gabriel with my blessin' if he makes a false move, but in the meantime, I'm dyin' to hear what's happened."

With no further ado, she opened the door. "Hallo, Gabriel. Where's our witness?"

Gabriel gave the wary Reynolds a friendly nod, and then followed Doyle toward the kitchen table. "I took her to the airport, and told her to hop on any outbound flight—she doesn't have to be listed on the manifest. I told her we'd let her know when the coast was clear."

"Good one," said Doyle, all admiration. "Although I don't think she knows much."

"They don't know that, though." Casually, he took a glance around the flat. "I was hoping to speak with your husband."

"He'll be back soon, but I'm glad you're here. I'll be needin' your help with a plan that I'm cookin' up, and I haven't much time to execute it."

With a raised brow, he sank into a kitchen chair. "Oh? I thought we were the blind leading the blind."

She gave him a look. "You're as sharp as can stare, my friend, and don't think that I haven't realized it. But I've got to nip down to the holdin' cells, and have a chat with the Santero. I suppose you might say that it's time to shake some of my own skulls."

For once, he seemed to be at a loss, and regarded her blankly. "What's this?"

Doyle repeated, "I need to speak with the Santero. And I need to do it in an attorney conference room, so there's no surveillance."

Gabriel shifted, and leaned an arm across the chair's back. "Well, setting aside the fact that your husband would strip me of my pension, if I helped you do such a thing, you can't just wander in and speak with a suspect, DS Doyle."

But Doyle had already considered this undeniable hurdle. "I can if he's got counsel present, and I know just the girl who's willin' to bend the rules a bit—Morgan Percy." She paused, thinking about it. "But I've got to make it worth her while, and since I can't hand Acton over to her, Williams will have to be the Percy-bait."

"I'll be your Percy-bait," Gabriel offered promptly. "It would be my pleasure."

But Doyle shook her head. "Percy's not mad for you, Gabriel. She's just tryin' to make Williams jealous."

"Well, that's a blow to my ego. But I am worried that Williams is compromised." He met her eyes.

Exasperated, Doyle blew a tendril of hair off her face. "No, he's not; he's just bein' Williams, and all noble-like. He needs a good shakin', is what he needs. I hope he gets here soon—I don't know how long Acton will be gone, and I've got to shake my stumps and save the day."

Reynolds cleared his throat. "Am I given to understand, madam, that you intend to depart from the premises?"

"I'm the get-away driver," Gabriel informed him cheerfully. "I'm not handsome enough for any other role."

"Don't worry, Reynolds—" Doyle began, but they were interrupted when the concierge buzzed to inform them there was an Officer Munoz in the lobby.

"Good—send her up," Doyle asked the servant.

Reynolds did so, and then was seen to hover near the door, so as to open it the moment Munoz knocked. "Miss Munoz; may I take your coat?"

"What's all this about?" Munoz asked without preamble.

Doyle decided there was no harm in summing it all up. "The ACC is bent, and they're tryin' to frame Acton."

The girl was seen to roll her eyes, as Reynolds reverently escorted her toward a seat. "Not a surprise—I'd guessed as much. They were trying to make me believe that Acton's working with Savoie, on some massive smuggling rig."

"Ridiculous," Doyle scoffed.

"They should have come up with a better story," Gabriel agreed with a smile.

Oh-oh, thought Doyle, with a healthy dose of dismay. Oh-oh.

"Do we have anything to eat?" asked Munoz, who was not above taking gross advantage of Reynolds' infatuation.

"No eatin' yet," Doyle declared firmly, trying to decide how to handle this latest setback. "Remember my security fellow? I need to give him the slip, and I need your help."

Whilst Reynolds made a small sound of acute dismay, Munoz's eyes narrowed. "Oh? And why is that?"

Doyle quickly discarded any explanation that would involve a clandestine affair—considering how swollen her feet were—and decided she'd little choice but to fall back on the truth. "Gabriel's goin' to take me to meet someone without Acton's knowin'. *Please*, Munoz; I wouldn't ask, except it's very important." She decided to add, "It has to do with spikin' the frame-up against Acton."

Thoughtfully, Munoz considered this. "How much time do you need?"

"Just long enough to slip by him, is all, although if you can divest him of his mobile phone, that would be a topper."

"No, Doyle, you idiot; that would raise a huge red flag." Munoz's dark eyes slid in a speculative manner toward Gabriel. "He's going with you?"

"Well, I can't be the one to distract the security fellow," Gabriel explained. "I'm not as pretty."

"Cheek," Munoz declared without rancor, and walked over to the windows. "All right. Trenton's below?"

"Yes, probably watchin' the entry. Don't pretend to be someone else, he already knows who you are."

"Of course, he does." The other girl seemed a bit affronted that Doyle would assume otherwise. "I'll do an enlistment diversion, instead."

An enlistment diversion was a tactic whereby the police officer pretended to need a civilian's assistance, so as to distract them.

"That is excellent, Munoz; go down to the lobby, and then wait for my signal—I'll have Reynolds buzz the concierge."

Munoz pulled out her compact to check her lipstick. "Got it."

"And if you see Williams, tell him we're comin' right down, so don't bother comin' up."

"Cheers." Munoz lifted her fingers to them, as Reynolds escorted her out.

"All right; time to move." Rising, Doyle made her way over to the laundry room, and glanced at Reynolds as he closed the entry door after Munoz. "Were you expecting Mr. Rooke, Reynolds? I hope he's not detained, again."

There was the barest pause, before Reynolds bowed his head, his expression wooden. "I should not be surprised, madam." Mr. Rooke was the visiting nurse they'd locked in the laundry room, on a best-be-forgotten occasion, and hopefully Reynolds had received the unspoken message.

Doyle reached for a small box that was perched high on the laundry room shelf, and since he was closest to her, Gabriel sprang up to help her. "Here, I'll get it."

"Thanks."

As he stepped into the small room to reach for the box, she drew back, and slammed the door shut.

41

He informed Savoie that the contingency plan was now underway, and then went to Layton's office, to secure the funds.

With a twist of her wrist, Doyle locked the laundry room door, and there was a small silence from within. "What's this?"

She called out apologetically, "I'm not sure I can trust you, Gabriel, and I can't be takin' the chance."

"Oh. Well, there's another blow to my ego. If this keeps up, I'll be sorry I came over. But you can trust me; Williams will vouch for me."

This was true, and rather surprising, since she didn't think Gabriel and William were more than nodding-acquaintances. Frowning, she contemplated the locked door. "I thought you were worried that Williams is compromised."

"I still am. But he needed an assist, and he didn't want to go to Acton, so I said I'd lend a hand."

This was also completely true, and sounded very much like something Gabriel would do. It also explained how he seemed to know so much about the ACC plot against Acton, since presumably, Williams was trying to find some way out of the web.

"I wouldn't trust him, madam," Reynolds offered in a low voice.

"That's unfair, Reynolds," Gabriel protested through the door. "I hope you're not prejudiced—I'm only half Persian, you know. And as a sign of good faith, I'll not pick the lock."

"Oh no, you won't; it's Acton's lock," Doyle explained. "Acton's locks are un-pickable."

Gabriel laughed. "Insult upon insult. You win; we'll wait for Williams."

As if on cue, the concierge buzzed. "There is an Officer Williams in the lobby, who says he is expected. He also states that he has declined the advice of the young lady to wait downstairs, and would like to come up."

Blowing out an exasperated breath, Doyle moved over to the intercom. "No—don't let him up. I'll be right down." Truly, it was like one of those raree shows, where everyone kept entering and leaving through various doors so that it was impossible to keep up. Exhausting, it was, to try to put all the pieces in place, and she didn't know how Acton bore all his own guileful maneuvering, except that she had a niggling suspicion that he very much enjoyed it.

Despite Reynolds' small gesture of alarm, she unlocked the laundry room door. "Come on, then, Gabriel. Williams is a stubborn boyo, and he's goin' to try to stop me from goin' anywhere. So now I'm the one who's needs an assist, if you won't mind turnin' coat on Williams, but I *promise* it's all for the best."

"I'm your huckleberry," Gabriel replied easily, stepping out of the laundry room. "Is Williams a level six?"

"No, he is not," she retorted, and tried not to smile. Police officers categorized the appropriate level of force in any given situation, and level six was the maximum—the suspect could be subdued by any means necessary.

As could be expected, William's brow looked like a storm cloud when they confronted him in the lobby. "Back upstairs, Kath. I'm under strict orders."

But Gabriel interrupted apologetically. "Then we have a conflict; DS Doyle has given me strict orders to take her over to holding." He gestured Doyle past the other man. "Sorry; I have no choice but to obey."

Doyle looked to Gabriel in surprise. "Do I outrank you?"

"Maybe."

It was no surprise that this was not true, and so Doyle curtailed any further discussion about who-outranked-whom, and said to Williams. "I'll explain in the car, Thomas, but it's *imperative* that I go over to holdin'."

"Who's in holding?"

"The Santero. Or he will be, soon."

For a moment, Williams stared at her, speechless, and no doubt remembering the last time Doyle and the Santero had shared the same space. "What's *this*?"

But Doyle sidestepped all explanations and brushed past him. "I have to go turn the tables—somethin' I learned to do at the feet of the master. Are you in?"

Reluctantly, Williams fell into step beside her. "No, but I'll go anyway."

This was a welcome surprise, and she glanced up at him as they headed to the garage lift. "Truly? And here I'd warned Gabriel that it may come to duelin' choke-holds."

Williams bent his head for a moment, as he pressed the button to take them down. "I'm coming along because I remember what happened the last time you wanted to take an unsanctioned field trip."

She smiled, because the last time the princess had escaped from her tower, they'd wound up at Trestles, just in time to save the day. "Now, there's a car ride I won't be soon forgettin'." For Gabriel's benefit, she added, "Williams and Lizzie Mathis were goin' at it, hammer and tongs."

Gabriel raised his brows. "Were they? Do you mean fighting, or having sex?"

She laughed, and even Williams chuckled as they emerged into the parking garage. Thus reminded, Doyle couldn't help but think it was a shame that Williams hadn't set his sights on Lizzie Mathis instead of William Blakney's wife, but there was no accounting for such things, which was why—thank God fasting—the fair Doyle had ended up with Acton, as an excellent case-in-point. "You're a good man, Thomas Williams. All will be well—my promise—but first I'll need your mobile."

He was instantly suspicious, as he helped her slide into the car's rear seat. "Why?"

Slouching down, she raised up the hood on her jacket. "Because I left mine behind, and unless Gabriel is a complete knocker, he's not carryin' one, either."

"I have a disposable," Gabriel admitted, as he joined Williams in the front seat. "I feel lost without one."

With no further comment, Williams handed Doyle his mobile, and then drove them out of the structure. "If you are phoning Acton, I may as well get on the Great North Road, and just keep going."

Doyle did not deign to reply to this sally, and instead scrolled until she rang up Morgan Percy's number.

It was answered immediately. "Hallo?"

Doyle lifted the phone to her ear. "Hallo, Morgan; it's not Williams, it's Doyle."

The girl laughed lightly, although Doyle knew she was disappointed. "Well, I can't say I'm surprised—he's been ducking me, lately. Should I ask how you got his mobile?"

"He's here, actually, since I'm not much of a driver. I've enlisted him because I have a secret errand to perform."

With a smile in her voice, the other girl asked, "Oh? Do I want to hear about this?"

Good—Doyle knew she was very pleased that Williams was at hand, which was an excellent start; now, there was nothin' for it—and here goes. "I've got to ask a favor of you, Morgan, and it's a doozy. I want to speak to the Santero, off the record." She paused, and then added in an undertone. "It's not really connected to his case; I need—I need potion advice. The woman who's mindin' his shop said the ERU took all his potions away."

Not surprisingly, Percy's first reaction was skepticism. "*Potion advice? You?*"

"Yes; it's—the shop-minder said he had a potion for stretch marks. You should see my stretch marks, Morgan—my belly looks like a map of the Amazon. I have to worry about my skin; Acton used to say my skin was—was lunimous."

"Luminous, I think you mean." There was a calculating edge to the remark; she was not exactly displeased to hear that Acton's interest was waning.

"Yes; well, it won't take more than a few minutes, but I'll need you there, since I can't very well just stroll in and ask him about it. Williams says he'll take you out for a pint afterwards, as a reward."

The girl laughed again. "Oh? Maybe the Santero can spare me a love potion, too."

Doyle appeared to be much struck by this comment, and replied with a forlorn undertone, "Oh—oh, I hadn't thought of that, but I suppose he knows a lot about such things. It wouldn't hurt to ask—mayhap he can let us know where he hides his stash."

"All right; but it can't be for long. I'll try to keep it off the record."

"We'll meet you in holdin'."

Doyle rang off, and into the silence, Williams noted, "I'm one step up from a prostitute, apparently."

"Needs must, when the devil drives, Thomas. But don't let her put anythin' in your drink."

"I'd be happy to drive that devil," Gabriel offered. "It's a shame she's not mad for me."

No, thought Doyle, looking out the window for a moment. But—interestingly enough— she'd discovered that beneath his casual manner, Gabriel was mad for Munoz.

Williams, being Williams, was trying to button down the details of his assignment. "Am I supposed to keep Percy busy for a specified time?"

"You could always go at it, hammer and tongs," Gabriel suggested helpfully.

"I'll let you know," Doyle hedged. It was very unlikely that the date would actually go forward, after her little *tête-a-tête* with the Santero, but there was no point in giving the other two this alarming little tidbit of information.

Gabriel gazed out the window, and remarked to no one in particular, "It's a shame the Santero doesn't accidently shiv himself in the back. I imagine that would solve all problems."

Annoyed, Doyle tucked her hair into the edges of her hood. "Stop conniving with Williams, Gabriel. You can't murder the Santero—I need him. And that's how everyone got into this mess to begin with—you can't just go about doin' shadow murders, willy-nilly, and hope it all comes out in the end. Leave retribution to God."

It's been my experience," Gabriel offered diffidently, "that God needs the occasional assist."

"No, God's got matters well in hand, and we can't muck about in the plan just to suit our own notions."

Gabriel slid her a look. "Remind me why we're going to pay the Santero an illegal visit."

But Doyle had a ready answer. "Because we'd like him to repent of his evil ways. That's miles different than wantin' to shadow-murder him."

"A fair point," Gabriel agreed, and turned to face forward again.

Williams offered, "Don't argue with her about this, you'll get nowhere."

"I'm not one to argue," said Gabriel. "Let us go offer salvation to the Santero."

"Oh no, you won't; you'll stay in the car," warned Doyle.

"Got it," he replied easily.

42

What was this? She'd checked in at Detention, of all places. Quickly, he wrapped it up, and headed over.

Percy was standing in the hallway and looking slightly amused as Doyle approached. Doyle couldn't decide if it if was good or bad that the holding area wasn't as jammed-packed as it usually was, and mentally girded her loins for what was to come.

"Where's your support officer?" the other girl joked, as she turned to signal to the guard at the door.

"Williams is not comin' in; he's worried if there were two of us, it would look worse than it does already."

"Good point. Make it quick," Percy warned. "I don't want to get into trouble, either."

This was not true, which came as no surprise—Percy was up to her neck in the ACC's doings, and therefore had no fear of exposure or recriminations. For a moment, Doyle felt a pang; despite all evidence to the contrary, Percy wasn't a bad sort. Hopefully she'd not go down with the ship that Doyle was determined to sink.

"You go in first, Morgan. I'll wait until you're alone with him— I don't want anyone else to hear what I'm goin' to say."

"Got it." Smiling, the girl lifted a brow. "Watch through the window, and come in when the coast is clear."

Doyle nodded, and watched through the door's reinforced window, as the guard escorted the suspect into the interview room. The Santero hadn't changed much since the last time she'd seen him—only now, she knew why he was such a seething mass of bitterness. It must be outside of annoying, to be framed for such paltry run-of-the-mill murders when you specialized in occult murders. It hurt the brand, so to speak.

And as had happened the last time, the Santero seemed to know she was standing behind the door. As his guard saw him seated at the interview table, the suspect's gaze skewed over toward her, the whites of his eyes showing.

Here goes, thought Doyle, taking a deep breath and summoning up her best bad-cop. Time to be that brassy shant that Harding saw when I had him arrested; it's a similar situation, after all. As soon as the guard exited through the far door, she slipped in through the entry door, and closed it behind her.

"My friend Officer Doyle wanted to ask a small favor—" Percy began, but she was interrupted as the Santero sprang to his feet, and backed away, frantically making the sign against the evil eye. "No! No—away!"

Astonished, Percy stood also. "Come, now; settle down—"

Doyle stepped toward him with as much menace as she could muster. "You will grass on everyone who's put you up to all this, or there will be no corner in hell for you to hide— you, or your stupid *orishas*."

"Ah," the man cried, covering his face with his hands. "No! Away, away!"

"Stop," Percy commanded. "What on earth—"

But Doyle loomed over the cowering man and threatened, "Call your solicitor in, and start confessin', or you—and everyone you care about—will pay a terrible, terrible price."

"Wait a minute—you can't do this—"

"No! Stop; stop—" the man sank to his knees, eyes closed; his head shaking slowly from side to side.

"Guard!" shouted Percy in outrage. "Guard!"

The guard burst through the door, and then hesitated, seeing the suspect collapsed and weeping on the floor. "Do we need the medics?"

"Yes," Percy improvised. "The suspect seems to be hallucinating, and should be medicated."

"No—" Doyle protested, but just then, the entry door opened, and Acton stepped through.

Into the sudden silence, Acton's impassive gaze swept the room, and came to rest on the Santero, who'd buried his face on his knees, and was rocking back and forth, moaning. "Do you have a report, Sergeant?"

Doyle swallowed, and then spoke in a rush. "Sir, the suspect is goin' to grass, and he's got an alarmin' tale to tell. He's been framed for a variety of shadow murders that were committed by members of the ACC, and by Judge Horne. He'd like to call in his solicitor, and make a full confession."

Acton stepped forward, then crouched down before the suspect. "This is true?"

After taking a last, fearful glance at Doyle, the Santero buried his face in his knees again. "Yes—yes."

Acton then looked up at Percy, who'd stood, pale and silent, since his entry. She's trying to decide which horse to back, thought Doyle. She's no fool, and the wind has suddenly shifted.

"Counsel?" Acton asked.

"Let me call the solicitor," the girl replied quietly.

"She's goin' to raise the alarm," Doyle warned, although if her husband hadn't figured this out for himself, she'd wash her hands of him.

"I don't think so." Acton stood, and pulled his mobile. "Because then it would be a simple matter to prove conspiracy."

Percy paused, and then asked bluntly, "Do I need to hire counsel, sir?"

"No," said Acton, lifting the mobile to his ear. "You do not."

"Do I?" asked Doyle in a flippant tone.

"You will come with me." Acton ushered her out of the room, signaling to the guard to stay with the Santero. Doyle then listened as he gave instruction to the desk sergeant over his phone—all available PCs were to meet him in the strategy room, because he was going to run a simultaneous sweep, and time was of the essence. "We'll need to prep the public relations department," he added. "Send them along, too."

"Oh—can I come?" asked Doyle, after he rang off. "Faith; we could have a front-page photo of the bridge-jumper, slappin' the cuffs on Judge Horne."

Acton scrolled for the next number. "Instead, I am going to send you home with Williams, and ask that you stay there, please."

"Oh—but I'm just gettin' warmed, up, husband; for my next act—"

Pausing, Acton met her gaze, and placed a soothing hand on the back of her neck. "It's all right, Kathleen."

She pressed her lips together, and made a mighty effort to regain her equilibrium. "I'm gabblin'. Sorry."

He pulled her under his arm and kissed her temple, in a rare display of public affection. Trust him to know that she was always unnerved, when she was forced to put her perceptive abilities on display. Safe in his embrace, she listened to him speak with Previ, the editor of the *London World News*, as his voice resonated against the bones in her face.

43

It was all very apt; hubris had brought on Até, as it al-
ways did. He'd have to be more careful, in the future. He'd
upset her.

"**I** can't believe you got me into so much trouble. You, of
all people."

Doyle and Percy remained in the holding area, sitting
on the battered hallway bench and waiting for Williams, who was
supposed to drive Doyle home, but was instead briefing a hapless
PC, who wouldn't understand why Williams was over-explaining
a simple arrest—the officer was going to round up one of the
smaller-fish at the racecourse, now that the bigger-fish from the
ACC were being swept up.

Doyle understood, though; Williams—naturally—had been
champing at the bit in his eagerness to accompany Acton on the
initial arrests, but Acton had met his eyes for a silent moment, and
Williams had retreated from the fore.

You've been sidelined, she thought; and with good reason—
let this be a lesson, my friend. Although there was no doubt that
Acton would carefully arrange matters so that the cloud that hovered over Williams disappeared—perhaps even a suggestion that
it was off-the-record undercover work that he'd been performing,

all along; after all, even the mighty Acton couldn't erase Williams from this plot entirely. Although—although after Acton had nailed down the Santero's statement, no one thought to ask Doyle for a statement, or even seemed to realize that she'd been in the interview room, in the first place.

Next to her, Morgan Percy was emanating waves of angry frustration, mixed with a healthy dose of fear. Doyle was mightily tired of saving the day, but decided she should make one last effort. "It will be less trouble than the trouble you were already in, Morgan. You can't dance with the devil, and expect it to work out well. If you don't think a blackleg like Judge Horne wouldn't turn on you in an instant, you are sadly mistaken."

"I don't know what you're talking about," Percy replied in sullen tone, and it was a lie.

"Well, it's all goin' to come crashin' down, and you'd be an easy scapegoat, considerin' who it is that we're dealin' with. Best be careful."

The girl was silent for a moment, watching Williams, and so Doyle suggested, "Make a clean breast; tell them you were blackmailed—or pressured, or somethin'—and then grass the livin' daylights out of everyone else. There's a different justice system for pretty young women—you know it, as well as I do. I can't imagine you'd do any hard time."

Percy refused to look at her. "It's not that simple. You wouldn't understand."

Doyle sighed with sympathy. "It's simple, indeed; it's just not easy, and that's always the rub, isn't it?" She thought of Acton, and his doings, and how he was the furthest thing from a simple creature imaginable. Mayhap I'm wrong, she admitted, quirking her mouth; mayhap it *is* like the Wild West, and those of us who stand in the background, timidly pointing at the rule of law, are rightly and roundly ignored. Aloud, she said, "I can't imagine that we're supposed to live every man for himself."

"No," Dr. Harding agreed.

With some surprise, Doyle realized that the ghost was seated on the bench to her right. "Oh—oh; it's you. Am I dreamin'?"

"No; but I thought I'd take the opportunity to bid you goodbye."

She smiled, slightly. "You've redeemed yourself, then?"

He crossed his arms. "In a manner of speaking. I've replaced myself with the Santero, and so now it is he who will testify at the criminal trials."

"Is that so? So—we've replaced one witch doctor with another?"

He didn't respond to the barb, but glanced around with an expression of mild distaste. "I don't have fond memories of this place."

"Well, there's some brass, for you—considerin' it's me, sittin' right here. This place was nothin' more than what you deserved. Faith, the irony is thick on the ground, isn't it?"

"No," he replied. "Nothing is ironic. It is only true."

With a knit brow, she thought this over, then gave up. "Fah; that's too deep, for the likes of me."

"Perhaps."

They sat in silence for a moment, and despite having said his goodbyes, he seemed disinclined to leave. She offered, "Acton's not strokin' my arms, anymore."

"Abreaction." He nodded. "Good."

Since they were on the subject, she thought she may as well ask, "D'you think there's any chance he'll be over his—his fixation, some day?"

The psychiatrist sank his chin into his chest. "It seems unlikely, to me. The child's birth is a pressure point, of course."

But she shook her head. "He's not goin' to hurt Edward. I'll not believe it."

"No, but it may trigger a crisis."

"Excellent," she said. "And here I was startin' to run low on crisises."

"Crises," he corrected. "And if you don't like dealing with crises, you've chosen the wrong husband, and the wrong line of work. It's a volatile mixture."

"I thank you for the advice," she replied with heavy irony. "It means a great deal, comin' from you."

"I remedied this situation," he defended himself. "Quite satisfactorily."

She decided that this was more-or-less the truth, and that she shouldn't berate him any further. "Well, now that the Até is bein' roundly clobbered by the Nemesis, shouldn't you be leavin', to go off and study the classics, somewhere?"

"In a moment."

Percy suddenly spoke, from Doyle's other side. "I was going to warn Acton before they tried to arrest him—warn him to stand down. Because you and I are friends."

Interestingly enough, this was true, and Doyle thought it best not to mention that no doubt an integral part of the "standing down" would involve Acton's being unfaithful to his wedded wife—which just went to show you that Percy was far and away out of her league, if she thought Acton would allow himself to be manipulated in such a way. Instead, Doyle replied in a mild tone. "I appreciate it, Morgan, but he's not someone who's the stand-down type. Mayhap it's you who should stand-down, instead. I don't think you're very happy, doing all this plottin' and manuver-in'. It's a way of compensatin' for abandonment issues—reactive attachment disorder."

The girl turned to stare at her. "What?"

"We're rather alike, you know—our fathers left us to fend for ourselves. But we handled it differently; you were desperate for men to pay attention to you, whilst I wanted no one to pay atten-tion to me. Both are common reactions."

The other girl frowned incredulously at her. "I don't need a psychiatry session, thank you very much."

"A psychiatry session may actually be helpful; abreaction may be very therapeutic."

Angry, the girl turned a shoulder to her. "How I manage my affairs is none of your business."

Surprised at herself, Doyle glanced to her right, but found that the bench was now empty. With a sigh, she leaned back, resting her head against the wall as she contemplated the ceiling. "No, I suppose that's true. You'll find someone, Morgan, but it can't be Acton, and it can't be Williams. You're like a bird, beatin' her wings against a window, trying to prove somethin' that doesn't need provin' in the first place."

The girl made no reply, although Doyle could feel a sudden jolt of sad awareness. There, she thought, and closed her eyes for a moment. I may not know the fancy names for things, but I know people.

Hard on this thought, another voice was heard. "Hey."

Doyle lifted her head to see that Gabriel now stood before them, his hands in his pockets. "I got tired of waiting in the car. What's up?"

Glancing down the hall, she could see that Williams was now speaking on his mobile, his attitude one of frustrated anxiety. "The boom is gettin' itself lowered," Doyle explained. "Like a mighty, winnowin' wind."

Lifting his brows, Gabriel followed her gaze. "Oh? Maybe I should go back to the car, then." He addressed Percy. "Are you grounded, or would you care to join me? I'm sure we could come up with some way to pass the time."

With an ironic smile, Percy declined. "No thanks; I have the lowering feeling that you were just priming me for information."

But Gabriel only flashed his charming smile. "What? Was that wrong? You were priming me for information, too."

"I suppose that's only fair," Doyle offered, hoping to avoid yet another clash, on this cataclysmic day.

"I enjoyed the priming, myself," Gabriel added. "Wouldn't mind some more priming, in fact."

Percy regarded Gabriel, her eyes narrowing. "I'm still not sure where you fit in."

But as always, Gabriel had a ready answer. "I'm on the team that doesn't want to wind up being a shadow murder."

"Amen," said Doyle fervently. "Aren't we all."

44

There; the parameters of the story were nailed down, and all should play out satisfactorily. There were a few troubling loose ends, of course, but nothing that could not be easily resolved.

When Williams escorted Doyle back to her flat, they were treated to the sight of Munoz, seated at the kitchen table and watching Reynolds as he served up a hot dish. The flat smelt of peppers, and Munoz was wearing Doyle's new boots.

"Reynolds," Doyle exclaimed, dropping her rucksack on the floor in outrage. "For the love of all that is holy, you can't be lettin' Munoz look through my wardrobe."

"Well, you can't wear them," the girl remarked, and propped the boots up on the opposite chair, one at a time. "Someone should."

Whilst Reynolds avoided Doyle's accusing eye, Williams pulled out his own chair. "I'll have some of whatever that is."

"It's *paella*, sir," said Reynolds. "Let me fetch a plate."

"It needs a side of *queso manchego*," Munoz offered. "But other than that, it's very good."

"It is difficult to procure *queso manchego*, locally," Reynolds apologized.

"Where am I?" Doyle groused, as she sank into the sofa. "Good God; I think I've gone through the lookin'-glass."

Reynolds regarded her with an assessing eye. "May I make you some tea, madam?"

"Tea is not goin' to do it, today—I'll have the coffee, instead, and Edward will just have to get over it. What's happened to Trenton?"

"He's still outside, and none the wiser," Munoz reported with an air of satisfaction. "Am I getting paid for this?"

"You're gettin' fed," Doyle pointed out crossly.

"May I bring you a plate, madam?"

"No thanks, Reynolds—I'd have heartburn for days." Sighing, Doyle leaned forward as far as she was able, and rubbed her temples. "Saints and holy angels; I can't *wait* 'till I can eat like a dock-man again."

"You'll have to go on a diet, once you have the baby," Munoz pointed out, savoring another bite. "All that baby fat."

Williams asked Reynolds, "You don't happen to have a spare beer?"

Doyle lifted her head and frowned. "Aren't we on-duty?"

Williams thanked Reynolds, and twisted off the bottle-cap. "I'll vote for no."

Munoz eyed him, as she accepted her own bottle. "You're in a state. What's happened?"

Williams seemed disinclined to answer, so Doyle offered, "They're doin' a huge sweep on the ACC, because the Santero confessed that they were pinnin' a bunch of shadow murders on him. It's a lot like the harrowin' of hell, only with flexcuffs."

Munoz brought her boots down, and sat up. "Really? Who's going down?" Munoz wanted details, and small blame to her; she'd been a pawn in their game, and it was lucky she'd never let her guard down—a wily one, was Munoz.

"I don't think I can say who's under suspicion—not until the sweep's been completed," Doyle explained, and carefully did not look at Williams. "But the prosecutors may want you to testify about how they were tryin' to frame-up Acton."

"That won't go over well," said Munoz, addressing her plate again. "The public will be up in arms—Acton's their hero."

And yet again, thought Doyle, the irony is thick on the ground.

Munoz paused to take a pull from her bottle. "Well, if you can't say who the suspects are, can you tell me who the victims were?"

"I don't know everythin'," Doyle admitted, "but I do know that the ACC was killin' people who'd twigged their involvement in the corruption rig. Remember the QC—the one that was killed in the alley? He was one." In deference to Williams, she didn't mention any others.

Frowning, Munoz reached for a piece of flat bread, and broke it in her hands. "And why would the Santero stand for that?"

This was, of course, an excellent question—all the more so, since it hadn't yet occurred to Doyle. There was no question that the Santero was a seething mass of resentment, so why had he signed on, in the first place?

Williams spoke up. "They threatened his girlfriend."

This was unlooked-for, and Doyle regarded him in surprise. "The Santero has a *girlfriend*?"

"Yes; the woman who was minding his shop."

"Oh," said Doyle, much struck. "Oh—of course she was." After all, the woman had sat in that miserable shop, day after day—not to mention that the Santero had killed her very inconvenient husband. "Well—knock me down. He didn't seem the romantic type."

Williams gazed out the picture windows, to consider the view. "That's how the corruption rig operated—they threatened female relatives."

There was a thread of constraint in his voice, and Doyle easily surmised that—aside from threatening to tell Mary about his role in Blakney's death—they must have threatened to harm Mary, or even the fair Doyle, herself, to get Williams to cooperate.

Poor Thomas, thought Doyle; they had him over a barrel, and small wonder he was desperate to get out from under—although she was mixing her metaphors, again. Hopefully, when Morgan Percy had passed along the information she'd gleaned from Williams, the girl didn't actually know the level of evil she was dealing with—but then again, perhaps Doyle was being naïve, which was her usual state of awareness. There were a lot of people out there who felt that the ends always justified the means, with Doyle's better half serving as an excellent example.

And Williams had been too ashamed to go to Acton, because then he'd have to confess that he'd succumbed to wicked Morgan Percy's wicked wiles. Not to mention he didn't want Acton to know about his feelings for Mary—or Doyle, for that matter. Foolish man; Acton knew everything—well, except for the parameters of this nasty ACC plot, but lucky for him, he'd a very useful wife, who was willing to throw around a curse or two, herself.

Her mobile pinged, and she saw that the text was from Acton. "Who?"

"M and W," she texted. "Eating something spicy."

"Home soon," he replied.

Thoughtfully, she rang off, wondering who it was that Acton was checking for. Percy, mayhap; or even Savoie himself, bold as brass—it would be just like him, to saunter into Acton's flat without so much as a by-your-leave. With this thought, she stilled for a moment. Whilst Acton may be working some miracle to avoid his own ruination, Savoie may not escape a similar fate; Savoie had instigated the racecourse smuggling rig in the first place, after all. For Munoz's sake, she hoped he'd escaped to the continent—hard to imagine Savoie in prison; they probably wouldn't let him smoke there, either.

"Acton's comin' soon," she warned. "The general debauchery should be toned down a bit."

Immediately, Williams looked up. "Did he say anything?"

"No," she replied. "Although he didn't make a snipers-to-the-roof order, so I'll take that as a good sign."

Munoz signaled for Reynolds to take her plate. "Should I go?"

"Not without Acton's say-so," Doyle cautioned. "You may still be in danger."

"Is that so?" asked Reynolds, pausing in alarm. "Perhaps I should make up the spare bedroom."

Doyle threw him a sour look. "Just put her in mine, Reynolds; that way she can look through my jewelry, if she wants."

"You don't have any decent jewelry," Munoz noted, as she regretfully unzipped the boots. "I already looked."

Acton's card could be heard in the slot, and the two detectives stood upon his entry, as Reynolds hurried over to take his jacket. Doyle didn't rise, as she was almost certainly on maternity leave, starting from the moment she'd exited the Santero's interview room.

"At ease," Acton said.

"We weren't sure if we were on-duty, or off-duty," Doyle explained. "Therefore, there was only some minor beer-drinkin', as opposed to serious whiskey-drinkin'."

"Off-duty," Acton decided. "Is that *gazpacho?*"

"*Paella*, rather," said Reynolds, with deep regret. "And I'm afraid we're all out, sir."

"Munoz ate it all up," Doyle disclosed helpfully. "Reynolds has been ministerin' to her, out of the kindness of his heart."

Munoz slid her a malicious glance behind Acton's back, and reached for her rucksack. "Do I have orders, sir?"

"Yes; there is a PC waiting downstairs who will escort you to headquarters. Please report to the acting superintendent as soon as possible; they'll want to hear what you have to say."

"Yes, sir," said Munoz, with a great deal of satisfaction.

As of yet, Acton had said nothing to Williams, and Doyle could see that beneath the young man's stoic demeanor, he was emanating massive amounts of anxiety. "Might I be of some use, sir? Perhaps I could escort DS Munoz—"

In a rare display, Acton placed his hand on the back of Williams' neck, the soothing gesture similar to the one he'd used with Doyle, outside the interview room. "Go home, and sleep. That's an order, Inspector."

45

She'd gone to church alone, which was unexpected.
Perhaps she'd heard the news, then.

Doyle sat in a pew at St. Michael's, watching as the new deacon went about turning on the lights in the empty church, as the evening fell. Hope he's a nice fellow, she thought; we're due for a change of luck—although if I were a decent RC, I wouldn't be counting on luck, which is superstitious, and would make me no better than the Santero's customers. Instead, I should be giving thanks in all things, even when the "all things" seems to consist mainly of bad luck. I wish there was a potion you could use against sadness.

Even without looking, she knew when Acton entered through the doors behind her, and so she didn't look up when he slid in to sit beside her.

"Everything all right, Kathleen?"

She blew out a breath. "No, everythin's not all right. I went to pay a visit to Morgan Percy, just now."

He was silent.

"Just tell me that it wasn't your doin', husband."

"No," he said immediately. "She was a problem, but I did not want her dead."

This was true, and she felt a small measure of relief—although she hadn't truly believed that Acton had killed Morgan Percy. She'd realized that in Acton's world, the few people that Doyle counted as friends were untouchable. "She'd hate it, lying there under the fluorescent lights. She was always so careful about her appearance."

"I will see to it that her release from the morgue is expedited."

Doyle nodded; it went without saying that the coroner would do whatever Acton asked. "They're sayin' she's another victim of the Santero's minions—a containment murder, like the QC—but you and I both know that the Santero wasn't behind this, because he's terrified I'll rain down hellfire on his poor head."

"No," he agreed. "Hers is a shadow murder."

She turned to look at him. "Do you know who done it, husband?"

Acton tilted his head. "Unfortunately, there are a variety of possibilities. She knew too much."

She noted that he hadn't answered the question, and decided to cast a line. "Gabriel wanted to drive her home, yesterday. At the time, I thought that he wanted to protect her, but now I'm not so sure—he's a hard one to read."

He contemplated his hands for a moment. "I suppose it hardly matters."

But Doyle turned to face the altar again. "No—murder always matters. That should be my motto, I think; I'll take up embroidery, whilst I'm sittin' at home, starin' at the walls."

"You can do research," he suggested gently, taking her hand in his. "And help out with my docket. We'll be stretched very thin, after all."

"Or I could go to Trestles, and get a start on my tinned kale. I could enlist your mother to swing a scythe."

He offered a small smile. "As appealing as that sounds, I should stay in town, until this unpleasantness is settled."

She quirked her mouth at this euphemism, and took the opportunity to give him a mild scolding—mild, because she knew he was in a repentant frame of mind already, sitting here beside her, and anyways, it wasn't anything she hadn't said to him a million times before. "You were sailin' a little too close to the wind, my friend. Let this be a lesson, and recall that if you wind up in prison, the conjugal visits will be few and far between."

"Point well-taken."

She rested her head on his shoulder. "Not to mention that all the stupid fuss about the stupid succession will have been for nothin'."

"That would be a shame," he agreed.

She couldn't resist her own small smile. "Although it was almost worth it—to see Savoie turn all those stiff-rumps upside-down. And you have to admit, it's all very symmetrical—the ACC was going to use Savoie to discredit you, in the same way that you were usin' Savoie to discredit Sir Stephen. Savoie is everybody's favorite false flag."

"Symmetrical, indeed."

He offered nothing more, but Doyle was suddenly alert, because there was something—something underlying what he'd said about Savoie—

"May I take you home?"

Lifting her head, she sighed. "Not as yet; I thought I'd say a rosary for Harding."

There was a pause, whilst she could feel his surprise. "Dr. Harding?"

"The very same. I'm supposed to forgive him, you know—it's in the rules."

There was a small pause. "All right. Do you mind if I stay?"

"You may. Shall I say one for your father, too? I'm game, if you are."

There was another small pause. "You may suit yourself."

"And Morgan Percy—I suppose she should make the list."

He brushed a gentle, admonitory hand across her back. "We may be here all night, and you need your rest."

Doyle shifted her bulky body to kneel, and pulled out her mother's rosary. "Small enough price to pay, I think. It's a long journey, through eternity."

He made no reply, but stayed by her side as the shadows lengthened, and the beads slipped through her fingers, one-by-one.

EPILOGUE

As he walked away at a steady pace, he checked his electronics. Good, all was quiet at home. Best to get back quickly; he didn't like to be away from her, especially now that she was near term. Perhaps he could convince her to stay abed tomorrow; he'd asked her physician about the broken blood vessel in her left eye, and had been assured that this was a routine side effect. Still and all, it was worrying.

As he left through the park's gate, he took one last, backward glance. The Santero lay dead on the pathway behind him, a small caliber gunshot wound to the back of his head. His murder would be chalked up to the as-yet-unsolved Maguire murders; it would be a simple thing to come to the conclusion that the vigilante killer was unhappy that this particular informant had been allowed his freedom.

He took a quick glance around, before he unlocked his car. At this time of night, there were no potential witnesses, and any trace of his presence would be carefully erased from the CCTV cameras. The Santero's death meant that the man would not be available to testify at trial, but this was just as well; the scandal would have taken a terrible toll, and those who'd perpetrated the corruption rig had been satisfactorily sidelined. Besides, it was important that he not have the spotlight, just now. The financial district murders were about to come to a boil.

No; it was more important that the Santero be buried and gone—he knew about Kathleen, and so he could not be allowed to live.

AC 1-11-18

EI 3-15-18

WH 5-17-18

ST 7-19-18

64

Made in the USA
Lexington, KY
07 November 2017

ST 7-26-18/4P